A gangster
A musician
And the lovely young lady
who brought them together
on

Staten Island
(Revised)

by
Phillips Wylly

Large Print Edition

This book is a work of fiction. Any resemblance to actual events or persons, living or dead, is entirely coincidental.

"Staten Island," by Phillips Wylly. ISBN 978-1-949756-45-6 (softcover); 978-1-94975646-3 (hardcover).

Dedication:

All my love
To Ruth, Flip, Chris and David who were there at
the beginning...

To Shirley, who encouraged me to continue and
who made it all come true...

Without you there would be no book.

Author's note:

The original version of "Staten Island", my first book, was published many years ago. It was cluttered with too much verbiage, too many side plots and confusion. But, hidden there under is a pretty good story. I hope this revised edition reveals that story about a Staten Island gangster, A mid western musician and a beautiful young lady. Please come with me now to New York's smallest borough.

Part One

The Gangster

1.

HE AWOKE WITH A START, damp with sweat. The dream always made him sweat. If only he could reach the lift... but in the dream he never did. And the dream kept returning.

Sometimes he would cry out and his shipmates would wake him. Sometimes, like tonight, he awoke himself.

Trembling, he forced himself to lie quietly in his hammock trying to put the dream out of his mind by thinking about tomorrow while he waited for the ship's gentle swaying to lull him back to sleep. Tomorrow the squadron would sail into New York Harbor and he and his teammates were going to box the team from HMS Scorpion... He tried to visualize the movements George Driscol had taught him:

"Wait for his opponent to come to him. Circle. Watch his eyes. Wait for him to make the first move. Duck, or dodge, then move in quick with a left jab. Hold the right hand for an opening, then hit hard..." Driscol was a good

instructor... he felt confident...
Sleep returned...

2.

A RAGGED CHEER WENT UP from the small crowd gathered in an open field near the top of Staten Island's Grymes Hill as the British ships came into view. The crowd undoubtedly would have been larger were it not for the fact that their arrival was supposed to be secret. However, because two of the ships were to be docked in Stapleton, the Richmond Borough President's Office had been notified and word had somehow got round to a few "insiders" with the result that, in spite of the morning's dismal weather... there had been heavy clouds with light, intermittent rain since just after midnight... thirty or more people, equipped with rain coats, umbrellas, goulashes, field glasses and telescopes, had made their way up the Hill to watch and feel part of an historic event. According to Waldo Harris, who was on the Borough President's personal staff, this would be the first time British war ships had entered New York Harbor since the war of 1812.

Rising majestically behind the waterfront village of Stapleton, on an island that was almost a forgotten part of New York City, an island populated mainly by middle and working class Italian and Irish families, five hundred foot high Grymes Hill - actually the highest point on America's eastern seaboard from Maine to Key West - had become a virtual preserve for some of New York's wealthiest families who had built summer homes there with breath taking views of New York Harbor, the Narrows and the Atlantic Ocean beyond. Indeed, the field upon which this morning's group stood was part of Sir Edward Cunard's 38-acre estate. An estate that, together with several acres from the neighboring Vanderbilt property, was about to become part of the campus of Staten Island's small but well regarded Wagner College

On April 6th President Wilson finally got, a formal declaration of war, and on this day, the 12th of April, 1917, the tragedies of war were far from the thoughts and minds of the excited group on Grymes Hill.

A man with a telescope shouting, "Here they come," was first to see them. Quickly all conversation stopped, all heads turned towards the sea. Eyes straining through the mist... Dark streaks at first, slowly materializing out of the clouds, gradually taking shapes... The shapes of British Men of War sailing slowly, proudly, through the Narrows, the two-mile wide channel between Brooklyn and Staten Island that is the entrance to New York Harbor.

Guarded to the south by Staten Island's Fort Wadsworth, originally built by the British in 1663, and to the north by Brooklyn's Fort Hamilton, also built by the British a year earlier, New York Harbor is one of the most land locked and best protected harbors in the world

.

Moments after the British squadron came into view, three New York City fire boats arrived on the scene and, much to the delight of the spectators on Grymes Hill, commenced shooting fifty foot high plumes of water into the air in welcome to Rear Admiral Cabot Spalding and his four ships.

The people on the hill waved handkerchiefs and hats and applauded and were quite unaware five workmen, who had been digging an excavation for a new structure to be built some two hundred yards away, had joined them. The workmen had taken note of the distinguished looking spectators as they began arriving earlier in the morning but had pretty much ignored them until they heard the shout, "Here they come!" at which point they decided to take a well deserved break from their job and see what the excitement was all about.

"Wha-chu look at?" a workman named Franco Tucci, who spoke better English than his companions, asked one of the on lookers.

"History in the making," the man replied. "That is a Squadron of British fighting ships come to say hello. Best damned navy in the world," he continued. "Won't be long now... we'll show those damned huns..."

Franco explained the situation to his pals and, for a few moments they watched in silence. But there really wasn't very much for them to see. The ships were a long way off. Without binoculars the waterspouts from the fireboats were hardly visible and they had work to do.

"Come on." Franco turned and headed back up the hill. He had no inkling of the influence the event he had just found less than interesting would have on the rest of his life.

3.

REAR ADMIRAL THOMAS SPALDING'S FLAG SHIP, the heavy cruiser H.M.S. Buckminster, and one of it's escorting destroyers sailed majestically up New York Harbor to berths at the Navy Yard in the East River but, because of limited space there, H.M.S. Mosquito and H.M.S. Scorpion, two "G" class destroyers which completed the squadron, had been assigned berths on Staten Island's north shore, just a few miles from Grymes Hill, in the town of Stapleton.

Nicknamed "Mediterranean Beagles," the sleek, three stack, high-speed "G" Class destroyers were among the few remaining coal-burning fighting ships in the British Navy. Numbering thirteen in all, the "Beagles" each carried similar armament: One 4 inch gun; three 12 pounders; one 3 pound Anti-Aircraft gun; one machine gun; and two 22 inch torpedo tubes. Each ship had an average top speed of 27 knots and carried a compliment of 96 men. HMS Mosquito was 276 feet overall, displacing 983 tons. HMS Scorpion was seven feet longer and displaced 987 tons.

"It isn't exactly New York City is it Percy?" Mosquito's Captain's voice clearly expressed the disappointment he felt as his ship nosed into Stapleton's Pier #6.

"Not exactly sir." Lieutenant Percy Stilton, who still maintained much of the enthusiasm and appearance of the Oxford student he had been before "joining up" adjusted his cap as he looked away from the dismal shoreline and grimy pier. "But the crew is looking forward to the boxing and some liberty and I'm told Stapleton's a fine place for all that."

"Is that what you've been told Percy?" Lieutenant, Senior Grade, Cyril Roberts cocked an eye at his executive officer. If Percy Stilton looked like an Oxford student, Cyril Roberts, although only four years his senior, looked very much like he might have been one of Percy's professor. As youngsters, neither man had envisioned naval careers. That was before the war came.

"Well, something like that Captain." Percy grinned back. "But you know what they say, 'any port in a storm'."

"I suppose," Roberts agreed. "Anyway, we shall make the best of it, though I should very much like to have seen New York City."

"Yes, that would have been nice." Percy Stilton's face mirrored the disappointment both he and his friend and captain were feeling, however Percy was not a man who long held on to negative thoughts. "But by Jove, Cyril, we're the first ships into New York Harbor. We'll get a great reception here on Staten Island. ...And if our lads should win tomorrow perhaps you and I will have an opportunity to pay a visit to that city we've heard so much about."

"You're right as usual, Percy," Cyril Roberts managed a smile. "And I'm betting our fellows will win. Driscol says they're very good."

Moments later Lieutenant Stilton signaled, "Finished with Engines" and deep down in the bowels of the ship Hugh Allan Crawford hung up his shovel and wiped the sweat from his face. They had arrived. It had been his father's dream that one day he would take his family to America. "Anyone can make a fortune there if-n he's willin' ta work hard," his father had said. Now his father and his mother and his brothers were gone, and here he was, in America.

And tomorrow, here in America, he would have a chance to prove himself, to make a name for himself.

4.

IN THE THREE PLUS YEARS since his enlistment at age fourteen, little had happened to bring Hugh Allan Crawford to anyone's attention. He had slowly risen three grades to Stoker 1st Class. He had listened more times than he could count to the "chunk"..."thud" of depth charges being dropped by the Mosquito as they hunted German submarines and each time he thought of the mine, his father and his brothers, and wondered if this would be the time the thin steel skin that separated him from the sea would suddenly implode with a flash of fire and tons of water.

In those years since his enlistment he had grown nearly a foot and a half in height and added almost three stone in solid muscle. The weight and muscle he attributed to his daily life of shoveling coal into Mosquito's massive fireboxes. The foot and a half he had grown were no doubt the legacy of his mum and his pa.

It was that combination of size and muscle

that a few weeks ago caught Lieutenant Stilton's eye during one of his infrequent inspections of the engine room.

Percy Stilton did not like the engine room. It was hot; it was dark, below the water line and smelled of perspiration.

"That man over there chief." Lieutenant Stilton jutted his jaw towards Hugh Crawford.

"Crawford, sir?" The engine room chief pointed to Hugh and beckoned him to step forward.

"Yes, he's the one."

Percy Stilton watched the young giant approach. Little more than a boy, he thought, still, he was big enough and if his bulging muscles were any indication, strong enough. And, covered in sweat and coal dust, he certainly looked fearsome enough too. "Crawford, is it?"

"Aye-sir." Hugh put the knuckles of his right hand to his forehead in a quick salute.

"Well Crawford, I've decided to put together a ship's boxing team. You look big and strong, would you like to learn the manly art?"

Hugh blinked in surprise but quickly answered, "Aye-sir. That I would."

"Good show." Stilton told him as he turned back to the chief, "Have him report to Driscol when he's off duty."

Before the war, Gunner's Mate George Driscol had been a professional "pugilist", as he insisted his former profession be termed. He was a head shorter than Hugh, did not weigh more than eight or nine stone, and, Hugh guessed, was at least twenty years his senior. But his first lesson with Driscol taught him the little man could hit hard enough to knock him down and was nearly impossible to hit in return.

Realizing there was much he could learn from the chief, Hugh became an attentive student. Now, only five weeks after beginning his training, he was about to have a chance to put his new found skills to the test.

Carpenters from both ships worked half the night constructing the boxing ring on the pier between the two ships. "The square circle," Driscol called it. Two rows of benches along opposite sides of the ring were set up for the enlisted men, while a platform, lined with chairs and covered by a canvas awning to protect from the morning sun, awaited the ship's officers. The high foredecks of the two ships afforded a view of the ring for those whose duty required them to remain on board.

From below decks, in the mess hall where

a temporary dressing room had been set up for the fighters, Hugh could hear the loud cheers from out on the pier. The first two fights had been won by his teammates but the third and fourth had gone to Scorpion's fighters. Now it was his turn and a shiver of anticipation ran up his spine. His fight would decide the tournament. Driscol slapped him on the back and said, "Let's go."

Loud cheers greeted him as he walked out on deck, descended the gangway and crossed the few feet of pier to the ring. The man he was to fight was standing in the far corner, waving to his mates and gesturing towards him. Gestures that said, "I'll finish him quick."

"Jesus, he's damn big ain't he Driscol?"

"Yes. Yes he's a big one," Driscol agreed. "But I'm thinkin' dats a lot-a beer fat he's carrying. You just fight like what I trained ya."

"I will," Hugh answered quietly. Then, acknowledging the cheers from his shipmates, knowing a win would give them the prize they all wanted - a 24 hour shore leave - Stoker 1st Class Hugh Allan Crawford climbed easily into the ring and waited quietly in his corner watching his opponent as he stood waving his arms, gesturing to his shipmates, shouting words like, "No trouble," and, "One round!"

"All right gentlemen..." Lieutenant Stilton stood in the center of the ring with his hands raised, calling for quiet. "Gentlemen.... Gentlemen...please.."

"I don't know Cyril," Scorpion's Captain leaned towards his friend and opposite number seated next to him. "That lad of yours hardly looks old enough to be a fighter"

"Not to worry, Dickey," Cyril Roberts smiled. "The lad's young alright, but he's mean as a shark, and just look at those muscles. I believe he can handle himself."

"Hummm... I don't suppose you'd care to put another quid on that would you old boy?"

"...Gentlemen..." Lieutenant Stilton was finally getting sufficient control of the crowd to proceed. "This final bout will decide things then..." Cheers from the men of both ships. "From H.M.S. Mosquito, at thirteen stone even, I give you Hugh 'The Crusher' Crawford."

Cheers from the Mosquito side.

"And from H.M.S. Scorpion," Stilton continued, "Weighing fifteen stone and three, here is 'Hammering' Harold Hawks." The descriptive nicknames were his own creation and his voice conveyed the pride he felt at his cleverness. He waited until the cheers from Scorpion's men began to die down then he nodded to Chief Cook Robinson standing alongside the "ring" and the man responded by striking an iron spoon against a heavy metal pot making a sound somewhat resembling a bell.

With his fists held quietly at chest level Hugh moved easily to the center of the ring as Hawks came menacingly toward him with arms and fists rotating in a style Driscol termed "windmill". The two circled briefly, then Hawks swung a powerful round house right at Hugh's head. Only Hugh's head wasn't there.

Straightening after "The Hammer's" fist sailed harmlessly overhead, remembering Driscol's teachings, Hugh stepped into Hawks to deliver a left hand to the man's stomach that doubled him over. A right uppercut to the jaw straightened him and was followed with stunning speed by a left cross to the side of his head then another right full on the nose as the man fell to the deck.

Shocked, Lieutenant Stilton looked at the fallen man for a moment before starting his count. "One... Two... Oh, I say chaps, I think it's all over."

"Good lord, Cyril. That was quick." Scorpion's stunned Captain groaned as he handed a pound note to his companion. "I guess its Liberty for you and your lads then."

"Yes, thank you." Cyril Roberts accepted his winnings, shook his friend's hand, then could not resist saying, "You will take good care on my ship while we're off playing, won't you Dickey."

5.

FOR THE MOST PART "Black Gang" members keep pretty much to themselves as do "topsiders," but on this night Hugh Crawford was champion of them all. Flush with the one-dollar American "shore money" each man had received, with beer at a nickel and whiskey ten cents, there was scarcely a saloon along Stapleton's waterfront where his shipmates did not buy him a drink. By the time Hugh and his pals reached Angelo's, his steps were far from steady. Nor were his companions in particularly better condition.

It was never quite determined who learned of the "house" across the street from Angelo's, nor who decided they ought to treat their hero, but a hat was passed and enough collected to pay for Hugh's first "all night," on a night that had turned surprisingly cold for April..

As the group of seven sailors stumbled out of Angelo's door, the cold air braced him slightly, but Hugh only vaguely realized he was crossing a street, supported by two pals who helped him up steps to a wide verandah and through the front door of a house he later learned was known as "Mothers." How he got from Mother's parlor to a bedroom would always be a mystery. The next thing he was aware of was waking up in a bed, with a fierce thirst accompanied by a desperate need to urinate. Then discovering he was not alone.

"Hello," a soft, wonderfully feminine voice said to him. "How are you feeling?"

"I've got ta piss," he answered.

"There's a pot under the bed," the voice told him.

As he swung his legs out from beneath the covers he became aware of two things. A dim light coming from a candle on a table in the corner of the tiny room that was hardly bigger than the bed, and the fact that he was naked. "I've got no clothes on," he said in surprise.

"Neither have I," the voice was even softer. "Have yer pee and come back to bed."

The sound of a strong stream of water hitting the side of the bucket assured her his first need was being cared for.

"Now if I just had a drink of water..." His voice was almost drowned out by the sound of his elimination.

"On the table next to the candle."

How could anybody pee this long and with so much force, she wondered. He finished at last, drank the full glass of water, got back into bed and immediately fell back into a restless sleep.

She wasn't sure how many sailors had come in - at least seven or eight - all bragging about Hugh's victory. "Mother" Donna Marie had asked if she felt ready to work and only moments later the sailors selected her to spend the night with their hero. As a loud groan exploded from the man lying next to her, she decided so far the job was a lot less challenging than she had worried it might be.

The dream was back: His mother was crying and he had never seen her cry before.

"Now, now mother..." His father put an arm round her shoulder.

"But he's so young, Tom. Do watch out for him."

He wanted to tell her he wasn't so young. He was six. All his friends were working. Why was she so upset?

"Not to worry, mother. He's just gonna be a donkey boy. No danger there you know."

He didn't know exactly what a "donkey boy" did, but his father said there was no danger and he was going to work with his brothers and his father and that meant he was grown up and his mother should not be crying...

The picture changed: His mother was dead. Something about her lungs he did not understand. He was eight and he knew he shouldn't cry. Still, after he and his brothers climbed into their bed, he couldn't help it... His oldest brother, Tom junior, told him to shut up and go to sleep but he thought for certain Tom was crying too...

Then he was standing on the lift: Even after eight years in the mines, even after he graduated from donkey boy to being a full fledged miner with his own shovel, he had never got over the terrible feeling that always came the minute he stepped onto the lift and the gate closed behind him. A feeling that grew worse as they started down. It was hard to keep from screaming when they dropped below ground.

Once they stopped at the tunnel level, six hundred feet below the surface, once everyone began to get off it was better, he was able to get control of himself. But, oh God, how he hated going down... down... down.

His father, his brother Chad, and several other men were working at the end of a side tunnel. He and his brother Tom junior, were pushing an empty cart towards them when the foreman called to him.

"Hugh, lad. Run back to the lift and bring us some more candles."

"Yes sir."

He had just reached the lift when the explosion knocked him to the ground. Crashing timbers... Falling rocks... Screams...

"Awwww." His cry woke her. He was sitting upright, thrashing around. It was not yet sunrise but enough light came around the window shade for her to see him and duck under his flailing arms. "They're dead. They're all dead."

"It's all right." She slid close to him and put her hand on his stomach. "It's all right."

She wrapped her arms around him as he fell back onto the pillow. "All right, 's all right," she whispered again and held him until his shivering stopped.

"Who are you?" He asked suddenly.

"Me name's Mary Catherine, but everyone calls me Mary Kate. I'm here to please you if you're thinkin' you might want to." As she spoke she slid her hand down his stomach until she reached his penis. It took only a moment for his answer to be apparent.

"Holy Jesus," he whispered after a while. "Tell me where I am and what I'm doing here?"

"You're at Mother's. You won a prizefight and your mates brought you here for a treat. An' you just had one I'm thinking."

"That I did." He put his hand on her breast. Although it was hard and callused his caress was surprisingly gentle. "Do you suppose we could do it again?"

She reached for him and was amazed to find he was more than ready. A far cry from old Mr. Murphy, she thought as he moved on top of her.

"Ohh...Oh Hugh." She had never experienced anything like this before. She had not realized women could. She dug here fingers into his back as he continued moving in and out.

"Ohhh. Jesus, Mary and Joseph. My God, Hugh..."

"Was it a dream you were havin'?" she asked after a while.

"Yes," he answered slowly. "A dream."

"Tell me about it then."

"No." He never told anyone about the dream.

Ignoring his answer she rolled towards him letting her breasts flatten against his chest. "I understand about dreams," she whispered. "I have dreams of me own. The whippings at the home was bad enough but then they sent me to live wid the Murphy's and the Mister begun coming into me bed..." It was her turn to shiver. "When I was old enough, I run away," she whispered. "I never knowed me mother nor me father. All the sisters ever told me was they found me in a cardboard box all wrapped up in a woolen scarf and left on the steps of St. Catherine's.

"That's your pit is it then?" Lying there in the dark, Hugh pulled her closer. "Mine's a coal pit." His voice was a whisper. "Me father and me brothers were trapped..." Remembering the explosion, for a moment he could not finish the sentence.

"...I waited around fer two days," he said at last. I waited 'till they decided not ta dig out the bodies then I went ta the pay master and got him ta give me the money pa and me an' me brothers was due. Then I went up ta Liverpool and enlisted."

"What about yer mother," she asked.

"Ah, me mother. She died when I was ten. Black lung they called it."

"Oh," there was a catch in her voice, "Then you're an orphan like me." She ran her hand tenderly down his cheek and across his jaw, "So how old were ya when ya enlisted?" she asked.

"I was fourteen when the war started and they was asking fer one million volunteers. I wanted to sign up then, but pa said, 'No, they need you more here in the mine.' He told me they'd have plenty-a soldiers an' sailors and what was gonna be needed most was plenty-a coal an' I should stay right there in the mine and the war would be over in no time. The explosion come just a few months later."

"My God, Hugh." She bent her head and kissed his chest. "And you been in the Navy ever since?"

"Ever since," he agreed. "I got our pay then hid on a train carrying coal up ta Liverpool an' joined His Majesty's Navy."

"And the dream?" she asked.

"Ahh, the dream, nightmare I call it. It begun the first time I heard guns firin'. They sounded kinda like that explosion..."

"Bad dreams never go way I suppose..." There was sadness in her voice. Then, brightening, she reached for him again. "But I believe this can help, if you think you're up to it."

A spoken reply was not necessary...

They had fallen back into a dreamless sleep when "mother" Donna Marie's voice woke them. "Time's up, gentlemen." They could hear her knocking on doors further down the hallway.

"Sorry, gentlemen but the ladies must get their rest. Time's up. Time's up."

"Oh Hugh." Mary Kate's voice caught in her throat. "Hugh. Will I ever see ya again?"

Hugh's reply was drowned out by "mother's" loud knock on their door. "Time's up Mary Kate. Time for that fellow ta leave."

Had she been able to hear Hugh's reply to her question, she would have heard him say, "There's no way of knowin'. This war might last ferever."

6.

WHEN GREAT BRITAIN ENTERED the war in August of 1914 it was commonly believed "It will all be over by Christmas." A month later, following the Battle of Aisne, English optimism began to waver. Then, with the first Battle of Ypres, fought along the Marne River in late Fall, stark reality set in:

Trench warfare. Hundreds, then thousands of men killed as the armies fought back and forth, gaining a few yards in one battle, loosing it in the next. It had become a stalemate, a war of attrition that seemed impossible for either side to win until the summer of 1918, a year after Hugh said goodbye to Mary Kate, when American Forces under General John J. Pershing began arriving in Europe in sufficient number to make a difference. Then, in less than six bloody months, it was over.

"GET THEM HOME FOR CHRISTMAS!" The Liverpool Guardian's banner headline urged on December 1st, 1918 and, as much as possible, His Majesty's Government was making every effort to comply with the popular sentiment. Each day since the Armistice dozens, then hundreds, then thousands of men had been released from the services with the result that Great Britain was literally awash in discharged service men and Liverpool, like many cities, was faced with a crisis in public transportation. There simply were not enough trains to take every discharged sailor or soldier where he wanted to go, when he wanted to go, but as the saying goes, "it is an evil wind that blows no good." Men with money in their pockets and time on their hands were a boon to the shops, theaters and pubs of Liverpool.

Six rows of nine-foot long tables and benches provided seating for more than four hundred sailors in the general mess hall next to Liverpool's Navy Barracks on Pier Four. The cafeteria style serving provided a degree of levity for men who been on shore for a day or two as they watched new arrivals struggle to maintain their balance as they carried trays of food from the serving counters to the first table they could get to where seating was available. When a man has been at sea for a long period of time it takes a while for his "sea legs" to deal with a surface that is *not* in perpetual motion.

Together with two hundred or more other recently discharged men who had already got back their "land legs," Hugh, his bunk mate John Ward and his friend and boxing coach George Driscol ate their suppers in the mess hall and chuckled as they watched "new boys," making their unsteady way across the unfamiliar mess deck. Once the last staggering sailor was seated and the fun over, like many of the others in the mess hall that night, their conversation turned to the subject of their futures: Would transportation home be available before Christmas only ten days away? And then, what next?

For Hugh, there was only one thing he was sure about. Having spent his childhood in the mines and more than four years shoveling coal in the bowels of a Navy ship, he was sure he did not want ever again to be below ground or sea level shoveling coal. For a time, after Stapleton, he thought about going back to America if the war ever ended. Since Stapleton he had been to whore-houses in a dozen or more cities where, as the navy saying went, "the worst he ever had was still pretty damn good," but those visits were nothing more than relieving pent up needs. Nothing had ever been like being with Mary Kate, and for a long time thoughts of finding her again were in his mind. But as the months passed, and the war went on and on, thoughts of Mary Kate began to fade away replaced by Driscol's insistence that, "Pugilism is the way fer ya ta go, Hugh. Ya can make a lot of money."

In the year and a half since Stapleton, Hugh had won eight more fights and become the pride of His Majesty's Atlantic Fleet. During that time he had gained another six centimeters in height and nearly two stone in weight. And, if Driscol was any judge, he still had more to grow. After all, he wouldn't be nineteen for another two weeks.

Tonight, much to John Ward's annoyance, as was so often the case when their conversation turned to the future, "pugilism" again became the topic of conversation. John returned his empty tea mug to the heavy wooden table with sufficient force to get their attention. "Hugh! Driscol! I'm tired a hearin' about yer damned puuu-ge-lis-um. Come on. Let's us go down ta tha pub fer a pint er two an' celebrate our freedom."

7

LESS THAN A MILE FROM THE NAVY PIER, The "Pulley and Cleat" had been in the same location on Seaman Lane, just off Wharf Road, for nearly one hundred years. In all that time very little had happened to change it's appearance. Gas lamps still provide somewhat minimal light. The low, exposed beams, hand hewn from solid English Oak, may have become darker from absorbed smoke over the years but the change had been so gradual no one could really notice. Years of hand rubbing and polishing had worm slight depressions in some of the tables and the bar itself, but these changes had also been so gradual no one could remember a time when it was any different.

During peacetime, the Pulley and Cleat's clientele was made up of sailors and merchant marine seamen in about equal number- the perfect mix for frequent confrontations. But since the war began, with the British Navy Piers so close and the tremendous increase in the number of men in uniform, the merchant seamen had become badly outnumbered and were smart enough to keep clear of the place. Nonetheless, their absence did little to reduce the frequency of physical conflict.

With black-gang against deckhand and marines against them both, there was adequate rivalry within the "oldest service" to insure few evenings would go by without fisticuffs. Not surprisingly therefore, the pub was often referred to as the "Club and Fist" by many of it's patrons. On this night however, the spirit of Christmas seemed to have reached even the "Pulley and Cleat." The pub was crowded, but there was a mood of warmth and togetherness not always common to its guests.

Near mid-night, Hugh, John Ward and Driscol were standing at the bar, finishing their second or third pints, when Driscol announced his need to visit the Loo. Neither Hugh nor John had the slightest idea how it started but seconds later a Marine Sergeant, with the neck of a broken bottle clutched in one hand, was standing over Driscol who lay crumpled on the floor with shards of bottle glass protruding from his bleeding scalp.

Almost simultaneously two other Marines jumped at John Ward knocking him to the ground while the Sergeant, now holding a knife in his hand, advanced slowly towards Hugh.

Fists fights were an acceptable form of entertainment as far as Hugh was concerned, but broken bottles were not very welcome, and knives... well knives quickly elevated the entertainment into something serious.

Hugh was waiting as the sergeant approached when an unexpected groan from Driscol took his attention. "Hugh... Ahaaa..."

Driscol's call distracted him for only a second but it was long enough for the sergeant to lunge at him.

The man knew how to use a knife. If it weren't for the reflexes Driscol had drilled into him - reflexes that had become automatic - the slashing blade would have done far more harm than the four-inch gash he received across his left arm. But Hugh's reflexes were more than equal to the sergeant's attack and as the blade flashed back towards his chest, he caught the man's arm and brought it down over his knee with a resulting "crack" that could only have been caused by a breaking bone. The man cried out, then tried to twist away from Hugh's grip and reach for the knife that had fallen to the floor. Before he could get to it, Hugh grabbed a handful of his shirt, lifted him to his feet then, holding him with his blood covered left hand, slammed two powerful rights into his mid section. As the sergeant started to double up from the blows to his stomach, Hugh released his blouse, stepped back slightly to give himself room, then, telling him, "This is fer Driscol," with all his strength, drove his right fist into the man's face. The force from the blow smashed the sergeant's nose and propelled him backwards until his head slammed into the edge of the bar where he collapsed onto the floor and lay motionless. His bloody head bent at a strange angle, his lifeless eyes staring up at nothing.

The results of the sergeant's attack on Hugh had taken the attention of the other two marines away from John Ward long enough for John to get to his feet, grab a beer mug from the bar and quickly use it against the head of one of them. John's second attacker backed away only to find himself locked in Hugh Crawford's blood soaked arms and almost immediately the recipient of a similar blow from the mug in John's fist.

"All right now..." picking up the sergeant's knife, Hugh turned towards the crowd of sailors and marines encircling them. "Anyone else?"

There were no takers. The bleeding, dead or dying sergeant lying on the floor was an overwhelming deterrent to further trouble.

Carefully carrying their semi-conscious pal Hugh and John made their out of the pub and up Wharf Road to the Navy Medical Office on Pier

Three where they waited for more than an hour until an ageing, gray haired nurse took a quick look at Hugh's bleeding arm and decided it was not life threatening. Telling the orderly to bind up Hugh's wound, she turned her attention to Driscol's head.

After carefully picking bits of broken glass from Driscol's scalp, the nurse told them he might have a concussion and would have to remain in sickbay until morning when a Doctor could look at him.

They thanked her, then, in silence, walked slowly to the three deck high, wooden Barracks Building #4 where they had been assigned side-by-side bunks on the first deck.

Entering quietly, so as not to disturb several men who were already sleeping, the two walked to their bunks. Hugh surprised his companion by picking up his footlocker.

"Come back outside with me," Hugh whispered as he headed towards the exit door.

"What are ya doin' Hugh?" Ward asked as the two reached the barrack's outside deck.

"I'm getting out of here John." Hugh put an arm over his friend's shoulder.

Ward was not sure he understood. "What are ya sayin'?

"I goin', John. There's not much they'll bother you or Driscol about, but if that bastard's dead like I think, they'll sure be lookin' fer me and I've no interest in seein' the inside of the brig."

"Hugh. 'Twas self defense. Besides they got no idea who ya are."

"Think a minute John. How long before they start checkin' hospitals fer a sailor what's got his head bashed in with a bottle? They'll know who we are in no time."

"But Hugh..."

"No, there's no 'buts' John. You been a good mate, a good friend. And Driscol... I owe him a lot. You tell him thanks fer me, will ya?"

"I'll do that Hugh... but where you goin?"

"I don't know that John." Hugh turned and started to walk away. "Wherever it is, I'll think a you and Driscol," he called back over his shoulder. "Maybe next war we'll run into each other again."

"Yeah, Hugh," John Ward said softly as he watched his friend disappear in the darkness. "Maybe next war."

8.

AFTER SEVERAL HOURS spent walking north from the Navy Pier, along the Crosby Channel almost to the town of Bootle, Hugh had decided the King's Arms looked to be a good place for some hot tea and a bit of breakfast before starting his hunt for a berth on an outbound ship. If he were to have a choice, he would pick one heading for America... best of all New York. But the important thing was to find a berth on any ship headed anywhere away from the authorities in Liverpool.

Shortly after Hugh arrived and ordered his breakfast, Terrance Pierson walked into the King's Arms and, quickly closing the door behind him against the cold, wind driven fog, made his presence known to the eight or nine men seated at tables or standing by the counter. "Me name's Terry Pierson," he shouted. "Third Mate of the beautiful Sea Glory here to see would any a you like to earn top pay leavin' ta-day fer a quick voyage to the beau-ti-ful city of New York in the

USA? This time-a year it's a Christmas paradise, an' I'll promise ya some liberty ta see it!"

Hugh looked up in surprise from his steak and kidney pie and raised his hand. He took the arrival of Third Mate Pierson to be a good omen indeed. "I would fer one," he told the ruddy faced, barrel chest little man standing at the doorway, and an hour later followed him up Sea Glory's gang plank and signed on, not surprisingly, as a member of the "black gang."

The Steamship Sea Glory hardly lived up to her name but worn out as she looked and was, three hundred seventy-two anxious American doughboys had boarded her. The men knew they would still be at sea on Christmas Day, but they had every hope of arriving back in "the good old USA" in time to celebrate New Year's Eve.

As the old ship made her way up the channel and out into the Irish Sea, Hugh thought about the promise he had made to himself not go below decks or below ground again, but as he pitched his first shovel full of coal into the ancient furnace of the "beautiful" Sea Glory he told himself this was an emergency measure and it would be the very last time.

Broad of beam and slow of speed, Sea Glory's

single stack belched a continuous stream of heavy, thick smoke over the dozens of sea sick soldiers who daily lined her railings as she pushed her way into a constant head wind and heavy sea.

Christmas came and went. What celebration there may have been up on deck was not shared by Hugh and his companions in the engine room below where, other than for an extra tot of rum with their dinners, little attention was paid to the holiday.

Seldom making more than seven knots, it was fourteen long days before, under a frosty gray morning sky that promised snow, Sea Glory steamed through The Narrows, into New York Harbor and made her tired way up the busy East River to a pier in the Brooklyn Navy Yard where a hero's welcome awaited her passengers.

It was not until they had docked and one of his mates said, "Happy New Year," to him that Hugh realized what day it was. Not only was it New Year's Day, 1919, it was his birthday. He was nineteen years old. He had been born just a few minutes after midnight, January 1st, 1900. For a short time, his mother once told him, they thought he was the first baby born in Wales in the new century and if he had been, they would have got a twenty-pound prize from the crown. But, as it turned out, there was a baby born in

Caernarfonshire a few minutes earlier. "No matter," his mother always told him. "We got the best of it... We got you!"

He loved his mother. He thought of her often. He wondered what life might have been like if she had not died when he was so young. Surely he would have stayed with her after Pa and his brothers were killed. Likely he would still be digging coal...

After the last American Doughboy had gone ashore, Sea Glory backed out into the river again and made her way further up stream to a pier on the Manhattan side where a return cargo awaited her. While Longshoremen loaded the cargo, Sea Glory's over worked crewmen each received a half dollar American as "shore money" and four hours leave to see the New York paradise Third Mate Pierson had extolled.

Third Mate Pierson, Hugh learned almost as soon as be became a member of the crew, was not only the Third Mate, but the Second Mate, First Mate, and the only mate Captain McShay had on board. For some reason Hugh could not begin to guess, Pierson always referred to himself as the "Third Mate."

"Come on Hugh, we're goin' ta O'Riley's." Just what or who "O'Riley's" was Hugh had no idea, but together with several of his shipmates, he followed Third Mate down the gangplank and across the pier to the dock master's office where they signed out.

Turning north on East River Street, they walked three blocks to East 96th Street and what Americans call a "bar," named "O'Riley's". A Christmas Tree decorated with lighted candles and chains of brightly colored paper rings, was almost the first thing they saw as they crowded through the doorway into the bar room which, as far as Hugh could tell, differed from an English pub only in the height of its ceiling. In most pubs back home, the beams were only a few inches above his head. In O'Riley's, the ceiling was well above where he could reach with his arm extended. But the beams seemed just as old and the gas lights just as dim, the air just as filled with smoke.

"Hello Sean, Happy New Year!" Third Mate Pierson called to the man standing behind the bar as they entered. "'Tis terrible cold out there and we're in need of some beer and whiskey."

"Beer and whiskey, is it?" The man Pierson called Sean came out from behind the bar and clapped his arms around Pierson. "Sure an I didn't know if I'd ever lay eyes on ya again an' all ya got ta say is Happy New Year, give us beer and whiskey?"

After returning the bartender's embrace, Pierson turned to his companions. "Any-a you as don't know, this fine gentleman is Sean O'Riley his self." Then looking back to O'Riley he told his friend, "Now Sean, we got damn little time, so let's stop with this love-making and start settin' up some drinks."

Hugh's mind was on things other than beer and whisky as he took a sip from the stein Third Mate had handed to him. "I need to go to the loo," he said to no one in particular.

"Back there," Sean O'Riley pointed towards the far corner of the room. Opposite the door to the loo, as he had hoped, there was a back exit to the street.

It was full dark outside when Third Mate took his watch from it's pocket, checked it against the clock behind the bar, then announced in a somewhat slurred voice, "Drink up lads, time to head back."

Over the crewmen's grumbling and Sean O'Riley's surprised, "So soon?" Hugh called out, "I'll be wit chu in a minute... I got ta take another piss."

Before leaving Sea Glory, Hugh had put on both the shirts he owned and stuffed his spare union suit and socks into the pockets of his pea coat. Aside from the money belt that never left his waste, these were his only worldly possessions. As he headed towards the toilet Third Mate intercepted him. "I'm thinkin' you'll not be coming back with us then."

It was not a question.

Before Hugh could decide what to say, Pierson took a small roll of bills from his pocket and pressed it into his hand. "You worked hard fer us. I know ya earned more'n dis, but it's all me and the Captain could come up with just now. It'll help you some."

Stunned, Hugh looked down into Pierson's eyes. He had known the man for only two weeks. He had never mentioned anything about his plan to stay in America. How did he know he was going to jump ship? Why would he and the captain give him this money?

"I got to go now," Pierson told him, breaking the spell.

"I don't know what-ta say..." finally managing to find some words Hugh grasped the man's shoulder. "I'll not be forgettin' this. One day I'll find a way to pay you back."

"Yes, alright." Pierson smiled and nodded his head up and down. "I'm sure-a that. Just like I'm sure Sea Glory's gonna make it back ta Liverpool in three days," he laughed. Then raising his voice loud enough for the others to hear, he continued,

"Go take yer pee, we must be gettin' back ta-da ship."

"I doubt the ship'll do that," Hugh spoke softly enough so only Third Mate could hear him. "But me word's me promise..." he insisted, then he turned and hurried to the back exit he'd discovered on his previous visit to the loo and quietly let himself out onto the street.

He was free from Sea Glory. Now, how to get to Staten Island? To a town named Stapleton, and a girl named Mary Kate.

9.

WALKING WEST ON 96TH STREET, away from
O'Riley's, the river and the Sea Glory, he was
amazed by the number of electric lights all about
him. Christmas lights streetlights, headlights,
lighted signs, lights shining from the windows of
houses and shops... And the traffic! It was what
New Yorkers called "rush hour." Automobiles,
lorries, horse drawn wagons of every sort
constantly coming and going and the further he
walked the heavier the traffic became, both
vehicular and pedestrian.

Several blocks away from O'Riley's he came to
a wide, north/south street with what he judged to
be railroad tracks running above it. A signpost at
the corner identified the street as 2nd Ave. Under
the railroad trestle, in the middle of the
intersection of 2nd Avenue and East 96th Street,
a bobby stood directing traffic... Policeman, he
reminded himself. In America they call 'em
policemen... The policeman would be the one to
ask for directions, but it looked to be nearly

impossible to get from the sidewalk to where the man stood without being run down. What made it extra dangerous, he realized, was the fact that these Americans drove on the wrong side of the road. It was hard to remember which way to look when you crossed a street.

After a moment the policeman spotted him and realized he was trying to get his attention. Raising his hands in both directions the policeman halted all traffic then called to Hugh, "All right boy-o. Come to me."

"Well yer at the right place sure enough," the policeman laughed in answer to Hugh's question. "You go to the corner over there," he pointed, "Climb up them stairs to the station and fer a nickel you can ride the El Train all the way down town ta the Battery and the Staten Island Ferry."

At the top of the stairs Hugh found himself standing behind a heavy set woman in a short line of people waiting in front of a booth of some sort. Inside the booth, behind a heavy wire screen, a small, dark haired man sat taking people's money and, in return, pushing coins back out to them.

"How does this work?" he asked the woman.

"You must be a stranger," she told him in a heavily accented voice.

"I am that," he replied.

"Well sure an it's the easiest ting in da world.

You ain't got no nickels fer the turnstile the man in there'll give you some fer whatever ya got. Then all you do is put one in the slot and in ya go."

By the time she finished her explanation she was next at the change window. "Here, watch me, it's like dis." She showed him the twenty-five cent piece she had in her hand before pushing it under the window to the man inside the booth. Almost immediately he slid five smaller coins back to her. "Like I tol-ya. Nothin' to it."

Selecting a ten cent coin from the money he had in his pocket, Hugh put it in the shallow, bowl like depression in the wooden counter beneath the screen as the woman had done and watched the clerk inside immediately replace it with two what the lady had called "nickels." Sliding one of his nickels into the slot on the top of the turnstile, he pushed against the heavy wooden arm and made his way onto the train platform.

Several minutes later two short, high pitched whistle blasts, announced the arrival of the El Train. Five passenger cars that roared into the station and with a great screeching of breaks, came to a jarring stop. The doors hissed open and he followed the lady into the car. Almost before he could seat himself on one of the hard but comfortable wooden benches lining both sides of the car, the doors closed and, with a sudden jerk that almost caused him to loose his balance, the train was again in motion.

The spotlessly clean cars were longer than railroad cars at home and seemed to rock from side to side more. Colorful pictures on placards advertising products and services he was not familiar with lined the curved juncture of the roof and the side wall above the car's wide windows: A big bowl of Campbell's tomato soup; A cute dog sitting with his head cocked, in front of an RCA Victrola; A bottle of Dr. Brown's Cough Medicine; A handsome man smoking a Lucky Strike Cigarette; A Remington Typewriter; A cute boy named "Buster Brown" holding a puppy in his arms; A Sears and Roebuck Catalog open to a page displaying Ice Boxes... All new to him, all fascinating.

Moments later screeching breaks announced a sudden deceleration and the train came to a violent stop at another station. As the start/stop process was repeated again and again, he realized that each station, no more than ten or so blocks from the previous one, was identified by the number of the cross street where it was located: 86th St.... 75th St.... 68th St. Each declining number served to reassure him he was indeed headed downtown.

Between each grinding, break screeching stop,

he was fascinated by glimpses of American family life behind the endless stream of lighted windows in the buildings lining 2nd Avenue. Children and Christmas Trees were everywhere. Men and women, who seemed oblivious to the passing train, were eating, reading, washing dishes, playing cards. A man reading to a young boy seated in his lap reminded him of how he had once sat in his father's lap. His father did not read to him. His father could not read, but he could tell stories. Wonderful stories about knights on horseback, or American cowboys. And about how someday they would all go to America... He missed his father, and his mother, and his brothers. He wondered if ever he would have such a family.

At each stop he could see more and more people on the streets below and more and more passengers crowded into the train. Some, choosing not to sit, clutched at hanger straps lest they lose their balance as the train accelerated away from the station. When eventually they reached 10th St. Hugh assumed he was nearing the end of the run to the ferry. But no, after the numbers ran out there were ever more stations with street names Hugh knew he would never remember: Delancy Street; Canal Street; Chambers, Fulton and Wall. Finally, almost three quarters of an hour after boarding the El at 96th

Street, the train arrived at the Staten Island Ferry Terminal.

The train ride had been remarkable. It was beyond anything he had seen before in smoky, foggy Liverpool, or London, or even on the one other occasion when Mosquito put in at an the American port, Boston. But nothing during the train trip prepared him for what came next.

Another nickel fed into another slot allowed him to pass through another wooden turnstile, similar to the one at 96th Street, and make his way on to a waiting boat with the name "Queens" showing in bold letters across the front of the small pilot's cabin perched above the top deck.

The ferry boat "Queens" was one of five similar boats, each bearing the name of one of the city' five boroughs, that had been commissioned in 1905 as Staten Island was becoming more and more a Mecca for Manhattan's businessmen seeking a rural atmosphere in which to raise their families. Each nearly 250-foot long boat had tunnels for vehicles on the first deck and a giant cabin for passengers on the second. In addition to the passenger cabin, there were covered decks around the periphery of each boat affording passengers both fresh air and spectacular views of the city and the harbor.

As the ferry's engines shuddered into life and the boat's propeller began to push it out of the slip, into the waters of New York Harbor there grew behind it the most beautiful sight Hugh thought he would ever see: Lower Manhattan's skyline. Thousands of bright, twinkling lights in hundreds of windows in buildings so tall the tops of some were lost in the clouds overhead. "Skyscrapers" he had heard them called and now he knew why. As if to make this extraordinary view even more wondrous, a light snow began falling. Little flakes, swirling in a gentle wind, translucent in the city's glow. Off to the west he could see the Statue of Liberty. Her lighted torch held high above her head. The torch made him think of the candle his mother always put on his birthday cake. While she was alive she always made his birthday special. She always baked a cake for him. In his mind he could hear her voice, "Happy Birthday Hugh darlin'..." She always wished him "Happy Birthday" when he awoke on New Year's Day.

"Ma, I wish you could see this..." he whispered softly as the spectacle of New York's skyline grew even more magnificent until, as the boat moved on through the dark water of New York Harbor, the lights began to slowly fade behind the deepening curtain of falling snow.

10.

SHINE? SHINE? Fi-cent. Shine." Oblivious to the falling snow that was beginning to collect on the shoulders of other passengers who, like Hugh, had been standing along the railing marveling at the view, a bootblack wearing a heavy black shirt, black trousers and a black cap, was slowly approaching. "Shine? Shine?"

"No," Hugh told the man. "But I'd be obliged if you could tell me how I get to a place called Stapleton."

The shoe shine man's heavy Italian accent made his instructions difficult to follow but Hugh understood the boat would dock in a place called Saint George and Stapleton, only a few miles away, could be reached by both Railroad and Trolley.

Having no real idea where Angelo's was located, Hugh decided the trolley running along Bay Street, Stapleton's main thoroughfare, would offer him the best opportunity to look for the restaurant, or Mother's, or something else he might recognize.

During the few moments it had taken him to make his way through the Ferry Terminal and find the trolley station, the snow that had begun falling lightly as the boat made it's way across New York Harbor, proved it had serious intentions. By ten o'clock, when Hugh finally reached Stapleton, an inch or more of the fine, fast falling, wind blown flakes had accumulated on the ground and it seemed likely a good many more could be expected. Stepping down off the trolley, he began to make his way up and down holiday deserted, poorly lighted streets running from Bay Street north to shoreline hugging Front Street. Most of Stapleton's businesses, closed because of the holiday, were to be found between those two roads.

The street lighting that impressed him so much in New York City had been electric, here in Stapleton, except for a few main intersections, the lights were still gas. Not bright at best, the increasing volume of falling snow reduced their light to little more than a warm glow which barely lighted the snow covered sidewalks.

After nearly an hour Hugh decided his memory of that night almost two years ago was not as accurate as he had thought. He could find no house that looked like Mother's and although there were closed saloons in every block, none he could find was named Angelo's. For all he knew Angelo's might have gone out of business or, for that matter, Angelo's might not have been the name at all. Right name or wrong, closed or open, the snow was falling so heavily now that it made walking difficult and, hunched down in his heavy pea coat, covered in white, Hugh was too cold and too tired to go on. A block or two back he had passed an unfinished building. That, he decided, would provide a place to spend the night. Tomorrow would be time enough to find Angelo's and the whorehouse called Mother's.

As he approached the building, light reflected off the falling snow allowed him to see a large canvas covering some bricks near the front entrance. "I have need for you," Hugh said out loud as he pulled the canvas loose. Locating a corner inside the building where the snow was not likely to reach, he rolled himself in the canvas and chuckled, "Not the best bed you ever had, nor the worst. Happy birthday Hugh."

11.

SIX HOURS LATER, something awakened him. He pushed the half frozen canvas away from his face and listened... Footsteps outside. Then a man's voice, "Where's me tar-po-lin?"

"I put it over them bricks like you told me," a boy's voice answered.

The two were startled when Hugh suddenly appeared in the doorway holding out the missing square of canvas. "I borrowed it for the night."

"And who said you could do that," the man growled. Then, looking at the size of the fellow approaching him quickly added, "Not that I suppose it done any great harm. Spent the night in there did ya?"

"I did that." Hugh agreed as he shook the few bits of snow that had found their way back to his sheltered corner off the tarpaulin and carefully folded it. "Where will I put it then?"

"Give it to the boy."

"You'll be the brick mason?" Hugh asked the man as he handed the folded canvas to the youngster.

"I am that," the man agreed.

"And the boy here, he's you're assistant?"

"My hod carrier," the mason corrected him.

"And a fine looking lad he is." Hugh smiled at the boy he took to be maybe seven or eight years old. "But I doubt he can carry that many bricks. Why don't you get rid-a him and take me on in his place?"

"Ha. You're a nervy bastard I'll say that," the mason chuckled. "No, I'll not be getin' rid a me son even if you're Samson himself. And lookin' at the size-a ya, you might well be."

Hugh grinned back at the mason then reached out and put his hand on the boy's shoulder. "Well, looks like you've no fear-a losin' yer job then. You're a lucky lad to work wit-chur pa. I did that once..."

A picture of himself riding on his father's shoulders from the street corner where he waited for him and his brothers to come home from the mine each evening came into his mind. Of course that was before he turned six. Before he started to work in the mine with them. After that he was too grown up to ride on his shoulders. He doubted this youngster rode around on his father's shoulders anymore either. It wasn't something you did once you were most grown and working a job.

"I'm the lucky one," the mason told him. "Lucky to have so fine a boy." Then, turning to the youngster, he added, "Now then son-a-mine, if you don't know it, the holiday's over so mix up some-a that mortar and just maybe we'll get a bit of work done here before the day's all gone."

"I will pa."

Hugh watched the boy head for the mortar trough. "Well, if you don't need my help do ya know if there's someone else around here who might?"

"A job is it yer lookin' fer"

Hugh nodded yes.

"Go up ta Bay Street there," the mason pointed. "Turn left, go a few blocks around a bend and you'll see a big job they're diggin'. The foreman has a shapeup every mornin' at six-thirty fer men with strong backs what's good with a shovel. Could-ya handle that?"

"Maybe not so good as I could handle yer bricks," Hugh laughed as he started off in the direction the man had indicated. "But I'll give it a try, and I thank ya."

"Don't dilly-dally," the mason called after him. "The foreman gets there right on time. If yer not there waitin' he'll not even look at chu." Hugh waved back at the man and picked up his pace.

12.

IT WAS STILL NOT FULL DAYLIGHT, but even at that early hour Bay Street was already snarled with traffic. Horses as well as motorcars were having trouble with their traction because of last night's snow and the low temperature that was preventing it from thawing. The resulting traffic jam slowed things enough for Hugh to reach the job site and join a group of waiting men long before the foreman stepped down off a trolley car and walked carefully across the icy street towards them.

"Good mornin' boys, let's see how many we got here today?" Making a quick count he continued, "I make it an even dozen and I'm thinkin' I can use all-a you. The ground'll be half froze so we'll need two picks ta each shovel."

Producing a large key ring from under the overcoat he had bundled around him, the foreman walked to a shed standing along side a wood ramp leading down into the growing excavation. "Lineup now, single file." He looked towards Hugh and another man also new to the job. "If you two don't know it already, the pay's two dollar a day. If you do a good job you get paid tonight when you turn in yer equipment."

One at a time, each man stepped to the shed door where the foreman handed him a tool. Pick, pick, shovel. Groups of three. Pick, pick, shovel. Hugh was the first man in his group. "You're new here but chu look big enough ta handle the job." The foreman told him. Then pointing with his jaw towards the man behind him said, "You work with Franco there, he'll show ya what to do."

"Aye aye, Cap'n." Taking the pick he was handed, Hugh nodded agreement then stepped aside to wait while Franco and the third man in their team were handed tools.

"Me an' you use-a da picks." Franco told him in an accent that was the equal of the bootblack's on the ferryboat. "Benito shovel-a dirt inta da cart." With no further instructions the big Italian led them down the ramp to a place along what would eventually be the north wall of the basement, spat on his hands, hefted the pick he was holding and began cutting away the frozen earth.

Pick and shovel work is hard, as hard and physical as work can get. Those who do this work take fierce pride in their strength and their endurance, a pride that makes every job a competition, a test to see who is the strongest. Hugh knew the game. It was the same game he had played in the mine and the engine room nearly every day for more than half his life. The two Italians were big and strong, but Hugh was bigger and stronger. They were tough, but Hugh was tougher. After an hour of steady work, it was Benito who said something to Franco who then turned to Hugh and announced, "Time-a to dump."

"Okay," Hugh replied. Looking into the cart Benito had been filling he knew it could take several more shovels full, but he also knew this break was the Italians way of surrendering. He had won the game.

Once a cart was filled, the three-man team had to push it up the ramp and onto a platform alongside waiting wagons into which they dumped their load. The empty cart was then rolled down the other end of the ramp, past a water barrel where they could stop for a drink and a brief rest before completing a circle which took them back into the growing excavation. Other than for a few words exchanged at the water, barrel, the men had little time or inclination to talk with each other.

In Stapleton, as in most factory towns, whistles announce the noon hour each day when workmen lay down their tools to eat their dinners. The aroma coming from Franco's dinner pail made Hugh realize he had not eaten since leaving O'Riley's Bar yesterday afternoon.

"Where's-a you food?" Franco asked as he bit into a huge sandwich.

"I didn't bring any," Hugh answered in surprise. These were the first words he had heard from the man since his, "Time to dump," announcement several hours ago.

"Here." Taking a second sandwich from his pail, Franco handed it to Hugh.

"No. I can't take yer food."

"You no eat you no work good. We slow down." Franco nodded towards the foreman, "He don't pick us no more."

Hugh looked at the food then into the eyes of the man offering it. "All right. And thank you. I'll pay you back."

Franco's only reply was a nod and a grunt as he bit into his sandwich.

Twenty minutes later the foreman blew his own whistle and the men returned to work.

13.

DARKNESS HAD RETURNED by five o'clock that evening when Stapleton's factory whistles again sounded. The end of another day. Up the ramp once more. Time for pay, time to go home, time to rest.

Lantern light at the tool shed. Picks and shovels returned to their proper places in the racks. Foreman watching, handing out pay as tools are returned. Two dollars tucked carefully into trouser pockets.

"Thank you boss. Can you use me tomorrow?"

"We'll see... we'll see. I'll know in the morning. Be here."

As he pays off the last man in line he realizes there is an open slot in the rack. A pick is missing. Tools are the foreman's responsibility and stealing is a constant problem. He is certain no one was carrying a pick when he left. It must be hidden somewhere in the hole where the thief can find it later tonight. It's already full dark. His wife will have dinner waiting but there's no help for it. Finding a missing pick will not be easy in the dark but he must find it, or pay for it. Such is the life of a foreman.

Picking up the ax handle he keeps for protection, he locks the racks, takes the lantern, closes the shed and goes looking....

As he starts down the ramp he hears a noise, the sound of a pick slamming into frozen ground. Someone is still working in the hole and that could mean trouble. He has the ax handle ready for trouble. Half way down the ramp the beam from his lantern reveals a man working on the far side of the dig.

"Hey you!" He calls. "What-a you think yer doin'?"

The man stops work and turns towards him.

"A little somethin' extra Cap'n. I thought maybe it would help ya-ta remember me in the mornin'."

"I'll be damned." The foreman loosens his grip on the ax handle. "What's yer name then?"

"Hugh."

"All right Hugh, I'll remember you. Now come turn in that pick and collect yer pay. I got to get home fer me dinner."

"I'd like to make you a deal," Hugh says as he reaches the tool shed.

The foreman again tightens his grip. "And just what kind of a deal would that be?"

"That bit of canvas I seen in the shed there."

Hugh angels his head towards a folded tarpaulin lying at the end of the tool rack. "I'd like the use of it tonight. You can hold me pay 'till mornin' case I don't bring it back."

"And what will ya be wantin' it fer," the foreman asks.

"I'm planin' on sleepin' in the hole here tonight an I'm thinkin' it's just the thing to help keep me warm."

Normally he is not a trusting person but there is something about this man the foreman likes. "All right Hugh, take yer pay and use the tarp. If ya don't bring it back in the mornin' I'll find you out and have the police on ya."

"It'll be here in the mornin' and so will I. One thing more," Hugh says almost as an afterthought.

"What would that be?'

"Can ya tell me if there's a place around here called Angelo's?"

"Angelo's is it?" The foreman's reply is almost a laugh. "Sure that's where all them sailors and dock fellas hang out." Nodding his head to indicated the direction he adds, "Go down Bay Street here fer four er five blocks to Beach Road, then ya turn left towards the harbor. Angelo's 'll be on yer left side almost all the way down ta Front Street. But chu be careful there, it's a bad neighborhood and a tough lot what goes ta that place."

Taking the canvas Hugh replies, "I'll watch out fer meself and thanks to ya. See you in the mornin'."

With his boots making crunching sounds in the frozen snow as he walks, Hugh arrives at Beach Road. At the corner a small grocery store is still open for business and he can see women with scarves over their heads standing in front of counters placing their orders. Next to the grocery store there is a small butcher shop with its share of customers as well and beyond that, a clothing store. Opposite the shops, on the other side of Beach Road, Hugh can see four houses with lights in their windows. For the next several hundred feet, on both side of the road, there is open land. Then, on his side of the road, he sees a sign illuminated by an electric light: "Angelo's."

Electric lights, especially outdoor electric lights are still a rarity on Staten Island, however Hugh's interest is not in the light nor in the restaurant beneath the sign, but in the single house across the street. A large, two-story, tan stucco house with a wooden railing around its wide front porch; the house he remembers as "Mother's."

Pulling the borrowed canvas off his shoulders, he tucked it under his arm, took the four steps up to the front porch in one stride and reached for the bell knob. A moment later the heavy front door swung open.

"Good ev'nin sir."

Hugh looked down at the small black boy smiling up at him. "Who are you?"

"I is Liddle Alvin, sir. Can I heps ya?"

Getting over his surprise, Hugh returned the youngster's smile, "Hello Alvin. I'm Hugh. Is this still "mother's" place?"

"Oh yas sir Mista Hugh, it surely is." Pulling the door further open, Alvin continued, "Please to come in and wait in de parlor. Miz Donna be wid ya directly."

"Thanks Alvin."

Donna Marie Prudenti, otherwise known as "mother" joined him less than a minute later but her news was not to his liking. "Mary Kate's not here tonight but I know you'll find somebody else..." As she spoke, Mother crossed the parlor to open a pair of sliding doors at the rear of the room behind which, in the back parlor, three scantily dressed young women were waiting.

"This is Maria, Angela and Tina." As Mother spoke the girl's names each nodded, smiled, and made a provocative gesture of one sort or another.

"Very nice," Hugh told Mother as he looked at the women. "But 'tis Mary Kate I wanted ta see. When will she be back?"

"I don't know that," Mother's voice sounded sad. "She's away on personal business." Then, brightening she added, "But I can see Tina already has eyes for you. Why don't chu get acquainted with her." As Mother spoke, the girl named Tina moved towards Hugh. Pressing her body against his, she reached up to tousle his hair. A feat she could accomplish only by standing on her tiptoes.

"No, no thank you." Blushing slightly, Hugh put his hands on the girl's shoulders and gently pushed her away. "I'll come again one day when Mary Kate's here." Turning to leave, Hugh was well aware Tina's attentions had not left him unaffected. He was glad for the pea jacket that hid the bulge in his trousers.

"Good night Mista Hugh." Mother heard Little Alvin tell him.

"Good night and thanks ta-ya Alvin," she heard him reply, then, after the youngster closed the front door and she could hear the man's footsteps crossing the front porch, she called to the boy.

"Alvin... What did you call that gentleman?"

"Mista Hugh, Miss Donna. Dats what he tole me."

14.

DURING THE FEW MINUTES Hugh had been inside "mother's," snow had begun falling again. It seemed to dampen all sound, or was it the roar in his ears that was causing his deafness? The door closing behind him seemed to have made no noise he could hear, nor did the motor of an automobile making it's slippery way down Beach Road.

Taking a deep breath he asked himself, "Have I come all this way just to see a whore I fucked a couple-a years ago? Is that the reason I've come all the way to America?" Shaking his head "no" in answer to his own questions, he crossed the street to Angelo's where the light from the sign above the entrance door lit his vaporizing breath and tantalizing but unfamiliar aromas made him realize how hungry he was.

Nothing about Angelo's seemed particularly familiar to him. The dark wooden bar running the full length of the left side of the large smoky room; the non- descript wooden tables and chairs scattered throughout were like every bar he visited in seaports on both sides of the Atlantic. .

Three electric lights mounted between the mirrors behind the bar and a dozen or so gas lights in the shape of ship's lanterns, mounted on the other three walls provided a minimum of light. The best thing about the place was that it was warm, almost too warm.

A waiter, a boy no more than thirteen or so, carrying a tray of food, approached him. "You gonna drink or you gonna eat?"

"Eat," Hugh grunted back.

"Take-a da table by da winda," the boy pointed with his elbow towards a table standing in front of a curtain covered window along the front wall, "I be wid chu in-a minute."

Hugh sat down on a chair facing into the room. The place was a good deal larger than he had first realized. Perhaps two dozen men were standing along the bar that easily could have accommodated twice that number, and of the twenty or so tables in the dining area, not more than half a dozen were currently in use. Not surprisingly perhaps, as far as Hugh could see, there were no women in the establishment.

True to his word the boy waiter returned almost immediately. "Special tonight is-a Osso Bucco. Wid it chu get-a soupa, pasta an-a some beans, coffee an-a pie. At's-a twenty cent. You wanna just pasta an-a sausage is a ten cent."

"Gim-me the pasta fer ten cents." Hugh told him. He was not at all sure what "pasta" was but wanting to save money and having spent a lifetime eating mostly potatoes, sometimes with bully beef, sometimes with fish, if he could eat something different for ten cents he would eat pasta whatever it was. Besides, he had no idea what Osso Bucco might be. "And bring me a beer," he added.

"Pasta an-a beer comin' up."

"Wait a minute," Hugh called after the boy as he started away. Pointing towards the slender, dark haired bartender Hugh asked, "Is that fella behind the bar there the owner, Angelo?"

"No. Dat's his son Tony. 'Ant-a-nee', the old man says we should call him." The boy angled his head upward toward the ceiling, "The old man's up-a stairs. He don't-a come down so much no more."

"Anthony." Hugh repeated the name. "All right then. Thanks to-ya."

Moments later the boy placed a huge bowl in front of him filled with what looked like slender yellowish colored worms covered in a thick red sauce. "You wanna parmesan?" the boy mumbled.

"Want what?"

"Cheese. You wanna cheese on-a you pasta?

"So dis is what you eye-talians call pasta, is it?"

"Yeah..." The boy was obviously surprised by Hugh's question. "Well, tonight it's-a linguini but it's all-a pasta. You never had it before?"

"No," Hugh admitted. "But it smells damn good."

"You gonna love it." The boy grinned as he pulled a grater and a chunk of cheese from his apron pocket, "But chu got to have-a da parmesan."

The first mouthful was so strange to his taste that he had trouble swallowing and quickly washed it down with a large gulp of beer. But something of the taste remained in his mouth and insisted he try another mouthful. The garlic caused a burning sensation in the back of his nose and made his eyes water much like mustard did when he first tasted it in the sandwiches his mother made for him to take to work. But this was somehow different. He did not know what he was tasting, but once over the surprise of the first mouthful, he wanted more.

He ate slowly, each mouthful tasting better. It had been a long time since his last restaurant meal and he was enjoying this one to the fullest. When his plate was nearly empty he realized he had forgotten his beer. He sat back, lifted the stein to his lips, took a long sip and wondered why he did not feel more satisfied with himself. He had done a lot in the past few days. He had gotten safely to America, found a job, and turned nineteen. But he had not found Mary Kate!

"No, I haven't found her yet," he told himself, "But I will."

Why is finding her so important, he wondered. After all, he had been with her for only one night. Not even that, he reminded himself. Most of the night he had been drinking or drunk. What was it that made it impossible for him to forget her? He didn't know, but he needed to find out.

She was still very much in his thoughts when he first noticed them. Three husky looking drunks with a "look out for us" attitude, turning away from the bar and striding into the dining area. Longshoremen most likely he decided. A veteran of more bar fights than he could remember, Hugh had a sixth sense for trouble.

He watched the three walking deliberately towards a table near the center of the room where two older men, sailors by the look of them, were eating their suppers. "Get up, we want our table," the obvious leader of the group growled.

"What-a-ya mean 'your table'?" the sailor with his back to Hugh answered. "It's first come first served here, boy-o. There's empty tables all 'round. If you want dis one you can have it when me an me pal finish our supper."

Without further discussion, the Longshoreman suddenly up-ended the table then knocked the startled sailor out of his chair. Before his companion could get to his feet the other two longshoremen grabbed his arms and threw him to the floor as well. Dazed the two men looked up at their attackers. It was obvious the two of them had no chance against the three younger men.

"A wise man knows when to fight and when not to," Hugh heard the man with his back to him say. With that the two got carefully to their feet and made their way towards the door to Beach Road. As they did, Anthony limped from behind the bar and into the dining area.

"Gentlemen, gentlemen, please..."

"Fuck you, Tony," the spokesman told him. "Get da kid ta clean up dat mess an get us some food." He pointed to an unoccupied table. "We gonna sit over there."

"Okay. Okay." Anthony forced a smile as he tried to calm the situation. "Food'll be right out."

Hugh watched an obviously discouraged Anthony Belinni slowly make his way back behind the bar. He had never been much for planning things very far ahead. For him things just seemed to happen and when they did he tried to make the best of them. Now, watching the three longshoremen demanding a drink "on the house," as the young waiter and a flagpole thin older man, Hugh took to be the cook, picked up the broken furniture and spilled food, an idea came to him. Easing himself out of his seat, he walked quietly to the end of the bar and waited until Anthony saw him and headed his way.

"Hi big-a fellah." Anthony looked up at him, "What'll ya have?"

Hugh was surprised by the man's calm attitude and seemingly genuine smile. "How come you let dem fellows get away wid that?"

Anthony Belinni normally controlled his anger very carefully, but Hugh's question cut deep and for just a flash his anger surfaced. "None a yer God-damn business."

"Whoa, whoa." Hugh raised both hands in make believe fright. "I'm not meanin' ya no offense."

As quickly as his anger had surfaced, Anthony's usual, self-effacing personality returned. Apologizing for his anger he offered Hugh a drink "on the house."

"You've a right ta be upset," Hugh told him ignoring the offer of a drink. "I'm just surprised ya don't make them pay fer the damage and chase dem out-a here instead-a treatin-em like royalty."

"Yeah, sure. The old cook, the kid'n, me wid my club foot, we just-a go tell them to pay up an-a get out!" He laughed bitterly. "Then, when they get through wid us, my father can-a look for a new bar tender an-a new cook an-a new waiter."

"Well maybe ya need a bit of help." Hugh put his hand on Anthony's arm. "Would ya like fer me to have a word wid-dem?"

"A word?" Anthony laughed again. "Just what word you gonna have wid dem?"

"Well, real polite like, I'll tell them to pay fer their suppers and drinks and the broken stuff, then I'll ask 'em to leave..."

"Oh yeah, yeah," Anthony's voice became sarcastic. "All tree-a dem. Why'nt you just-a go do-dat."

For an answer Hugh pointed to the pieces of broken chair the cook had put behind the bar. "Gim-me one-a dem chair legs an I'll take care-a it right away."

Not believing Hugh, but somehow frightened he might actually do something foolish, Anthony hesitated a moment before deciding to hand him the chair leg and call what he was sure was a bluff. "Aw-right wise guy. Here. Let's see ya do somethin'."

Walking casually between tables Hugh reached the longshoremen almost before they were aware of his approach. With all the speed his ring days had given him he swung the chair leg down over the head of the leader. As the man next to him started to rise, Hugh swung back toward him with a bone shattering backhand blow to his knee. Before the scream of pain could reach his second victim's lips, the third man found himself, chair and all, pushed over and pinned beneath Hugh's left foot, looking up at the chair leg club held threateningly just above his head.

"Now laddy," Hugh's voice was low, cold. "It's time ta pay yer bill and leave. What I want chu ta do is collect all the money you and your pals has got and give it to me, then you get yerself and them two bastards out-a here. Can ya understand that?"

"Yeah... yeah," the man's voice quivered as he looked towards his two mates. One doubled over clutching his leg, moaning in pain, the other, their leader, not moving nor making a sound.

"Is Charlie dead?"

"It's hard to tell and I don't much care," Hugh answered. "Now get the money from dem and get the fuck out-a here else I'll do it fer ya an I promise I'll not be gentle about it neither."

"Christ Almighty," Anthony Belinni moaned as he watched the uninjured longshoreman carry first one then the other of his companions out the door and deposit them on the snow covered sidewalk. "This'll start a war for sure," he said as Hugh handed the chair leg back to him. "We'll be ruined."

"Ruined you say?" Hugh laid nine dollars and thirty-seven cents on the bar in front of Anthony. "I'll take a dollar of this fer me trouble. The rest ought to cover yer damages and leave enough for a good tip to yer waiter there," he nodded towards the young boy, "And the cook too," he added. "Now tell me about how you'll be ruined."

"Those guys'll be back." Anthony's voice was one of defeat. "Probably bring some of their friends and they'll tear the place apart."

"Is that it then?" Hugh laughed. "Well Anthony, I'm Hugh Crawford and I think ya best hire me and me mate to watch over things around here."

The temperature had dropped far below freezing by the time Hugh left Angelo's and, even wrapped in his tarpaulin, the snow, pushed by what had become a howling wind, stung his hands and face and made footing treacherous. Ten minutes of fast but careful walking brought him to "the job" where he found the entire excavation now covered by four more inches of fresh white snow. Making his way carefully down the slipery ramp, he slid under the highest section of it and there, with it serving as a roof to shelter him, he wrapped himself in the borrowed canvas and prepared for sleep. He was pleased with the arrangement he had made for a room, food and three dollars a night to split with his partner. There was just one problem, the partner. Franco, the man he had worked with today, would make a good partner, but would the big Italian go for the idea? "Well, that's tomorrow's worry," he said softly to himself as he rolled over and went to sleep.

15.

WHAT WAS TO BECOME one of the heaviest snowfalls in Staten Island history had covered the excavation with another five inches before Hugh awoke. He had no idea how or why, but he had always been able to wake up at whatever time he needed to and this morning it was to be in the six-thirty shapeup. It took him only moments to wash his face with a handful of snow, then make his way up the ramp to where several shivering men with turned up collars and pulled down hats were already gathered. Hugh quickly determined that Franco was not among them.

"A damn fool time a year fer a buildin' ta start," someone complained.

"Yeah but ain't-chu glad fer it? Where else-a ya gonna find-a work?" another answered.

Three blocks away lightening like flashes of electricity arcing through the snow announced a trolley rounding the curve in Bay Street and heading towards them. "Here come-a da boss I bet," a thickly accented Italian voice told no one in particular.

Bay Street had been one of the first avenues on Staten Island to be "electrified" with an overhead cable which provided power to trolley cars equipped with a spring loaded mast that ran from the car's roof to the cable above. Bumps, swaying or sometimes even hard gusts of wind could and did momentarily break the contact, causing electrical flashes. In wet or snowy conditions the flashes tended to be bigger, brighter, of longer duration, and sometimes strong enough to kick the mast away from the cable. A situation which made life difficult for the brakeman who's job it then was to climb up onto the car's slippery roof and, frequently under a shower of sparks, struggle with a rope that allowed him to pull the mast down and swing it left or right until he could get it into position to re-make contact with the cable. Yes, electricity was a wondrous thing, but not all trolley men were pleased to see the horse drawn cars being slowly replaced.

Still no sign of Franco, Hugh thought as he looked up and down Bay Street for the third or fourth time. Concerned that Franco might not come today, he looked over the other waiting men. None of them near as big or strong as Franco. He had been counting on him being here and on being able to convince him to join him.

The trolley came to a stop just opposite the job site. Seconds later, as it pulled away, Hugh was relieved to see both The Boss and Franco starting to make their careful way across the icy street.

"I'm thinkin' we wont get a lot done in all this snow and ice," the foreman told them as he walked to the tool shed and unlocked the heavy wooden door. "Line up everybody, I'll be needin' all-a-ya today."

Stepping next to Franco, Hugh told him, "I was thinkin' maybe you wasn't gonna be here today."

"Why you worry? I'm-a here everyday," Franco answered. "What's it to you anyhow?"

"Well," Hugh smiled. "It's quite a lot ta me and I'm thinkin' maybe to you as well. Somethin' come up last night might interest ya." Hugh accepted a pick from the foreman before he continued, "I'll tell you about it when we have our dinner."

By mid morning the snow had become a full fledged blizzard making it difficult to see anything more than a few feet away. The weight of the snow, added to the problems of frozen earth and slippery footing, was making it nearly impossible for the men to push loaded carts up the ramp.

Finally, about ten-thirty, the foreman blew his whistle. "That's it fer today," he yelled. "You've all worked hard so even though 'tis only the middle-a the mornin' I'll pay ya a full half day."

In spite of loosing half the day's pay, the men were glad to be done and grateful to the foreman for being willing to pay them that much. Some, they knew, would have paid nothing for their morning's work.

"Ya want that tar-po-line again?" The foreman asked as he took Hugh's pick and gave him a dollar in return.

"No, I'll not be needin' it tonight." A grin warmed Hugh's face. "I've got me a place to stay now, but I thank ya fer the offer."

Stepping aside he waited for Franco to receive his pay before approaching him. "Franco. Will ya walk with me a bit and listen to what I've ta tell ya?"

With slow, deliberate action, Franco pulled a leather purse from his trouser pocket and pushed his dollar bill inside while his suspicious eyes searched Hugh's face. "Why for I wanna do dat?"

"Because I've a proposition you might be interested in hearin'," Hugh answered.

"Prop-a-gician?" Franco had trouble with the word. "What's-a dat mean?"

"It's about makin' some extra money. A job I think the two of us can do." Hugh let just a bit of irritation creep into his voice. "You wanna hear about it or don't cha?"

"I wanna hear." Franco replied.

"Okay, then come walk wid me." Hugh turned and started down Bay Street.

"You look like a fella what can take care-a his self in a fight," Hugh said as Franco caught up. Surprised by the remark, Franco squared his body towards Hugh and moved his arms forward, ready for an attack. "It-sa fight you look-a for?"

"Don't be daft, man." Hugh laughed and began walking faster. "I'd beat the crap out-a ya in no time. But there's this here Eye-talian saloon down on Beach Road where you could maybe find a bit of a scrap if that's what yer wantin'. Angelo's, ya know the place?"

Franco nodded, "Yeah. I been dere."

"Good. Well, they're havin' some trouble wid-da gobs and da grunts..."

Franco frowned, "What-sa-da god? What-sa da grump?"

"Ah, no. It's not 'god' ner 'grump,' it's 'gobs' and 'grunts'," Hugh explained carefully. "Gobs and Grunts. That's what we call sailors and dem stevedore fellows what work on the docks. They're all-a time fightin' and breakin' up things at Angelo's, so you'n me is gonna be wardens and stop all that trouble and save a lot of money fer Anthony and he's gonna' give us three dollars a night, supper, breakfast and a place ta sleep in the pantry behind the kitchen."

Hugh stopped to look directly into Franco's eyes. "So "what-a-ya think?""

"It's-a no for me," Franco answered, then turned and started back towards the job site.

"Hey. Wait a minute," Hugh called after him. "Why fer Chris-sake not? It's a dollar and a half a night fer ya!"

"I work-a for da boss an after da job I go home wid my wife an-a my bambinos is why."

"Oh. Yer married are ya." Hugh's voice revealed his disappointment. "I hadn't thought-a that. Let me think on this a minute."

Franco and Rosa were a storybook romance. Both were six years old when they first met on Ellis Island where, together with their families, in 1895 they had waited three days for entry into America. Both families went to Staten Island where Rosa's uncle Pietro had already established himself. Together they found places to live in the same apartment building on Vanduzen Street, in Stapleton.

Rosa and Franco were quickly enrolled in the neighborhood school where he remained until finishing third grade when, at age ten, he joined his father working in a black smith shop operated by the Staten Island Transit Authority. Rosa stayed in the school until 6th Grade before she started doing housework with her mother for well to do families in St. George.

From the time Rosa and Franco first met, until they married at age nineteen, neither had ever looked at another person. Since their wedding, they had been totally devoted to each other and to their two children... Franco Junior and Pietro, named after Rosa's uncle.

Franco looked at the man standing in front of him. He was a good deal younger; three, maybe four inches taller but near enough to the same weight, he judged. "You tink you can-a beat me?" he asked unexpectedly.

"Oh hell yes, with one hand," Hugh smiled. "Listen, fer two years I been heavy weight champion of the whole fuckin' British Navy. And I tell ya, I had ta beat some mean bastards too. But you're near strong as me and what chu don't probably know about scrapin' I can learn ya."

For a moment Hugh was not sure if he would have to prove his statement as the Italian looked hard at him before breaking into the first smile Hugh had seen on his face. "I tell-a you this, you got-a big-a-da, big-a-da balls. But I'm-a no interest."
"Well, a wife and kids are a problem, I can see that."

Hugh put an arm around Franco's shoulders to urge him to continue their walk along Bay Street.

"Look," he said after a few more steps, "The most likely trouble is gonna be tonight. I had-a rough up three-a dem grunts last night. Like as not them an their pals 'll be back looking ta get even. That's when I might need help. Come wid me tonight an I pay you two dollas. Can ya miss a little sleep 'n supper with yer family fer an extra two dollars tonight?"

Franco thought a moment then began to nod his head. "Yeah, I can-a do dat. When-a ya wanna start?"

"Six o'clock tonight. An' bein' as how there's no more work here today, you can go home now and have yer supper with yer wife and the kids first.

"Okay." Franco agreed, "Six o'clock, I see you."

"That's settled then." Hugh clapped his new partner on the back. "Now, I'm gonna give you yer first lesson."

Franco cocked his head suspiciously. "Yeah? What?"

"Don't never let nobody yer not sure of put an arm round yer shoulders like I been doin'. If I was wantin' ta, I could grab you by da throat, like this," Hugh put his hand gently around Franco's

Adam's apple. "And when you reach fer me hand, like yer doin' now, you're openin' yerself up fer a bloody awful blow ta yer kidney."

By evening, what was now officially being termed a "blizzard," had brought traffic throughout all of Staten Island to a standstill. Anyone who had anywhere to go went on foot.

As six o'clock neared Hugh wondered if Franco would be able to get there. "A bloody fuckin' mess," he muttered as he pulled on his pea coat and stepped out into the storm. Flailing his arms and stamping his feet as the snow hit him, he looked up the street. He could see almost nothing beyond the glow from the electric light above the sign overhead. Then, slowly, he became aware of a figure moving toward him.

"How come you stand out-a here?" Franco asked as he came into view.

"I was lookin' fer you." Hugh grinned and started to again put his arm over Franco's shoulder. He was satisfied to see him turn instantly out of his grip. "Well, you learned that," Hugh chuckled. "Come on, let's get out of this fucking snow."

Once inside, Hugh explained his plan. Franco was to sit at the table next to the entrance door with Hugh's chair leg club close at hand. Hugh would position himself at the near end of the bar.

Then, as patrons arrived he would walk to the doorway to greet them... and look them over. It was nearing nine o'clock when Hugh's prediction proved to be correct as Charlie and his stevedore buddies returned.

16.

THE ENTRANCE DOOR TO ANGELO'S opened outward and was really only wide enough for one person at a time to enter comfortably. By squeezing, two could make it through side by side if a third held the door open. It was in this way two angry looking men suddenly appeared a few minutes after nine o'clock.

Nodding to Franco, who was seated at the table, Hugh quickly headed towards them. Taller than either of the two, he could see Charlie - his head swathed in bandages - standing behind them, holding the door. Behind Charlie, there were several more angry looking men seemingly anxious to enter.

"That's the bastard," Charlie shouted. "Get da prick!"

Having recognized the trouble coming, Hugh did not slow his approach. Instead, as the man to his left raised his arm with an iron pinch bar in his grip, Hugh grabbed him around the neck and pulled him close enough to effectively prevent him from striking with the pinch bar. Tightening the headlock, he slammed a fist into the man's stomach then, holding him, and leaning his weight against him, he kicked the second man in the groin. As that man double in pain, Hugh slammed an open hand chop to the back of his neck rendering him momentarily unconscious.

Turning his attention back to the first would be attacker, who was struggling to get loose from the headlock that was incapacitating him, Hugh used the same open hand chop technique to the area just above his kidney.

All this took place so quickly none of Charlie's other companions had started to squeeze through the door. By the time they began to realize what was happening, Franco arrived in front of them holding Hugh's second victim who was bent double, vomiting, and holding his aching testicles. Throwing that man into those trying to enter, Franco grabbed Charlie on either side of his bandaged head and twisted it towards his stunned partners. "Tell-a dem ta back off or I crush-a you God-damn skull."

"Aw-right. Aw-right!" Feeling extreme pain from Franco's grip, Charlie screamed at his men, "Quit. We quit."

Holding the pinch bar in his right hand and dragging the semi conscious body of the first man with his left, Hugh joined Franco on the sidewalk in front of Angelo's. "Charlie lad," Hugh's voice was low... threatening... "I want you should listen careful to me."

Franco twisted the longshoreman's head back towards Hugh. "He's-a listen."

"Yes, I do think he is." Hugh jammed the pinch bar into the pit of Charlie's stomach. "But is he payin' attention is what I want ta know."

"Yes!" Charlie screamed again from the double pain of Hugh's jab and Franco's increased pressure to the sides of his damaged head. "I'm listenin', I'm listenin'."

"All right boy-o. Hear what I'm tellin' ya then."

Without taking his eyes off the others, punctuating his words with prods from the iron bar, Hugh leaned closer to the man. "If you, er any-a these other lads what ya brung wit-chu, show up in this bar or even on this bloody street again, me an Franco here'll kill you. Understand? I mean kill you fuckin' dead!"

Hugh leaned closer to Charlie and pushed the end of the pinch bar into the soft flesh above his Adam's apple, forcing his head up and back. "Am I makin' meself clear, Charlie?"

"Yes... yes."

"Alright then." Raising his voice now so all could hear, Hugh continued, "I'm givin' ya about thirty seconds fer you an your pals to get clear-a here before I start showing all a you just what this here now pinch bar can really do!"

Three hours later, midnight, Angelo's had to close. A "blue law" had been passed in New York City required all bars and restaurants to stop serving alcoholic beverages from midnight Saturday until 9AM Monday morning.

Yawning, Hugh walked with Franco to the door where they shook hands as Hugh paid him the two dollars he had promised. "Thank you Franco. I'm sure glad you was here wid me, and thanks to that new law what gives us Sunday off.

"Yeah," Matching Hugh's yawn with one of his own, Franco folded the bills and pushed them into his pocket before adding, "Ya know Hugh, I tink we pretty good team."

"That we are." Hugh put his hand on his friends shoulder and gripped it firmly, "That we are."

"Yeah. So maybe we should-a try-n stick-a together. What-a ya think?"

"I think it's a hell of an idea

On Sunday the weather began to clear and by Monday morning a bright sunshine was warming the job site. When the noon whistles sounded, Hugh and Franco headed for the tool shed where The Boss ate his dinner. Work was again going well and The Boss, seated comfortably on a toolbox, was in a particularly good mood.

"Boss, can we talk wit-chu?"

"Sure. Bring yer dinner pails 'n eat wid me if you want."

"No, no. We wont be botherin' ya that long," Hugh assured him. "It's just a question we got fer ya."

"Sure-n I'm all-ears."

"Well," Hugh squatted down so that he was on a level with The Boss. "Me an Franco here think we're pretty good workers..."

A trace of suspicion crept into The Boss' voice, "You are that."

"Right. Well, me 'n Franco's got ourselves a night time job that pays us good only it keeps us up fearful late. So we was wondering if we could work half a day fer you. We could start right after noon and probably do as much as the rest-a them do in a full day anyhow."

"If ya got such a good job how come ya wanna work fer me at all?"

"Two reasons," Hugh answered. "First, we need to make as much money as we can and we like workin' fer ya. And second, we need to keep our muscles in shape."

"I make that three reasons but no mind..."

The Boss chuckled. "How come yer thinkin' about yer muscles?"

"Aw well, it's this job we got now, keepin' order down to Angelo's. A lot of toughs come in there, so we got-a keep strong an' nothin' makes muscle as good as shovelin'."

"Sure and there's truth to that," Boss agreed. "And just what did-ya think I would pay you fer this half a day you're proposin'?"

Hugh was surprised at the question. "Well, seems ta me half pay fer a half day. A dollar each."

The Boss took a large bite of his sandwich and chewed carefully before answering. "I was thinkin' more like seventy-five cents."

"Why ya think-a that?" Franco's surprise was genuine as he spoke up for the first time..

"I'll be setting a precedent Franco," The Boss answered easily. "Pretty soon every one a dem fellows'll be wantin' ta work half days and I'll be gettin' nowheres with the job."

The Boss shook his head from side to side. "No, if I'm gonna start somethin' like this, I've got to have a financial incentive. Seventy-five cents."

Hugh shook his head, "No. Ain't fair. Me an Franco 'll find another place to keep our muscle." "Jesus, Yer a hard man, Hugh," The Boss sighed. "But I guess I'll have to go along wid chu then. I don't wana lose the two-a you. A dollar it is."

"One thing more." Hugh knew when to push an advantage.

"And just what'll that be?" Resigned, The Boss took another bite of his sandwich while he awaited Hugh's demand.

"At quitin' time one-a us'll bring our tools and collect fer the both-a us. That way the other one can get ta Angelo's quicker."

17.

WORD OF THE "FRIDAY NIGHT WAR", as it was being called, spread quickly throughout Stapleton. Not unexpectedly, the next few days brought to Angelo's several bullyboy types, looking to prove their manhood. Each, in turn, learned that such attempts could be dangerous to one's health and each incident only served to enhance the reputation of "Angelo's boys," as Hugh and Franco were becoming known throughout the neighborhood. But it wasn't until ten days later that Hugh began to realize just how much of a reputation he and Franco had acquired.

As he arrived for work one evening, Anthony called him over to the bar and introduced him to a man named Joe Nuzellese.

"Joe own-a da bakery down ta the corner-a Front Street," Anthony explained. "He want-a ask-a you somethin'."

"Hello Mr. Nuzellese..." The man seemed nervous as Hugh reached out to shake his hand.

"Can I do somethin' fer ya?"

"I been-a talk ta Tony about dose fellas you been dealin' wid…"

"Charlie Carlyle and his pals yer talkin' about?"

"Yeah…" The man hesitated. "Da ting is, some of dem come inta my place on da way ta work in da mornin'. Dey swipe a few rolls, or a loaf-a bread. I tell-a da cops, dey don't do nothin' then I get a brick through my winda…. I don-know what to do. So I talk-a to Tony about how he got-a no more trouble and he say maybe you could-a look in-ta my place a couple-a times. Dey think you look out-a fer me, dat scare dem off."

"I tell-a Joe you don-a get up so early, but maybe a couple-a mornin's you could walk down-a dere," Tony explained. "Dey see you talk-a wid Joe, maybe dey go someplace else."

"Yeah?" Hugh nodded his head up and down thoughtfully. "Maybe I could do somethin' like that."

"Tony say pay you a dollar…"

"A dollar seems a lot fer what we're talkin' about Joe. Maybe fifty cents a couple-a mornings, and we see how things go."

A little after five-thirty the next morning, Hugh waited at the corner of Beach Road and Front Street until he saw three men cross Front

Street and enter Nuzellese's Bakery. He recognized one of them as the man he had kicked in the groin. The man still walked with a slight limp to remind him of the experience.

Moments after the men entered the bakery, Hugh arrived as one of them was trying to engage Nuzellese in conversation while the other two slipped several rolls into their pockets.

Hugh made his presence known with a loud, "Good Mornin' to ya, Joe."

With a smile of relief, Nuzellese waved, "Mornin' Hugh. I'll get chu some coffee..."

"No hurry, Joe. These fellas probably wanna pay you fer the rolls and things so they can get ta work."

Several quick back and forth glances between the three was followed by the fellow who had been trying to talk to Nuzellese taking some money from his pocket and handing it to him. "Yeah, here, three rolls..."

They turned to leave.

Hugh was blocking the door.

Looking hard at the man with the limp, he said slowly, in a low voice. "You're awful close to Beach Road, boy-o. An you know what's gonna happen to ya if every I find you there, don't chu."

"Yeah... yeah, I know. I ain't goin' there." The terrified man looked quickly to his companions, "Come on, we be late to work."

"I'm not that sure I like seein' ya bother me friend Joe here neither," Hugh added before he stepped aside to let them pass.

"Yeah... Right," one of them muttered as they made their way around him and out onto the street.

18.

OVER THE NEXT FEW WEEKS it became apparent to old Angelo there were definite changes in his business as well as the entire neighborhood. Four more businesses along Front Street were now happily paying Hugh a dollar a week to "visit" them from time to time, with the result that everyone's business in the area seemed to be getting better and better. In his restaurant, bar and food receipts were growing, expenses for breakage were dropping and the number of unpaid bills had fallen to almost zero. And there had been subtle but definite changes in his clientele as well.

Stapleton's population was predominately Italian, but many Irish lived there as well. For reasons Angelo never understood, particularly on St. Patrick's Day, the Irish and the Italians, like oil and water, did not mix. Instead they fought. Three years ago, on the last St. Patty's day Angelo's had been open, the fighting resulted in damages that kept the place closed for five days and cost nearly one hundred dollars for repairs. But now, with the example of a Welshman, who many thought to be Irish, and his Italian partner keeping order in the place, customers were beginning to find the common ground of friendship far more enjoyable than the frequent black eyes and busted heads of the past. As a result, as St. Patrick's Day drew near, Angelo decided they would once again open for St. Patty's Day.

After ten consecutive days of warm sunshine, St. Patty's day arrived cold and rainy. "Not a great day fer the parade," Hugh said to no one in particular as he arrived at the job. Men who worked on jobs such as The Boss's did not go to St. Patrick's Day Parades, they worked!

"Yeah. 'Sa crappie day," Franco grumbled as he joined Hugh at the tool shed. This was the third excavation they had worked on for The Boss since starting their half-day schedule.

"Not fit fer man ner beast," Hugh added with no premonition of what the day was yet to bring.

Although the cold rain had not abated, Hugh's afternoon suddenly brightened an hour later as he and Franco pushed their first loaded cart along the platform to a waiting wagon. "Hey Hugh," a voice called. Hugh looked down to see where it came from.

"It's me, Jeff... Jeff Flannigan..." A slender, sandy haired young drover they scarcely knew, seated on the wagon they were about to dump into, waived to them. Hugh and Franco up ended their cart and the noise covered whatever else Jeff Flannagan had to say.

Once the cart was empty and the noise had stopped, the young drover called again, "Hugh, can I have a word wit-chu?"

"What's on yer mind, Flannagan?"

"Hugh, I've got me a big date fer tonight 'n I'm wantin' to make it special like. I was wonderin', workin' two jobs like ya do, if maybe ya could spare me the loan of a couple-a bucks. I'd pay ya back end-a-da week."

Mistaking Hugh's thoughtful silence for a potential rejection, Flannagan quickly added, "I'll pay ya back three fer two on Saturday, just like the barber gets."

"The barber? That fellow what cuts hair?" Hugh was not sure of Flannagan's meaning. "Ya borrow from him and pay three dollars fer two?"

"Yeah. That's the goin rate, Hugh."

Hugh thought for a second, then told him, "Tell you what I'll do, I'll loan ya the two dollars and you'll pay me back two dollars and fifty cents on Saturday. How'll that suit chu?"

Two thoughts flashed quickly through Jeff

Flannagan's mind: Somethin's fishy, and don't look a gift horse in the mouth. "Why would chu do that Hugh?"

"Because yer goin-ta tell all yer friends that I'll loan 'em money fer a better rate 'n that other fellow does, is why."

Hugh reached into his trouser pocket and pulled out a handful of coins. Carefully selecting two silver dollars, he put them in the man's outstretched hand. "But Flannagan, you'll tell 'em if-n I don't get me money back on Saturday, I'll bust 'em up real good. And that goes fer you as well."

19.

SHORTLY AFTER ST. PATRICK'S DAY, 1919, completing its fifth voyage as a troop transport, the one time luxury liner S.S. Sea Shark arrived at the Brooklyn Navy Yard with a "cargo" of nearly seven hundred returning soldiers. Walter Sinchak and four companions who had served with him were among them.

When the ship arrived, Walter and his buddies were among the last to disembark because they were engaged in a poker game which, when it finally broke up, had netted them thirty-eight dollars and forty-five cents. That, added to the money they had collectively won over the past nine days of almost continuous play, brought their total winnings for the crossing to nearly six hundred dollars. "Not bad," Walter said to his buddies as their lieutenant told them it was time to pack up and leave the ship.

Walter Sinchak had been born on the 4th of July, 1896, at his father's pig farm in Secaucus,

New Jersey. As he grew up his mother always insisted, "The reason Walter is so independent is because he was born on Independence Day." Perhaps because of his independent spirit, Walter had long ago decided that when the war was over he would have nothing more to do with pig farming.

Not that growing up on the pig farm had been all bad. Because of it, he served in the army as a butcher and never got closer to the fighting than a cook tent several hundred yards behind the front lines. Walter was a good butcher, but he'd had enough of butchering and pigs and anything to do with farming. During the twenty months he spent in Europe he had discovered other things he was good at. Things like handling details and dealing with other men, as his promotions to the rank of Tech Sergeant testified. Even more important, in Walter's mind, was the discovery of two unsuspected talents upon which he intended to build his civilian career... First, he was a superb card player with an innate sense of how to tip the odds in his favor. And second, he had an uncanny ability to procure women for himself and others to fuck.

No one would consider Walter handsome. In truth, he was a very plain looking man with a rather large nose and thinning black hair. Other than these, he had almost no distinguishing features except for a deep, resonant voice, yet women seemed drawn to him. Especially in war ravaged French towns where they would do almost anything for a bit of food, and food was Walter Sinchak's world. Food enough to satisfy all the lust Walter could summon as well as that of anyone who would pay him two dollars for the temporary companionship of one of "Walter's Pussies." A fee he waived from time to time for his companions, Boris, Harry, George and Johnny Hayes.

Most of the arriving soldiers striding down Sea Shark's gangplank were greeted by joyful, excited, cheering family members, but only one person awaited Walter, his younger brother and only living relative, Stanley.

Shortly after Walter had shipped off to the war in France, their father had fallen in a pig enclosure and been stamped to death by the frightened animals. Since his death, eighteen-year-old Stanley had done his best to run the farm as their bereaved mother directed. Then, three days after the signing of the armistice, she had succumbed to influenza. Following her death, while awaiting his brother's return, Stanley had tried to continue the normal daily routine she had established.

"Go home and sell the fuckin' place!" were almost the only words Walter spoke to his brother before climbing into a wagon that would take him, his pals and twenty of their companions to Brooklyn's nearby Fort Hamilton to await their discharges.

20

THE THIRTY-FOUR SQUARE MILE ISLAND of Manhattan is a microcosm of the world. By the year 1919 large Jewish and Italian communities adjoined each other on the lower east side next to a growing Chinatown. Further north, with the exception of the German colony around 80th Street, the island was heavily Irish until reaching largely black Harlem.

The west side was less well defined. Much of the mid and upper west-side was home to many socially prominent New Yorkers, the lower west-side, sometimes called "Hell's Kitchen," was quite the opposite, and considered a dangerous place to be after dark. There, countless saloons catered to Merchant Seamen off the ships moored at piers along the Hudson River and the thousands of soldiers and sailors just returned on the ships they sailed. Cheap rooming houses and hotels abounded and prostitution was rampant.

After waiting in Fort Hamilton an interminable three weeks for the Army's discharge mechanism to function, it was there, in Hell's Kitchen, that Walter Sinchak decided to set up business in a small hotel on Charles Street, a tiny lane located between 10th and 11th Streets, ending at Pier 46 on the Hudson River. Not surprisingly the hotel was named the Charles Hotel.

No less than five saloons lined the block in which the Charles Hotel was located, and at least two dozen more within a stone's throw on 10th Street and 11th Street. Saloons that served as temporary social halls for merchant seaman and lonely service men awaiting transportation to their homes in Iowa and Michigan, Alabama and Illinois and most of the other forty-eight.

With their uniforms serving as introductions, Walter, Boris, George, Harry, and Johnny took turns visiting the bars each evening where they befriended likely candidates and invited them to a friendly game of poker in their hotel room. For Walter and his pals, the result of each night's game was the same. They won. They won anywhere from ten or fifteen dollars to as much as thirty or even forty dollars. This was not just a matter of luck. Walter had devised ways to rig the game.

But, there in Hell's Kitchen, it soon became apparent Walter's other talent was not much in demand. The first bar tender they had talked to, in the first saloon they visited, had presented them with the address of "the best house in the neighborhood" as he served them their first drinks. Clearly no one needed Walter to find available pussy. But learning of this did not discourage Walter who prided himself on his ability to deal with the unexpected. If he wasn't going to make money finding girls to work for him, he would find a way to make money from girls who were working for someone else.

"It looks like every God-damn bartender around here knows at least one place where you can get some pussy," he told the boys one night after the poker game broke up. "So we're gonna find a couple-a them houses and sell 'em some insurance."

"What-a ya mean 'insurance', Sarge?" Johnny Hayes wanted to know.

"What I'm talkin' about is maybe you and Boris go ta one-a dem houses, do some fuckin', then rough 'em up a little, take their money and run. Then next day me and Harry and George go see 'em and sell 'em some insurance." Walter sat back with a satisfied look on his face. "So what-a-ya think?"

"Insurance? I don't understand," Johnny answered.

Sometimes Johnny Hayes was too dumb to believe. "Insurance." Walter repeated slowly. "I tell them my company will protect 'em. If anybody bothers 'em again we'll find em, beat the crap out of them and get their money back... with interest. That's what I mean."

"So what if they don't want insurance?" Johnny persisted.

"Then we give 'em more trouble until they do. You unerstan now?"

"...You mean we go back... "

"That's right Johnny. You go back!"

"Okay! Yeah. I get it." His sudden enthusiasm brought smiles to everyone's face. "Sounds good to me."

The following evening Boris and Johnny set off on their first "expedition".

As the evening began, all went well. The girls were good looking and expert at their jobs. Things couldn't have been better until it came time to put the arm on the madam. Then, out of nowhere, a small swarthy man with a large pistol in his hand appeared.

"You boys must be plain crazy," the madam laughed. "You think I could operate a place like this without protection?" She reached out and gave Johnny Hayes a little pinch on the cheek. "Now I know you boys just got back from winning' the war so Joey is gonna show you out with no trouble. But do ya-selves a favor, boys. Don't come back here no more. And if I was you, I wouldn't fool around no place else neither. Not everybody is patriotic like me."

The failure of the expedition did not please Walter Sinchak. The idea that someone else was making use of what he considered his own idea seemed unfair. "I probably should have checked things out before sending you guys," he told them when Boris completed his report. "I better look into this for myself."

"Yeah," Boris agreed. "You ought-a check it out. It's kind of expensive Sarge, but worth it. Where we were they got some great lookin' pussy."

Walter pulled on his uniform tunic and headed for the door. "We'll call it research."

"Okay Sarge," Boris called after him. "You'll find they got some great lookin' 'research'."

Another of Walter Sinchak's talents was his ability to judge people, an ability he made good use of at the house on 11th Street he went to . The girl he picked was not only a great mechanic in bed, she loved to gossip if given the chance. In little more than an hour Walter copulated successfully with her three times and learned all he needed to know about the men watching over the house.

"Boys, we run into a bad situation here," he announced when he returned home.

"We figured that out Sarge." Boris' sarcasm was deliberate. "But at least you got some good 'research', right?"

"That I did." Walter stretched contentedly as he eased himself out of his army tunic. "And I also learned a lot in case yer interested."

"Yeah. We're interested." Usually silent Harry Sauerhoff answered for the group.

"Okay. What I learned is that a bunch-a Eye-talians got things pretty well tied up around here. All the girls kick in part-a what they make to pay 'em fer 'protection'. My 'research' told me she was thinking about going back to Staten Island..."

Where?" Boris expressed the surprise they all felt. "Staten Island!?"

"That's what she told me." Walter nodded his head vigorously up and down to emphasize his point. "She said she used to work at a house in some place called Stapleton where they didn't get as much for a trick but they didn't have to pay no protection and they didn't have to service no Eye-tallies for free neither."

"Jesus," George Ganter said to no one in particular. "I didn't think they would even know what fucking is on Staten Island."

Walter joined in the laughter. "I'm not sure they do" he admitted. "But what she told me, I think Staten Island might be a virgin field in a manner of speaking."

"You think we're up to virgins Sarge?" Harry Sauerhoff asked innocently.

"Maybe," Walter grinned, then his voice took on a serious note. "But I think we ought-a look into it, only this time I think we put the fear a God in em right from the start." He thought for a second or two then added, Johnny, you and Boris could got to the place in Stapleton, George, we'll find a place in St. George for you and Harry.

Next day, Walter's young brother Stanley arrived to join them.

21.

THE TRIP TO STATEN ISLAND seemed endless to
Stanley Sinchak. Under other circumstances the
ride to South Ferry on the 10th Avenue El would
have been exciting. Stanley had never been on an
El Train before. Under other circumstances the
ride on the Staten Island Ferry would have been
even more exciting. He had never been on the
Staten Island Ferry before. He had ridden on the
Hoboken Ferry from New Jersey to Manhattan
once when he was a kid, but it was nowhere as big
or as grand as the Staten Island Ferry. Under the
present circumstances however, nothing but
getting his first "nookie" had any place in
Stanley's mind.

It was almost dark by the time they reached
Staten Island where they got on a railroad train
and traveled to Stapleton. From the Stapleton
station they walked a block and a half to Beach
Road then, at Johnny Hayes' insistence, they went
into a saloon across the street from the "house"

for a couple a beers.

"What-a-ya think, Boris?" Johnny asked after guzzeling half his first stein of beer. "Ya gonna get laid or you gonna have "French?"

"I don't know," Boris answered. "French is pretty good. I'll probably have both."

The two men were deliberately trying to tease young Stanley and were doing an excellent job of it.

"What are you guys talking about?" Stanley asked. "What's 'French'?"

"Oh, that's something the French girls do," Boris answered. "They suck your cock."

Stanley's eyes exploded. "No Shit!"

"Yeah," Johnny Hayes added. "You might wanna try that."

"Oh, fuck guys. When can we go?

Boris stretched and leaned back in his chair. "No hurry, it's just across the street. Let's finish our beers first."

Maybe they don't need to hurry, Stanley thought, but getting laid for the first time was not something he wanted to put off any longer. "Aw, come on guys. Let's go."

It was almost ten o'clock when a terrified Little Alvin burst into Angelo's and threw himself into Hugh's arms. "Mista Hugh. Mista Hugh.

Come quick! They killin' 'em!"

"Alvin. Alvin!" Hugh scooped the trembling boy into his arms and held him. "Easy now, easy. Tell me what's wrong."

"Dem mens! Dey got guns. Dey hurtin' Miss Donna."

"Alvin," Hugh's voice was soft, but stern. "Stop it now. Stop yer blabberin' and tell me what's happened."

"Yas-a Mista Hugh." The boy choked back a sob. "Da men. Tree-a dem, Mista Hugh. I let dem in like I spose ta, an dey grabs me, an den dey grabs Miss Donna . Dey got a knife an-a gun. Dey grabs de udda ladies too, an Miss Donna, she tell me ta get dem mens some whiskey in da cella. She say, 'Get Mista Hugh's whiskey,' an I knows she mean I was ta come get-cha. I come out da cella doah..."

"All right, boy. All right." Hugh tried to comfort the youngster.

"Come on-a Hugh." Franco had overheard the boy's words. He handed Hugh the chair leg club and headed out the door.

Shouting to Tony that he should call the police, Hugh quickly followed his partner. "Hold up, Franco," Hugh said as he caught up with him. "Best not run in there with out a plan. The boy said dey got a gun."

"Me too!" Franco reached into his pocket and

produced an old, six shot Colt pistol.

"Holly shit!" Hugh looked at the weapon in Franco's hand. "Is that thing loaded?"

"It's-a no fuckin' good if'n it ain't," Franco answered. "Come on."

Testifying to Willie's haste, the hatch covering the outside steps leading down into the basement was open, as was the door at the bottom. The cellar was pitch black except for a slight glow some distance away.

"That'll be the stairs over there," Hugh whispered. "Do ya know how ta use that weapon-a yours?"

"I know," Franco assured him.

"All right." Hugh continued. "Come on. When we get ta the top-a the stairs there's a hallway. The door ta the back parlor where the girls wait 's right across. I'll take that one. Up front there's slidin' doors in-ta the front parlor. You go there. We'll go in on my signal... Don't shoot unless ya gotta."

"Okay," Franco answered.

At the top of the stairs Hugh quietly opened the door to the hall, then, pointing to the left, he let Franco slide past him and move stealthily up the hall towards the front of the house and the partially open double doors leading into the front parlor.

Once Franco was in position, Hugh carefully turned the knob of the door to the back parlor, then slowly opened it just a crack. A sudden moan, followed by muttered, indistinguishable sounds of passion told him there was somebody in the room.

Nodding "go" to Franco, Hugh pushed the door open. Just inside a man sat in a chair. A woman wearing only what appeared to be a black slip, knelt between his legs. The man's head was turned upwards and the sounds Hugh heard were coming from his partially open mouth.

Holding his pistol in one hand, Franco leaned sideways far enough to see into the front parlor. Two men were in the room. One, holding a knife in his hand, had Mother on the sofa. The second, with a revolver in his hand, was holding a girl over the back of an easy chair.

As Hugh stepped into the back parlor the man saw him... so did the girl between his legs and at the same instant Hugh swung his club towards the man's head the girl bit down as hard as she could. A piercing scream came from the man's mouth. A scream, that ended abruptly with the sound of club meeting bone.

Before the scream ended, Franco stepped into the front parlor. Boris was the first to react. With a look of frantic surprise on his face, he pointed his revolver at Franco. Franco did not hesitate. Aiming his pistol at Boris' head, he pulled the trigger. While the deafening explosion was still reverberating in the room, before the man with Mother could get to his feet, Franco aimed the pistol at him and fired again.

Moments later Officer Howard Quinn and two other policemen arrived.

"Oh Howard," Donna Marie said to him as she climbed over the body of the man who had been using her. She crossed to the policeman she had called Howard and took his arm for support.

"'Tis all right, Mother," Officer Quinn assured her. "Now just what in the name of God is goin' on here?"

"...These men, Howard." She pointed to the bodies on the floor. "If it hadn't been for Hugh and Franco there, I think they would've killed us all."

The damage to Stanley Sinchak's penis, caused by Tina's teeth, was massive. "My God. How did this happen?" Doctor Randall asked the police officer who accompanied the unconscious prisoner into the emergency operating room at

Staten Island Hospital.

"He was forcin' a woman... ah... a novitiate mind you doctor..." The officer was embarrassed. How was he supposed to tell this kindly, straight-laced old doctor the man was getting his cock sucked? "Forcin' her to...ahh. Well, doc, she bit him if you understand my meanin'."

"Good Lord." The very idea of a man and woman engaging in such behavior was abhorrent to Thomas Randall, MD. That a man would *force* a woman to do such a thing was beyond his understanding. A man who would do that....

Possibly in the hands of a more skillful surgeon, or perhaps a surgeon less devoted to his staunch Baptist upbringing, Stanley Sinchak might have faired better. But skillful or not, Thomas Randall, MD, was most thorough in removing all that remained of Stanley's lacerated penis.

It was not until ten o'clock the following morning, when a loud knock on his hotel room door awakened him, that Walter Sinchak began to learn how badly his Staten Island Expeditionary Force's adventure had turned out. A New York Police Officer, with notebook in hand, stood waiting in the hall.

"You Walter Sinchak?"

"Yes..." Walter rubbed sleep from his eyes and began to feel an uncomfortable sensation in his stomach.

"You got a brother named Stanley Sinchak?"

"Yeah. What's up officer?"

"You know a man named Boris Schuman?" the officer continued ignoring Walter's question. "And a man named John Hayes?"

"Yes." Something told Walter to be careful, "Yes, they're friends of my brother's. What's happened? What's the matter?"

"Mister Sinchak," the officer looked up from his notebook. "It's my duty to tell you your brother's in police custody in a hospital on Staten Island. His friends, Schuman and Hayes are dead."

"Good Christ!" Walter grabbed the door jam to keep himself from falling.

Late that afternoon a Staten Island Police officer admitted Walter into his brother's hospital room. "Walt. Jesus Walt. She bit me!" Tears filled his eyes. "Somebody was shooting and she bit me. You didn't say nothin' about this."

There was not much Walter could say to comfort his brother. Tears filled his own eyes as he put his arms around him. "I know... I know," he murmured. "Don't worry, Stan. We'll get things fixed. I promise."

Four weeks after the raid on Mother's, Walter Sinchak sat in a Saint George courtroom watching and listening as his brother went on trial.

In perhaps the most emotional testimony, Lil' Alvin tearfully related how he had escaped through the cellar and run across the street to call "Mista Hugh and Mista Franco."

Donna Marie and Tina, each wearing non specific habits, testified that Stanley Sinchak and two other men had forced their way into their home at gun point, raped them and, they believed, had it not for the heroic actions of Hugh and Franco, would surely have murdered them.

Hugh and Franco, wearing suits borrowed from a neighborhood-clothing store, told of the rescue they had performed and basked in the glow of hero hood.

Finally, as members of the Stapleton Precinct of the New York City Police Department, men who had long known of Mother's establishment and, from time to time, been "guests of the Mother Superior," testified the house was a religious school for young women, Stanley began to wonder if his brother's information about the place had been correct.

Few questions were asked by the defense attorney Walter had engaged to defend his brother. Indeed, there were not many questions he could ask. At the attorney's urging, and with Walter's approval, Stanley entered a plea of guilty and begged for mercy in view of his tender age and the terrible price he had already paid.

Judge Lawrence Miller, however, was not a merciful man. Five weeks before his eighteenth birthday, Stanley Sinchak was sentenced to ten years in Sing Sing Prison.

Leaving the court room Walter Sinchak began thinking of a way to get even.

22

A FULL MOON SHOWN DOWN on Beach Street as Hugh stepped out onto the sidewalk in front of Angelo's for a quick breath of fresh air. What a beautiful night, he thought, so warm. And the moon, nearly full, it lit up the whole place. He looked across the street. Things had changed since the raid. Word was Mother's business was bad. Not a surprise, who wants to get laid in a place where two guys were killed. It's been more than a month, but people are still scared.

Stretching, he took a deep breath of the cool night air. It's a quiet night. Franco can go home early and maybe take Rosa for a moonlight walk. He's a lucky man with a wife who loves him and two fine sons.

His mind returned to the moon as he watched an automobile come slowly down Beach Road. It's a Ford, what they call a "fliver". There are lots of automobiles on the roads these days. He didn't know much about any of them, or how they work,

126

but he knew some day he would have one. Maybe just like that one. The way the loan business is going he could probably buy one now if he wanted to. But that would mean spending some of the money he was saving and he was not ready to do that.

He watched the "fliver" slow, then stop in front of Mother's. A man carrying a large box got out and, carrying it carefully, walked slowly up the steps to the front door. It is then that his attention snaps from thoughts of the evening to what is happening across the street.

Little Alvin opening the door... The man pushing the package into the boy's arms, then turning... running back to the automobile.

"Alvin. Drop it. Run!" Hugh shouts. As he turns towards Angelo's door and calls, "Franco. Trouble!" He heads for the automobile. Tires squealing, it moves away. Little Alvin standing on Mother's porch with the package in his arms... then everything dissolved into a flash of yellow/white light.

An unseen force knocks him backwards onto the street. The automobile bouncing... twisting as it gathers speed. Bits of burning wood and globs of something warm and wet hitting him.

"Oh Christ."

Nothing left of the porch. Nothing left of Little Alvin. The globs are bits of the child.

Nothing he can identify. Little Alvin has ceased to exist.

"Hugh. Hugh!" Franco's shout brings him back to awareness. "You okay?"

"It was a bomb!" Hugh answers as Franco grabs his arm to help him to his feet. "It was a bomb."

"Yeah," Franco answers. "A bomb!"

People from Angelo's are beginning to gather in the street looking at the wreckage that was once Mother's front porch.

Hugh gets to his feet and starts towards the house. Mother and Tina appear in an opening that once was the front door. "Are you all right?" Hugh shouts.

"Yes... yes I think so..." Mother's voice is tentative. "What happened?"

Hugh turns to Franco. "That automobile was from the city. I saw da plate. NY 3 somethin''. NY, that's a city plate, right?"

"Yeah, I think so," Franco answers, then asks again, "Are you aw-right?"

"Yeah. My ass is kind-a sore but I'm okay." Hugh grabs Franco's shoulder and starts to run. "Come on. We'll get the train. If they take the ferry back to New York we can catch them."

Running all the way Hugh and Franco reach the Staten Island Rail Road station just as the 11:34 pulls in.

"Wait! Wait!" Hugh shouts to the conductor as he and Franco run down the stairs.

"Take it easy," the conductor raises his arms and shouts back. "No rush. We're here early."

Eighteen minutes later the train arrives at the Staten Island Ferry Terminal. If all works as the schedulers planned it, the train's passengers will have time to make the mid-night boat. But all too often there are laps between schedules and reality.

Hugh and Franco make sure they are first off the train.

The boat is there. Breathless, they arrive on the upper deck just before the heavy gates slam down.

The ferry shudders as her propellers start to churn water, pushing her out of her slip into the harbor. Hugh and Franco walk slowly to a stairway leading down to the lower deck; the vehicle deck. Two lanes that run from stern to bow, far from filled, maybe ten automobiles, half again as many horse drawn wagons, on their way to Manhattan.

"You see it?"

"No." Hugh answers. "We ain't even looked yet."

Together they walk between the lanes of vehicles. Half way to the bow Hugh stops, "There." He points. "That's it."

The automobile is empty. "Maybe dey gonna leave it here," Franco suggests.

"Maybe." Hugh walks to the auto. "Then maybe not. One of them left a jacket."

Franco looks over Hugh's shoulder. "Yeah. Maybe not."

Hugh takes a folding knife from his pocket, opens the blade and drives it into the side of the front tire. A horse harnessed to a wagon in the next lane whinnies, and shies away from the loud pop and hiss.

"See anybody?" Hugh asks as he watches the tire collapse.

"No. I tink everybody out on-a deck, watch-a da moon. Let's go see."

It is indeed a wondrous night. The kind of night people take boat rides for. Moonlight turning the harbor into a silver spectacular. Passengers in groups of twos and threes standing along the railings, enjoying the air, marveling at the beauty of the night.

"Those two," Hugh says quietly and points towards two men standing by themselves a few steps back from the railing.

"You fellows got the Ford back there wid-a jacket in it?" Hugh asks as he approaches.

The unexpected inquiry surprises and

frightens both men. For a moment neither responds, then Harry Sauerhoff looks back over his shoulder. "What's it to ya?"

"Nothin'," Hugh answers easily. "Only if'n it's yours you got a flat tire needs fixin' so folks can get off."

"Oh shit," Harry mutters, "Come on George."

"Ya think there's a spare tire?" George asks as they walk away.

Franco watches the two men head back down the tunnel. "Nice-a dem to say thanks."

"I though so meself," Hugh agrees. "Let's me and you see if-n we can't help 'em."

Walter Sinchak had waited patiently until three AM before he began to worry. George and Harry should have been back by one o'clock, maybe one-thirty if they ran into traffic and missed a boat. Is it possible they were arrested in the stolen car? That isn't likely unless they were stopped for running a traffic light or something. But they talked about that. He warned them about that. Red lights were kind of new. None of them were all that used to red lights. They talked about being careful, driving slowly.

Maybe the car broke down. Maybe they had a flat tire. That made more sense. He was worrying about nothing. Still the feeling something was wrong wouldn't leave him. Ever since the second Expeditionary Force... ever since Stanley went to jail, every thing seemed to be going to shit. What if another cop comes knocking on his door? They believed him last time when he said Boris and Johnny were his brother's friends and must have talked the kid into going with them. But if Harry and George get into trouble what would he tell them this time?

At four o'clock, Walter decided not to wait any longer. Not for Harry and George or another policeman.

There is not much to pack. He wears his uniform. His money and his bankbook for the account at Dime Savings is in the money belt he never takes off. Aside from that he has only some skivvies, a couple of pairs of socks and two shirts. All fit easily into the shopping bag he has kept since bringing it home filled with nuts and pretzels for the poker game.

At four-thirty in the morning he leaves the hotel. Maybe the room clerk is asleep, maybe he went to the crapper. The good thing is, he's not there to see Walter leave.

Outside the hotel there is a hint of light in the east and 10th Avenue is already crowded with wagons and trucks. At an all night diner down the street Walter orders eggs and ham and lots of coffee. What should he do? Common sense tells him there is no reason to worry but instinct says otherwise. Something is very wrong.

He should get away from here. But what if the guys came back? They would have a right to be sore if he runs away. Maybe he should get a room somewhere else. Later he can telephone the Charles Hotel and ask for them. Good idea.

At noon, after a few hours of trying to sleep, Walter heads back to the diner. On the way he buys a late morning edition of the Daily News. "Fucking papers used to be a penny before the war," he growls at the newsboy as he hands him two cents. The boy gives him a "so what d-ya want me to do about it?" look.

Walter orders bean soup, and starts to read his paper.

Page four:

STOLEN AUTO FOUND ON FERRY

According to the paper, a Ford automobile, that had been reported stolen, was found shortly after mid-night on a New York bound Staten Island Ferry Boat. The abandoned auto had a flat tire. Except for a man's jacket found on the seat, there was no trace of the person or persons who were driving it.

It has to be the Ford they stole yesterday afternoon, Walter tells himself. Okay, it makes sense they would dump the damn thing if it had a flat tire. In fact it was a good a way to get rid of it even if it didn't have a flat. But how come they left a jacket? How come they are not back yet?

Two days of worrying later, Walter learned the answer. This time the headline was on page one:

BODY FOUND IN NY HARBOR!
Victim identified as Corporal George Ganter.

Walter read the short article twice. There was no mention of Harry Sauerhoff, but if Harry were alive he would have contacted him.

Thirty minutes later he boarded a ferryboat that would take him from Manhattan to Hoboken, New Jersey.

Sea air and ocean voyages can relax tensions and provide time to think. This can be true even on a voyage of as short duration as ten minutes, across an "ocean" no wider than the Hudson River. At least that was the case for the man who boarded the "City of Hoboken," in New York, as Walter Sinchak, only to disembark in New Jersey as Walter Simms. "Walt," as he now wished to be called, had not only a new identity but an entirely new plan for the future he was about to begin.

23.

THREE DAYS AFTER THE BOMBING, Anthony told
Hugh, "Me old man wants ta sell the place."

Hugh's eyebrows lifted in surprise. The
morning had started out like every other
morning. Carlo had stuck his head around the
corner and told him "Bon Journo" just like
always, then handed him a cup of coffee just like
always. He would never understand how a man
who made his living cooking could be so skinny.
Carlo was tall, almost as tall as himself, but he
could not weigh more than a hundred twenty-five
or thirty pounds, yet it seemed he never saw the
man when he wasn't tasting something he had
cooking on the stove, and there was always
something cooking on the stove, putting
wonderful smells into the air. The man ought to
gain weight just from those smells, Hugh told
himself as he took the coffee and told Carlo
"gratzi," just like always, then "just like always"
changed.

"Mr. Ant-a-ney in-a da res-ta-rant," Carlo told

him. "He say afta you get-a you coffee, you go see him." That definitely was not "just like always." Since he and Franco began working at Angelo's, Hugh could not remember ever seeing Tony before late afternoon. He wondered how Tony would look in sunlight. He pulled on some clothes and took his coffee into the restaurant to find out.

Tony was sitting at a table, looking not much different than he did at night, reading the Staten Island Advance and chewing on a piece of toast. As Hugh approached, Tony looked up from the paper and told him of his father's decision.

"Sell the place?" Hugh couldn't believe what Tony said. "Why would he do that?"

"The killin's... the bomb. Mother decide to give up-a so no more rent, an-a you know dat place is a mess too." Anthony's voice was flat. Emotionless. "An-a now he realize Prohibish really comin'.... He jus-a don think-a dis where he wan-a be no more."

Prohibition definitely was soon going to be the law. Hugh was surprised people like Angelo and even his partner Franco didn't believe it. But Hugh could not imagine any law that could keep a man from having a drink if he wanted a drink. And if that was true, as he had told Franco, somebody would find a way to provide that drink and there wasn't any reason why it shouldn't be the two of them.

"Did he make a deal yet?" Hugh asked Tony...

"No. No not yet Hugh. He only just decide. He wan-a to sell an-a go ta Chicago, be wid-a his sister an-er husband. Dey got a restaurant an poppa wants us ta go work wid dem. I wanted ta let-a you know right away. You an-a Franco."

"Thanks Tony. That's good of you." Hugh thought for a moment. Was there a way he and Franco could buy Angelo's?

With his Navy mustering out pay and most of his father's savings and now the loan business the neighborhood watching plus what he was earning at the job and at Angelo's he had saved quite a lot of money. It might just be possible.

"Tony, can you ask yer father to wait a day er so on this. I have an idea he might like ta hear but I need to talk with some people first. Do ya think he would do that?"

"I don't know Hugh. I could-a ask him."

Hugh waited until they were pushing their first full cart up the ramp to tell Franco about old Angelo's plan to sell the restaurant and his thoughts about buying it. Other men at "the job" worked in three man teams, Hugh and Franco worked by themselves. Nonetheless, the two of them could fill a cart as quickly, and push it up the ramp as fast as most three-man teams could. An accomplishment Hugh had more than once pointed out to the boss

"Where you get-a-da money?" Franco wanted to know.

"Well, I got some thoughts on that," Hugh answered. "First off, I got near a thousand dollars saved up."

"Pheeew." Franco whistled. "Dat's a lot-a money. You tink dat's enough?"

"No. I'm thinkin' two thousand, maybe more."

Franco whistled again as they reached the half empty wagon, dumped their cart and pushed on to the water barrel. "Rosa and me, we got-a five hun-ret nineteen dollar save... But that-a don't make-a no two thousant."

"I don't think we should use your money no how," Hugh replied. "That's money fer the house you an' Rosa are wanting ta buy someday."

"If-a you tink da res-a-rant is good idea," Franco said slowly, "You take it. Den maybe some-a-day we can-a buy a big-a-da house, but chu still no got-a 'nough."

"No... But that would help. And maybe..." Hugh wondered why he hadn't thought of this before?

A large sheet of canvas had been nailed up to cover the area where Mother's front door and windows had been. There was almost nothing left of the front porch and the canvas made it impossible to see just what damage had been done inside. But in back, the house looked as it always had. Hugh skirted the hatch cover over the steps leading down to the cellar door and could not help remembering how he and Franco had crept down there just a few weeks ago. The bomb had obviously been a pay back for the two men they had killed and the one who had been sent to prison.

He thought of Little Alvin and the pieces of his flesh that had splattered him. The bombers had paid for that, but that was of little consolation. He missed the boy. He had asked Donna Marie if he could help Alvin's mother only to learn that Alvin, like himself, had been an orphan. His mother had done house work for Donna Marie and when she died, Alvin had come to live at "mother's."

All right, enough of this he told himself as he climbed the steps up to the kitchen door. He blinked what might have been a tear from his eye, then knocked and pushed the door open calling, "Donna Marie?"

She was at the stove pouring coffee into two

cups she had set out. "Hugh. This is a surprise. Come on in and have some coffee with us." As he pushed the door open further he saw "us" was Mary Kate seated in the breakfast nook with a tiny girl standing on the bench next to her.

The coffee Donna Marie held out to him fell to the floor as his knees almost buckled from the shock. "Mary Kate.." He could hardly get the words out...

"Mornin' Hugh." she said casually. "Say hello ta me daughter Kathleen."

"Your daughter!" .

"Yes. We come to see Mother. She's had so much trouble..."

"...Yes..." Hugh was still to overwhelmed by her presence to think clearly. "Yeah, yeah, she has."

"Now you come to see Mother and it's time to get back to me waitress job." Scoping up her tiny daughter Mary Kate headed for the door. "I'll keep in touch, Mother," she said as stepped out, "Good to see you Hugh."

And she was gone.

It was too much for Hugh. He stumbled, grabbed a chair and sat down. "Mary Kate... Mary Kate... Mary Kate," he almost said the words out loud. Then he did, "Mary Kate!"

"Yes," Donna Marie agreed. "Doesn't she look well?"

"...She's married," Hugh said softly.

"No." Donna Marie shook her head. " No I don't think she is."

"But the baby...little Kathleen...her father?..."

"She may not know," Donna Marie looked at Hugh, "That's a question girls in this business sometimes have."

Hugh gazed at the door Mary Kate had just left through. He had come to America...to Staten Island to find her. He couldn't find her. Then suddenly, this morning...here she is...here she was...

"She's a waitress?... You know where?

"Some fancy hotel in St. George, I think" she said. "Now have some coffee, Hugh." Donna Marie placed a fresh cup on the table next to him, "And tell me what brings you here this early in the morning.. You know we ain't open fer business."

Slowly Hugh's mind began to re-focus. "Yes. I mean no, it's business I come to see ya about, but not the kind yer talkin'. What I come fer ... I come ta see ya about a loan."

"A loan?" The smile returned to Donna Marie's face. "I'm not lookin' for a loan Hugh. Specially not from you at the rates I hear you charge."

It's surprising how pretty she is when she smiles, Hugh thought. Even at her age... she must be in her late thirties, maybe even forty. When she was young she must have been pretty as Mary Kate.

"No... no. I'm not lookin' ta loan you money Donna Marie." Hugh returned her smile as he put his cup down and reached into his pocket for a piece of paper. "Long as you been in business I'm thinkin' you must have put some money aside..."

"Yes. I saved some money." Hugh could detect a note of suspicion creeping into her voice. "I won't starve if that's what you're thinking."

"Well that's good news, but it's not yer starvin' I'm thinkin' about neither. It's a business deal I got in me mind." Hugh unfolded the sheet of paper and held it out to her. "I want the loan of a thousand dollars. I wrote out this note that says I'll pay you back a hundred dollars a month for twelve months. That's twenty percent interest."

"Twenty percent it is," she laughed. " And that's good interest Hugh, but I hear you loan your money for twenty percent a week."

"Well that's true Donna Marie, but this is a different thing all together. I'm just loanin' a few dollars here 'n there." He hoped he sounded convincing. Hoped she had no way of knowing that last week alone he and Franco had made almost thirty dollars from loanin' money. "What I'm talkin' about is real money... real business."

"Business?" The suspicion in her voice gave way to a tone that was cold... calculating. Donna Marie remembered a time when another man had asked her to loan him money. It had cost her dearly. Not only had he stolen her money, he had broken her heart as well. She did not plan to make that kind of mistake ever again.

"For a real business loan there's need for real collateral, if you know what I mean Hugh. Not just your good looks and a bit of friendship."

"That's as it should be." Hugh's voice became more business like. "And if you read that note you'll see I've pledged co-lateral."

"I don't see that at all, Hugh." She carefully reread the paper. "I see where it says, 'As collateral for this loan I put up...' There's nothing but an empty space after that."

"Yes, that's true," Hugh agreed. "The thing is, if you agree ta the loan maybe I can make a deal that'll give me the collateral. Before you give me the money I'll fill in that space. If you don't think it's good enough you don't do the loan."

Without lifting her head Donna Marie looked up into Hugh's unflinching, steel blue/gray eyes. She saw strength there. No uncertainty. No backing down.

Her mind went back to the night of the raid.

If it hadn't been for him and Franco there was no telling what might have happened to her and the two girls. If you can't trust a man who put his life on the line for you, she told herself, then I guess you can't trust anyone. "All right Hugh. I'll loan you a thousand dollars... if your collateral's good," she quickly added.

24.

THE HOTEL IN ST. GEORGE... the "fancy" hotel in St George was very much on Hugh Crawford's mind as he left Mother's. But first things first, he reminded himself and headed for the outside stairs at the rear of Angelo's.

Stairs that led up to the apartment where Angelo Belinni lived.

At the top of the stairs he found a small landing in front of a windowless, solid looking oak door. There was no knocker or bell. Tony had said he should just open the door and walk in. His father was expecting him.

"Mister Belinni?"

No reply.

"Mister Belinni..." Hugh called again then pushed the door open and stepped into the large room.

"Hugh? Is-a dat chu? Come in, come in," a soft voice called to him.

The old man was sitting in a comfortable looking easy chair facing one of the windows along the north side of the large room. Without turning, he waved an arm in Hugh's direction, "Come. Sid-down. Ant-a-nee say you wanna talk-a bis-a-ness."

"Yeah, Mister Belinni, that I do." Over the old man's shoulder Hugh could see a panorama of Stapleton's piers and the New York Harbor. Hell of a view he thought, too bad the old man is half blind and probably can't see it.

"Aw-right, aw-right. You call-a me Angelo," the old man told him. "Sit. Sit, an-a we talk-a bis-a-ness."

"Angelo it is then." Hugh smiled. "Angelo, I hear you wanna sell this place and the house across tha street... what's left of it anyway, I wanna buy them from you."

The old man closed his eyes and began nodding his head up and down slowly. For a moment Hugh thought he was falling asleep, then realized he was deep in thought.

The decision to sell had not been an easy one for Angelo to make. This had been his home for many, many years. He had just turned fifteen when he and his twenty year old brother Amato, left their native city of Florenza and emigrated to the United States. Their father's brother, Guido, had gone to America before the Civil War commenced and, from time to time, sent back glowing reports of the money he was making fishing the waters off Staten Island. As his two nephews grew older, Guido's letters began urging his brother to send his nephews to join him in the new world where opportunities were plentiful, and futures assured.

Although there were three sisters between Amato and Angelo, their mother was not anxious to have her only sons go so far away but their father decided the opportunities for them in America outweighed his wife's objections. In May of 1872 he arranged passage to New York for the boys aboard a cargo schooner.

Fishing off the shores of Staten Island and Long Island with uncle Guido during the long, hot summer of 1872 was hard but not unpleasant work and the Belinni brothers quickly became proficient at their new trade. However, their enthusiasm for the fisherman's life began to diminish as summer gave way to fall and came to an end with the first frozen rain in November. On many nights, following a long cold day of fishing, Amato and Angelo climbed into their bunks in the bow of their uncle's boat that also served as their home, and talked about different futures that might someday be theirs.

"Someday" came more quickly than either brother expected.

"Someday" was actually a pitch-black night in early December. Freezing temperature and heavy snow blown by a strong wind made things on deck treacherous. Uncle Guido did not approve of either of his nephews drinking spirits, but this night was so cold and dismal that he allowed each to have a small sip from his bottle of Rye whiskey, "To keep-a da blood movin in-a ya veins," he told them. Not so concerned about his own consumption, Uncle Guido helped himself to several larger swigs.

Shortly before midnight on a south, southwest heading for their mooring in Staten Island's Great Kills Harbor, the wind began to grow in strength and Guido ordered the boys to take another reef in the mainsail. Perhaps the cold made the boys slower than usual, perhaps the alcohol Guido had consumed inflamed his patience, for whatever reason Guido suddenly tied off the tiller and went to do the job himself. Neither Amato nor Angelo saw what happened. All they knew was the sudden cry, almost a scream, and turning to see their Uncle falling over the side.

The wide beam, forty- foot long gaff rigged sloop Florenza was seaworthy but slow to the helm. It took several minutes for the two brothers to unlash the tiller, bring her about and headed back in the direction from which they thought they had come. Sailors with more experience would have known the impossibility of their search, but the brother's gave no time to such thoughts. Although by day break they were actually several miles from the spot where Guido Belinni fell overboard, the boys continued their searching until another boat came near enough for them to tell of their situation.

"You must put in to port and tell the Coast Guard," they were instructed.

An inquest found no reason to hold the brothers responsible for their uncle's death and, as Guido Belinni's only relatives in the United States, the Florenza was determined to be theirs.

Boat owners though they had become, neither Amato nor Angelo wanted anything more to do with fishing, or the sea. In Florence their father worked as a cook and he had taught each of his children some of the mysteries of Italian Cooking. If they could sell the boat, they decided, a restaurant would be much more to their liking.

On March 1st, 1873, "Tratoria Florenza" opened its doors, half a block from the waterfront, on Beach Road. Almost immediately the restaurant became profitable, but over the years, the restaurant's success was tempered by a series of tragedies which befell the Belinni family:

In 1885 Amato Belinni contracted pneumonia

and died.

In 1889 Angelo married only to have his wife die a year later giving birth to their son, Anthony, who was born with a clubfoot.

In 1910, Angelo began loosing his eyesight and was forced to turn more and more of the business over to his crippled son.

As an ever-increasing volume of shipping in New York Harbor pushed a greater number of ships to Staten Island's piers, the restaurant changed gradually from a family eating place to a dock worker's saloon. The changes were slow at first but by 1914, as war broke out in Europe, the establishment, long since renamed "Angelo's" but little changed in appearance, was catering almost exclusively to longshoremen and sailors. A fact that did not altogether please its owner.

Hugh sat quietly watching the old man, awaiting a response to his statement. All at once his head stopped nodding and he twisted his body to face him. "An-a how much-a-ya gonna pay?"

"Two thousand dollars." Hugh answered.

Hugh had told Franco he thought they could buy the place for two thousand or more. but as he thought further about it he guessed it would be "more". With Donna Marie's loan they had two thousand five hundred dollars available, but he had decided not to offer the old man that much to start with. Starting with two thousand left him room to negotiate.

"Two tous-ant dollar." Angelo repeated.

"Cash," Hugh added.

The old man turned back towards the windows. After a moment he looked down at his left hand and, using his thumb as a pointer, began counting on his fingers.

At's-a not enough." He said after a while. "I need-a tree tous-ant."

I don't have three thousand." Hugh said slowly. "I could pay you two thousand five hundred. That's all I got."

"No, I need tree tous-ant," the old man told him. "You good fella, Hugh, an' I like-a ta sell-a you da place, but I need-a da money. You smart. You find how ta get-a da rest what chu need. I give-a you ta Saturday before I sell-a ta somebody else."

"All right, Angelo. I'll try." Hugh got to his feet. He started to offer Angelo his hand but decided against it. Time enough to shake hands when a deal is made... if a deal could be made. Somewhere he had to find another five hundred dollars.

Tony Belinni was waiting for him at the bottom of the stairs. "So what did you and poppa talk about?"

"I told him I wan-a buy the place," Hugh answered

"Yeah. Dat's-a what I was thinkin' ya wanted." Tony had a habit of nodding his head up and down just like his father did. "So? What's-a happen?"

For a moment Hugh hesitated. Should he tell Tony about his offer and Angelo's terms? Tony had often complained the old man never discussed business with him. Telling Tony might fuck up the deal. Then again, Tony was a friend. Why shouldn't he know. Maybe he could even help with the old man. "I offered him two thousand five hundred... Cash."

"...Peewee" Tony's whistle was almost identical to Franco's. "That's a lot-a money Hugh."

"Yeah, but your father says he needs three thousand." Tony's eyes widened as Hugh continued, "Thing is, I ain't got three thousand. He gime 'till Saturday ta see if'n I can find the rest."

"Let's me an you walk up-a da street."

Tony's suggestion surprised Hugh. Walking was not something Tony did much of. His club foot embarrassed him and made walking difficult, but he led the way up the dirt path to the front of the building then turned to the right and started up Beach Road, away from the harbor, away from his father's view.

"Hugh, I could put five hundred in-ta the deal if that would help, and I'd be sort-a a silent partner."

If he took five hundred from Tony he would have enough to pay Angelo's price. But what about having a silent partner? "Tony I don't know. Why would you wanna put in yer money anyway?"

"I was born here Hugh." Tony's voice suddenly became choked. "An' my mother, she'a die here. Right upstairs where you and poppa was talkin.". This place been in-a my family fer years an-a years an years. I wanna keep a part of it."

This was something Hugh could understand, and he liked Tony. Tony was a good guy, and a friend. Small, not strong, and Hugh guessed the clubfoot had always made him timid, but he was smart and had always been fair.

"All right, Tony," Hugh said after a moment. "If you want that, me and Franco would be proud to be partners wit-chu."

On September 1st, 1919, Hugh accompanied Tony and his father to Grand Central Station located at Park Avenue and 42nd Street in New York City. Before the turn of the century "Commodore" Cornelius Vanderbilt had purchased a railroad yard that extended from

42nd Street to 48th Street, between Madison Avenue and Lexington Avenue and, not long after work was begun on what was to be the terminal for his New York Central Railroad . A tunnel extending all the way north to 96th Street was constructed. Tracks that were previously at street level were placed underground and the huge new terminal officially opened in 1913 and by 1919 the sale of "air rights" above the now underground tracks had paid for its construction and created a new commercial and residential center for the growing city. .

Hugh, Tony and old Angelo entered the terminal and stood at the top of the enormous marble stairway leading down to the main waiting room. It was the first time Hugh had been inside the 650 foot long, 100 foot wide building.

"Holly Jesus Tony! I never seen anything like this! You could put fifty buildings the size a Angelo's inside here... maybe a hundred of 'em."

"Yeah, it's-a big. An-a-da trains... all underground. Wait-a you see dat."

Not interested in looking at or discussing' the building, holding carefully onto the hand railing, Tony's father started down the magnificent stairway. They were nearly an hour early but the old man was nervous about being on time. He would not be comfortable until he and his son were on the train and in their seats. "Ant-a-nee, you got-a da ticket?" he called back over his shoulder.

"Yes poppa." It was the third time the old man had asked in the past fifteen minutes. "Come on Hugh, poppa wan-a-ta get on-a the train."

Stairs were not something Tony was too comfortable with either and, like his father, he also took careful hold of the handrail as they started down the seemingly endless flight of steps. He stepped down with his good foot, the left, then dragged the right off the step he was leaving. If he were not careful the dragging foot could catch and trip him. Hugh started to take his arm but quickly realized he would resent his help.

Tony was right about the countless tracks, platforms, and trains beyond the main waiting room. The train to Chicago they were seeking was to be on track 31. As they walked to it they passed a red carpet leading down the platform for Track 23 where the 20th Century Limited, an all Pullman Car express that was the jewel in the crown of the New York Central Railroad, awaited passengers.

Tony had hoped to travel on the famous Limited, but his father had no such grandiose ideas. Coach seats on the regular Chicago train were more than good enough for him and far less expensive. And if this train took twenty hours to reach Chicago instead of fifteen, as the Limited did, it was okay with Angelo... he had nothing else to do anyhow.

Hugh realized the beautiful Limited was obviously for very well to do folk. Someday I'll ride a train like this, he told himself... And wouldn't it be wondrous fine to take Mary Kate. He had not seen her since the morning he went to talk to Donna Marie about the loan but now it's time to fix that..

"High class hotel," Donna Marie had said. As far as Hugh could tell there were only two hotels in St. George that would qualify:

The restaurant in the St. George Plaza Hotel had an unblocked view of New York harbor. The host intercepted Hugh before he had hardly a chance to see it. "I'm sorry sir," his condescending voice told Hugh. "We don't serve gentlemen not wearing a coat and tie."

"Oh, I'll remember that," Hugh told him. "But it's not service I'm lookin' fer. I'm wantin' to know if a lady named Mary Catherine works fer ya?"

Obviously annoyed, the man rolled his eyes upward before looking back at Hugh and telling him, "No sir. We have no one by that name working here."

Several thoughts ran quickly through Hugh's mind but he dismissed them all, said, "Thank you," and walked away.

The Park Hotel was two blocks further up the hill. This place probably has an even better view, Hugh told himself as he approached the entrance to the Vendome Room. Here the Head Waiter was a "Maitre D', Hugh learned.

"Sir, I'm sorry..."

"All right," Hugh interrupted. "I'm not looking to eat here. I just wanna know if a lady named Mary Catherine works here."

"I do not have that information. You might go around back and inquire at the service entrance."

The Service Entrance was somewhat less pretentious but a uniformed guard sat at the doorway opposite a time clock and turnstile.

"I'm lookin-a see if a lady named Mary Catherine works here," Hugh told him.

"And who wants to know?" the guard asked .

"Me name's Hugh Crawford an' I'm an old friend."

The guard looked at him carefully, then deciding he looked alright glanced down at a list on his desk... "Mary Catherine... Yeah, she works eleven-ta three."

Hugh glanced at the clock on the wall over the guards desk. Almost two o'clock.

"So she's working now?"

"Yeah. She's checked in."

Hugh thanked the man then walked to a bus stop bench half a block away. From the bench he could see the Service Entrance. He could also see New York Harbor. The bus stop bench had it all over the Vendome Room, Hugh decided. It had an even better view of the harbor, and a large clock he could keep track of the time with..

Watching ships moving through the harbor Hugh's mind turned quickly to his first visit.. To meeting her. How could all this time have passed and he still remembered her, wanted her, loved her. Now he had found her. This time he must not let her go. Remembering...thinking... he almost lost track of the time. Suddenly he realized it was three o'clock...

And there she was, just coming out of the building. "Mary Kate. Mary Kate," he shouted as he jumped to his feet and began to run towards her.

"Hugh Crawford..." The surprise, the shock really, was written all over Mary Kate's face.

"My god Hugh...What?.. Why?..."

"I have at talk at ya Mary Kate.

"Talk?" The surprise was still in her voice. "If you be quick. I must take the bus there to pick up Kathleen. What is it you want to talk about?"

"Us," he answered slowly.

"Us?"

"Yes, us. Will you marry me Mary Catherine?"

25.

WITH FRANCO AS HUGH'S BEST MAN and Donna
Marie as Mary Kate's Maid of Honor their simple
wedding was held in the chapel of St. Mary's
Church, on Prospect Street, just a few blocks from
Angelo's. Following the service, Rosa and Franco
held a wonderful reception for the newly weds in
their tiny apartment. In addition to their two
sons, Franko, Jr "Frank", and Peter, the guests
included Rosa's uncle Pietro Donnitelli, Carlo the
cook, Joe Nuzellese, and Jeff Flannigan who was
going to drive the giant Packard automobile Hugh
had hired to take him and his bride to New York's
famous Plaza Hotel at the corner of 5th Avenue
and 59th Street.

The Plaza Hotel opened on October 1st, 1907,
and almost immediately became perhaps the most
famous hotel in all of the United States, if not the
world. When Hugh revealed where he had
reserved a room for their wedding night, Mary
Kate had almost refused to marry him. "My God,

Hugh. That's fer rich swells and royalty. We ain't goin' ta no place like that!"

"Yes, we are me darlin'," he told her. "Ya only get married once, it's time to splurge a bit. We'll be savin' come tomorrow."

When Jeff drove the Packard up to the hotel entrance they were welcomed by a uniformed footman and a doorman. Two immaculately dressed bellhops were quickly summoned to carry their luggage and they were escorted up the stairs to the hotel's grand entrance and into the elegant lobby.

Decorated in what was termed "Second Empire Baroque - Late Medieval French Chateau", the ornate archways, pillars and marble floors literally overwhelmed Mary Kate. "How can they keep these floors clean?" she whispered.

"Not fer you to concern yerself about," Hugh whispered back.

Proudly, Hugh signed the register "Mr. and Mrs. Hugh Allan Crawford," and they were quickly escorted to a spacious room on the eleventh floor, overlooking Central Park.

Hugh gave the bellmen a dollar to split between them, then, after they left, he took Mary Kate's hand and led her to the window where he bent slightly to kiss the top of her head..

For a response she reached up and pulled his

head down until their lips met...

They made love all night.

In the morning, after room service brought them breakfast, Mary Kate put her hand on Hugh's shoulder and said to him, "Hugh, there's something I must tell you."

He was surprised by the serious tone her voice had taken on. He had a sudden fear she had changed her mind about being married to him.

"Do you remember when you first came to Mother's?" she continued. "The night after you won yer fight?"

"Remember? I thought about it ever since Mary Kate." Hugh put down his fork and took her hand in both of his.

"Why do you think I come back after the war if I wasn't thinkin' about that night and you? You was like a magnet."

"Well Hugh, you were my first client at Mother's. Before that night Donna Marie had me doing housework and putting out clean towels for the other girls. Then, after you left, I told Donna Marie I couldn't do that for money anymore. You were the only client I ever had... "

He realized she was trying to tell him something but he was too wrapped up in the moment to realize what.

"I was at 'mother's' more than a month before

that night," she continued. "It was back in April, when the president said we was going to war that I run away from Murphy's." She slid her hand out from between his and used it to push her hair back.

"Mary Kate, there's somthin' here you're tryin' ta tell me but I'm a bit to slow ta know just what it is."

"Well, you think on it fer a while." Her voice was so soft he could hardly hear it. Then suddenly she brightened, "Now pass me some of that wonderful looking jam."

Taking the jam, she spread some on a piece of toast and handed it to him then re-filled his coffee cup, watched him bite off half the slice of jam and toast then wash it down. A moment later he looked at his watch. "Time ta be gettin' out-a bed," he told her. "Time at get back-ta' Angelo's. Franko an me is gona start fixin' up Mother's old place."

"He climbed out of bed and looked around the room. It was nice, but twelve dollars a day! Sweet Jesus! That was more than most people earned in a week. Well, he thought to himself, it's our honeymoon and if I can't spend me money on our honeymoon... well what the hell is money for anyhow?

"I'm fer takin' a shower." He told her then

added, "It's so big there's plenty room fer two in there…"

"Why Hugh. Do I seem dirty to you?"

"No. But then ya can't never be too clean neither."

Hugh had been in showers before but not any like this one. The tub was the biggest he had ever seen and the showerhead above it was as large as a saucer. Even so, they had to stand close together for them both to be under the spray. He put his arms around her and felt his desire grow as she rubbed soap on his chest. Carefully he lowered himself down in the tub. She needed no urging to follow.

Sitting on him. Joining with him. The hot water drenching them. Her breasts where he could kiss them. Their bodies lubricated by the water and the soap…..

Spent, they rested with heads on each other's shoulders… Eyes closed… Fulfilled….

His mind turned to little Kathleen. He was certain she would be all right while they were away… Rosa would take good care of her. Rosa and Franco. Franco is a great father, he thought. I hope I can do as well for Kathleen.

Then it hit him! "Jesus Christ!" He lifted his head from her shoulder.

Alarmed, she looked up. "What is it Hugh?"

"What you were saying before. About Mother's and me being yer first one."

Mary Kate tilted her head slightly and looked into his eyes.

"She's mine isn't she? Kathleen's me real daughter."

"Yes Hugh, she is your daughter." Tears filled their eyes as they leaned forward to kiss...

26.

WITH CHURCHES and a growing women's movement leading the way, the Temperance Movement in the United States had been gaining momentum ever since the end of the Civil War. During the early nineteen hundreds a number of states passed laws limiting the sale and use of alcoholic beverages, but for the most part the laws were ignored except in rural areas where people strongly believed in them. And their belief had been sufficient to produce the Volstead Act; the 18th Amendment to the U.S. Constitution: "Prohibition."

Termed "Noble in motive," by President Hoover, the 18th Amendment would become the law of the land on January 16th, 1920. Noble or not, it was a law which was immediately and constantly violated by seemingly everyone in America. It was a law that overnight would create bootlegging, a theretofore almost unknown business, and hundreds of hidden saloons that came to be known as "speakeasies."

Jeff Flannigan had become much more than just a client referral for the loan business. He had become a friend and willing helper as Hugh and Franco rebuilt Mother's house. With that job completed the three men turned their attention to the saloon where Hugh decided they should build a partition that would divide the room into two sections: the bar on the left; a dining room on the right; a dining room that, at Mary Kate's insistence, would have lace curtains in the windows and white cloths on the tables.

"I don't know why we build-a dis wall Hugh," Franco complained. "We gonna get-a-da prohibish, we got-a take out-a-da bar."

"Well, I was thinkin' we would keep the bar and use it fer people who jus wanna sandwich and things like that, you know, stuff ya can eat quick. Then on the other side we have a real dining room... with Mary Kate's table cloths."

Something about Hugh's expression caught Franco's attention. "You got-a more'n fast eatin' on-a you mind," Franco told him. "What-a you thinkin'?"

"I'm not sure I know meself," Hugh answered before turning his attention back to the nail he was pounding.... "But people who wanna drink are gonna drink, an' we got-a find a way ' ta help 'em."

By Friday afternoon Hugh, Franco and Jeff had completed the inside partition and were up on the roof finishing the new sign when a fish wagon drew up at the curb in front.

Looking down at the driver Franko called, "Ciao Pietro." Turning back to Hugh and Jeff he said proudly, "Rosa is make-a Blue Fish tonight, how 'bout you two an Mary Kate come for dinner?"

"Not me," Jeff answered quickly. "I got-a big date over in Jersey."

How 'bout you and Mary Kate?" Franko asked Hugh.

"Yeah...yes ." Hugh answered slowly as he waved to the man below unloading a basket of fish. "I'm sure she would like that...." then he added, "You never told me Pietro's a fisherman. He got-a boat?"

"Sure he got-a-da boat," Franco laughed. "The Rosa, for his sister. How da hell you think he's-a gonna fish wid- no boat?

With a thoughtful look on his face, Hugh turned his attention back to the new sign. "Original Angelo's," he read aloud. "I think Tony will be happy we're keepin' the old man's name." He looked at the new sign for a moment longer then turned to Flannigan, "Jeff, we sure couldn't-a done all this with out chu. Come down to the bar,

I'll pay you and we'll have a drink ta celebrate. ...And tell me this, you think yer brother what works on the docks would do me a favor?"

The following day Jeff Flannigan's brother left word for Hugh that Sea Glory was scheduled to make port in New York Wednesday next week. Hugh knew Sea Glory well enough to know there was no certainty she would actually arrive on Wednesday. But when she did, if Third Mate Pierson was still a member of her crew...
If he was, he should be able to contact him through O'Riley's. ...If there was still an O'Riley's. Saloons and bars were closing down all over the place now that prohibition was almost here. Sean O'Riley didn't seem the kind of man who would close his place down but the only sure way Hugh could find out was to go see for himself.

Saturdays were too busy for Hugh to even think about going to New York but on Sundays Angelo's was closed. O'Riley's probably would be too but if he went there he could leave a note. If he could reach the Third Mate....

The Volstead Act prohibited any foreign vessel carrying alcoholic beverages from entering the Three Mile Zone - the distance from shore the US claimed as part of this country. But, Hugh reasoned, if he and Franko and Pietro were fishing outside the three mile limit and happened to encounter Sea Glory, and if Sea Glory happened to have booze on board that needed to be dumped before entering US waters...

27.

THEIR FIRST RENDEZVOUS with Sea Glory, only three weeks after Prohibition became law, was close to a disaster. A strong nor'easter had been blowing for two days building huge waves that would have kept lesser seamen than Hugh Crawford and Pietro securely tied to a mooring in a sheltered harbors. The same storm lengthened Sea Glory's normally slow passage even more, with the result that she reached their meeting point almost fourteen hours later than they had expected.

Nearly exhausted from the job of holding the ROSA on station as they waited and watched, the task became even more difficult when Sea Glory finally did arrive. Communicating through megaphones, Hugh and Third Mate Pierson agreed it was not possible for ROSA to come along side for the transfer of two cases scotch whiskey and two kegs of beer. It was finally decided the kegs and cases would be tied onto a life raft that Sea Glory would try to drop into the sea..

Perhaps more by luck than skill, Sea Glory's crew was able to drop the raft with its carefully strapped down cargo into the heavy seas and Hugh somehow managed to snare the tow rope out of the water with a ten foot long gaff hook.

After that there was nothing to do but keep ROSA pointed into the storm until it blew it self out so they could turn and head for home.

With their liquor stored carefully under the floor in the bar, it was Hugh's intention to serve drinks to their regular customers. The restaurant would be open for breakfast and lunch as before, but in the evening only patrons with "reservations" would be admitted. He believed in this way the beer and liquor they had pulled from the sea would last at least two months, ample time for Sea Glory to travel back to England, and return.

And then Donna Marie offered to pay Hugh double what he had paid Sea Glory for a case of Scotch she wanted to serve to clients in her new establishment in the heart of swanky St. George.

And then Jeff Flannigan told him his girl friends brother was working for a man who wanted to buy beer and whiskey for his place in

New Jersey.

And then, as Hugh's eyes were opened to a brand new opportunity to make money, he sent a cable to Sea Glory: "DOUBLE NEXT SHIPMENT."

28.

THE DRIVE NORTH, along the Hudson River, was truly awe-inspiring and Walt Simms intended to enjoy it fully. Frequent rains in April and May had made the spring of 1925 one of the wettest on record which resulted in silvery, fast flowing little streams that tumbled down hill sides covered with verdant green grass, thousands of wild flowers, beautiful dogwood and wild berry trees and an overall look of nature at it's best.

Making nature even more beautiful, an endless collection of small sailboats, with pristine white sails reflecting in the sky blue water, moved gracefully back and forth across the river below. A Hudson River Day Line Cruise Boat heading up stream and three river tugs towing barges loaded with sand, bricks, lumber and other cargoes hidden under huge canvas covers, completed the scene. It occurred to him that some of them were probably carrying booze. Almost everything carried booze these days.

"What-a ya think Snake? Beer on that big red

one?"

"Naw. Nobody gonna carry beer up da river. Whasss da point?. Dey make it everywhere. If dey got anything itssss Sssscotch."

Roy Yeager was cursed with a speech impediment, a sibilant "S". He could not pronounce any word with an "S" in it without drawing the sound out into a prolonged hiss. His handicap provided him with his nickname, "Snake".

"Yea, I guess," Walt agreed. "How much further?"

"I don't know Walt, ten, maybe fifteen milessss. Enjoy da ssscenery. Like you sssaid, we got plenty-a time. We get dere when we get dere."

"You're right. They don't let him out until two o'clock and it's only eleven-thirty. Maybe if you see a place, pull over and we'll get somethin' ta eat, huh?"

"Sssure bossss."

Walt relaxed against the soft, rich leather of the Cadillac's rear seat. When he was growing up on the pig farm who would have thought one day he would own a Cadillac? Who would have thought one day he would own a building in Secacus and have almost two hundred thousand dollars salted away in three different banks? Five years of prohibition had made him a rich man. Five years that his kid brother had spent in prison. Well, he was in a position to make it up to the kid now.

He had not visited his brother with great frequency, actually visitation was not permitted very frequently, but on the rare occasions when he did, the little town of Ossining surprised him. The home of Sing Sing, the most famous and feared prison in America, Ossining was a great looking little town that made you think of home, mother and apple pie.

Today, Walt thought, with the sun shining, the birds singing, and every fucking flower trying to look better than the next one, the place was beautiful. Hanging baskets of flowers adorned the light poles as well as the entrances of many of the little shops along Main Street. He guessed if your town is best known for a prison, you probably did your best to make it look pretty and try to forget it.

Actually Ossining had done a good deal more than hang flowers on its lamp poles to try and forget the prison. Originally the little village on the banks of the Hudson River had been named Sing Sing. A name taken from the Sint Sinck Indian Tribe that had lived there many year ago. Wanting to divorce itself from the prison that had become infamous for its cruel treatment of prisoners, the town had changed its name to Ossining in 1901.

Snake parked the automobile in the Visitor Parking Lot near the main gates and watched his boss get out and walk to the Reception Office.

"I'm Walt Simms," he told the uniformed officer behind the bared window in the visitor's reception room. "I come ta pick up Stanley Sinchak. You know what time he gets out?"

The officer ran his finger down a list of names, "Sinchak... two o'clock." He looked up at the clock over his desk, "It's ten to now. He'll be along pretty soon."

"Thanks." Walt nodded his head, turned, and walked back to the automobile. "Just a few minutes I guess," he told Snake.

Although Stanley would be unlikely to agree, he had been fortunate to start his term when he did because he had arrived at the prison just shortly before Lewis E. Lawes became its warden. Lawes was a humanitarian and appalled by conditions at the prison.

Construction of Sing Sing was begun in 1825. One hundred convicts from a prison in Auburn, New York, had been brought down the river to the village of Sing Sing and forced to work in deplorable conditions, digging and cutting granite from nearby quarries, then constructing the prison itself. Eventually they built two parallel, four story high buildings containing a total of eight hundred one man cells measuring seven feet in length, three and one-half feet in width, six and one-half feet high.

Prisoners sent to Sing Sing were not permitted to talk with one and other. They were not permitted to have visitors. They were given bibles and told that reading them might be their way to salvation. The slightest infraction of the rules subjected them to lashings, bindings and other forms of torture.

During the day, they were forced to work at manufacturing a variety of products for outside companies that paid the prison for their labor. Money that did not go to the prisoners, money that was supposed to go to the state but often found its way into the pockets of the prison's authorities.

By 1900 improvements in the prison's condition and the treatment of prisoners began to make life a bit less horrific for the inmates. Cells were enlarged and eventually lighting installed in them. No longer did the prisoners have to sit in the dark when not at work. In time books were allowed, conversation between inmates permitted and occasional visitations by family members allowed. Warden Lawes was quick to further improve the conditions in which the prisoners lived and worked, none the less, life in "The Big

House," was still truly doing "hard time."

It was actually almost an hour before Walt heard a loud metallic clang from someplace behind the wall, then, a few seconds later, three men in ill fitting suits, escorted by two uniformed guards, arrived at the main gate. The men waited patiently while another officer, carrying a clip board, came out of the Reception Office and asked each man to sign his name on a release form. Finally, the outer gate opened and the three walked through it to freedom.

The ride from Sing Sing back to New Jersey was not what Walt had envisioned. His brother seemed distant, not much like the eager young man he remembered. True, Stanley had usually been less than friendly on the rare occasions when he had found time to visit him, but he had always charged that up to the prison atmosphere. Now that he was out, Walt expected... well, he didn't know exactly what he expected but certainly not this aloofness. Not this seeming indifference that bordered on anger.

"Stan, we got some good things goin' for us now." Walt reached his arm across the top of the back seat and tried to put it around his brother's shoulder but his brother pulled away. "Stan, listen, we got what they call a Speak-Easy and a

card room and a crap table. We got some of. .."
Oh shit, Walt thought to himself, I almost told
him about the pussies. Christ he ain't got no
pecker. The last thing he needs to hear about is
girls.

"The money is rollin' in kid," he continued.
"Your gonna have everything you want."

"What I want is ta go ta Staten Island and find
that fuckin' bitch what ruined me!"

"Ahhh... I can understand that Stan." How do
I handle this? Walt asked himself. "Thing is
though, we gotta be damn careful about Staten
Island. Snake gets our booze from people on
Staten Island and we don't wanna fuck that up.
"The cops and the Feds don't even know Staten
Island is part of the world. We don't want to start
any trouble over there that will get them lookin'
around, it could be real bad for our business."

"Fuck business Walter!" Stan's voice was
almost a shout. "I'm gonna find that bitch and
carve her up in little pieces. You know what I
mean?"

"I understand. But we can figure out how to
even the score with her and still not fuck up our
liquor supply, so let's don't do anything crazy,
huh?" Walt slapped his brother on the shoulder.
"Right?"

"Fuck off Walter!"

29.

TWENTY-FOR HOURS LATER, in spite of his brothers pleading, Stanley Sinchak stood on Beach Road looking at a restaurant named "Original Angelo's." and the three houses across the street where he remembered there being only one. Several little girls were playing on the porch of the house that looked vaguely familiar, although this house was painted white. The one he remembered was brown. "That ain't no fuckin' whore house," he told himself. "Maybe they know somethin' in the bar."

But a bar it was no longer. Nothing looked familiar to him. Where he thought there was a bar was actually a food counter with seats. Four comfortable looking wooden tables and chairs completed the small "Grill Room" that was separated by a partition from the larger "Dining Room" where he could see clean white tablecloths and napkins.

Aw fuck, Stanley told himself. This don't look

like da place we was in neither. While I been up da river dey did dis prohibition shit and the whole world changed.

A young man approached him. "Welcome to Original Angelo's. My name's Frank, you want the grill or the Dining Room?"

"This your place?"

"No, no," the young man laughed at the idea he might own such an establishment. "I just work here."

"Yeah? So what-a ya know about the place across the street?"

"Across the street?"

Can this fuckin' kid be as dumb as he sounds? Stanley asked himself... "Yeah, Frank. The whore house they call 'Mother's'."

"Gee," Franco, junior laughed. "I've never heard anybody around here talk about anything like that." Hugh and his father had trained him to be aware of his instincts, and his instinct told him this unfamiliar visitor might very well be trouble.

"Oh?..." Stanley took a cigarette out of his pocket and put it between his lips. Before he could find his matches the young man was holding a lit match for him.

"So, there's no whores across the street. You know where they went?"

"The whores?" The boy laughed again, nervously this time. Obviously "whores" was not a word he was comfortable with. "Gosh mister, I don't know. I don't think anybody around here would know. The most exciting thing that's happened since I been around was last summer when one of the kids across the street fell playing hopscotch and broke her arm. They sent for an ambulance and a police car came. "

Stanley decided the kid was never going to shut up. It was apparent he didn't know anything about "Mother's."

So what the fuck am I doin' here? he asked himself.

Nothin', he decided. Without saying "thanks", he turned and walked out the door.

That evening young Frank reported the afternoon's visitor to Hugh and his father.

"Good work Frank," Hugh clapped him on the shoulder, then turning to Franco added, "I have a bad feelin' about that fellow. I have a feelin' he just might be the lad what got his prick cut off."

Instead of returning to Port Richmond and and the ferry that connected Staten Island directly with New Jersey, Stanley Sinchak went to Saint George and took the ferry to New York City. Ever since he was a kid he had heard about Times Square. Guys at the Big House talked about Times Square. It was time he saw Times Square for himself.

When he reached the city he got on the new 7th Avenue Subway and road it all the way uptown to 42nd Street. Riding underground like that was scary. The tunnel walls were so close, and the train traveled at such an incredible speed. Looking out the window made him feel dizzy and when they came to a curve he almost fell off his seat

The distances between stations seemed enormous. After a while he began to worry he had somehow boarded the wrong train, or missed the station he wanted... Finally he asked a man sitting opposite him.

"No, you're all right," the man told him. "Times Square is three more stops,"

He didn't know exactly what he expected to find when he got to Times Square but it wasn't what met his eyes when he climbed up the stairs and stepped out of the kiosk on the corner of 7th Avenue and 42nd Street. The sidewalks were crowded with people and the streets seemed jammed with traffic. He could see four, no five trolley cars. More horse drawn wagons than he could count and motor trucks and automobiles bumper to bumper.

Opposite the corner he was standing on, the building where 7th Avenue and Broadway crossed was three sided and had a giant electric sign with moving lights that spelled out words... news headlines, he realized! "Yanks Beat Cleveland 6-3. Ruth Hits 2."

Giant billboards, advertising Camel Cigarettes, Dr. Brown's Cough Medicine, Ford Automobiles and Buster Brown Shoes looked down from the tops of the buildings all around him. And there were theaters everywhere. It wasn't yet dark but all of the theaters had hundreds of electric lights flashing around their marquees. The old Nickelodeon in Secaucus didn't look much like these places.

He decided he wanted to see a movie. It had been years since his last trip to the Nickelodeon, and there were no movies in Sing Sing. Here there were dozens he could choose from. He finally decided on a new movie called "The Gold Rush," staring someone named Charlie Chaplin.

Unlike the elderly woman who played the piano in the Secacus Nickelodeon, the music in this theater was provided by a four piece orchestra: a piano, two violins and, something he was not familiar with, a big violin that rested on the floor and was held between the player's knees. There, in the darkness, for a while he forgot about Sing Sing and about the whore who bit off his cock. But then he was forced to return to real life. He had to go to the toilet.

Stanley could not stand at a urinal and piss

like every other man did. He had to go into a stall and sit down like a woman. And that more than anything had made life in prison a living hell.

It was nearly eleven o'clock that night when Stanley stepped off the train in Secaucus and walked the three blocks to "Walt's Diner." It was hard to keep his anger in check when he looked at that sign. Somehow, while he was in prison, his fucking brother had made enough dough not only to buy the little restaurant but the whole Goddamn three-story building.

He had a "speak" in the basement, whores on the second floor, and a gambling room on the third. His Goddamn, son-of-a-bitch brother was fucking his brains out with them whores and all he could do was think about it. Shit! Who needs this?

The trouble was, he did. Walt had plenty of money and wanted him to be "part of the organization." So what else was he gonna do?

"Christ Stan, where you been all day?"

"I been to New York, Walter, if it's any-a your fuckin' business."

Walter tried to put his arm around his brother, but he pulled away. "You had anything to eat? Lemme get you somethin' to eat."

"I ate already." Stanley couldn't help his unpleasant tone of voice. His brother was the cause of all his troubles. To this day, he still wasn't fully convinced that it hadn't all been a terrible mistake; that the place called Mother's actually had been a church home of some kind. It was really tough trying to be friendly with Walter.

"All right. That's good you ate. What-a ya say we go down stairs and get a drink?"

A drink was a good idea. "Yeah. Okay Walt. Let's get a drink."

"Snake" Yeager looked out through the peephole in answer to Walter's knock then quickly opened the door. "Hi-ya bossss.... Ssstanley."

The room was smoky, noisy, and more than half filled with men and women "having a good time!" Being "daring!" Breaking the law.

Before Prohibition women just did not go to saloons. Now, speak-easy hopping was the thing to do, the delight of all socialites.

"Try some-a this scotch." Walt said as he went behind the bar and picked up a bottle. "This is the really good stuff."

"Naw. I don't like that shit." Last night was the first time Stanley had tasted scotch. In the pen the guys made something they called gin and they made wine. The wine they made was pretty good. So good in fact that some of the guards would swap them beer for their wine once in a while.

But whiskey, especially scotch whiskey, was foreign to Stan's taste. "Gimme a beer."

"Beer comin' up." Walt was trying to be nice to the kid, but he knew the time was soon coming when he would loose patience with his rotten attitude. He was sorry for what had happened to Stanley but for Chris-sake... Enough of this shit is enough.

"Here ya go." Walter topped off the stein he was filling, handed it to his brother, then called to Snake, "Keg's about empty."

"Yeah, we're runnin' low but we got one left an I'm makin' a pick up tomorra night."

"Beer's pretty good." Stan took a longer swig, "A lot better-n the stuff we was gettin up the river."

It was the first time Stanley had said anything positive since they had picked him up at Sing Sing and Walter was so pleased he spoke without thinking. "Staten Island's finest."

"Staten Island? No shit, this comes from Staten Island?"

Oh Christ!" Walter winced. Me and my big mouth, he told himself. I didn't need to bring up Staten Island again. "Yeah, I think so. Snake found us a bootlegger years ago. He ain't never told me much about him. He thinks it's job insurance if I don't know where he's gettin' the stuff, but I think maybe it's from the Island."

It would be good to change the subject now, Walter thought. After all, Staten Island isn't exactly the land of good dreams for the kid and he seems to have it in his mind to get even with that whore. But I don't need for him to go fucking around over there, botherin' my bootlegger, trying to find the bitch.

Stanley switched his mind from his brother and the beer to Snake's Staten Island bootlegger. A bootlegger ought to know what's going on in his territory, he told himself, and a whorehouse gotta have liquor. "What's this pick-up Snake's talkin' about Walt?"

"Well..." Walter knew what was coming. He never should have brought up Staten Island. "Every so often Snake picks up a shipment of booze over there."

"I wanna go wid him." Stanley announced.

30.

WITH THE WORDS:

Donitelli Fish Company.
The fish you eat today
Slept last night in Princess Bay

proudly mounted above her cabin, it was an unusual day when the ROSA did not return in the evening with a good catch of Blue Fish, Striped Bass, Eels and Flounder, all carefully iced down and stored in her hold.

If Sundays meant early mornings for the ROSA and Uncle Pietro, some Mondays, like this one, meant late nights for Hugh, Franko and Mary Kate. Today ROSA carried more than fresh fish. Today ROSA also carried several cases of whiskey and barrels of beer.

In addition to selling fresh fish to anxious housewives and restaurant owners at the several stops ROSA would make on her way to Tottenville, an after dark stop at an old boat pier in lonely Lemon Park was schedule as well.

It was on days like this one that Hugh did not

want Mary Kate to come along, but she came in spite of Hugh's protests.

Kathleen was safe at home with "Aunt" Rosa and she believed her place was with her husband. She knew the presence of a woman on board made it seem obvious they were going to sell fish and she was a far better salesman than either of the men. She prided herself in the fact that they never returned home with unsold fish in the hold.

Half an hour after leaving Seacacus Snake braked to a stop on the ferry boat that would carry them across Arthur Kill to Tottenville. The boat's wide, flat deck had room for perhaps a dozen wagons and automobiles. On the starboard side, below the wheelhouse, there was a narrow cabin which could hold upwards of twenty passengers, but at this late hour there were only three foot passengers who, foregoing the cabin, were standing on deck chatting with the driver of the one other vehicle on board, a horse drawn farm wagon loaded with fresh tomatoes.

"Should we get out an stretch our legs?" Stanley asked.

"You can. Ssss-only ten minutesss acrossss. I'm gonna keep the motor runnin."

"Okay. I'll stay wid-chu."

Moments after the boat moved out of it's slip, Snake bent forward to reach under his seat then straightened up with a pistol in his hand. Stanley felt his stomach turn over...

"You know how to shoot?" Snake asked.

"I ain't never used one," Stanley admitted with a sigh of relief.

"It's easy." Snake showed the gun to him. "You cock it like this." He pulled back the hammer. "You point it and you pull the trigger." Snake carefully lowered the hammer and handed the huge, single action '44 to him. "Just be careful. It's loaded. You cock it an it's gonna go off, so don't fuck wid it 'less you mean to shoot somebody. Usually just pointin' it at-em will do the job. We aint never had no troble wid des pickups," Snake added, "But it pays to be ready fer anything.

Stanley nodded in agreement, then took the pistol. It felt heavy in his hand. He rested his finger on the trigger and put his thumb on the hammer. He thought it would be easy to cock until he tried to pull the hammer back. There was so much resistance the gun twisted in his hand.

"Christ! Don't wave that thing around." Snake reached over and took the pistol from him and again carefully held the hammer back as he pulled the trigger, then let it down gently before handing the gun back to Stanley.

"Put it in yer pocket or stick it in yer belt like I do wid mine. Just keep it handy... Just in case," he added.

A hundred yards from shore Hugh cut the engines and let their forward way and the incoming tide carry them to a gentle meeting with a small wooden floating dock that was mostly used for swimming. As the bow touched, Hugh put the helm over hard and Franco jumped onto the dock with the bow line which he looped around a piling while the ship's momentum and the tide slowly brought her stern around until she was facing back out to sea and Hugh could step onto the dock with another line. Quickly, and silently, ROSA was securely moored.

31.

AS THEY DROVE OFF the ferryboat Stanley caught sight of an illuminated clock on the side of the small ferry office building. "Twenty past twelve...like you said Snake, ten minutes across. When we supposed ta meet 'em?"

"One aclock," Snake answered as he spun the wheel expertly to avoid the one auto waiting to board the boat for the return trip to Perth Amboy. "Dumb ssson-of-a-bitch. Musss be drunk." He resisted the temptation to shout at the driver as they rolled past him and turned onto Hylan Boulevard.

"Maybe he's a fuckin' Limey. Dey. drive on da wrong ssside-a da road."

"Yeah maybe." Stanley tried to laugh but the gun in his pocket seemed to have dulled his sense of humor.

Hylan Boulevard runs from Tottenville, along Staten Island's southeastern shore, all the way to Fort Wadsworth. Although it is never more than a half mile from the shore, the heavy woods running from the road side all the way down hill to the sandy beaches below, gave travelers very little opportunity to see the nearby ocean.

A few moments after turning onto Hylan Boulevard, Snake slowed to a speed not much faster than a man could walk.

"Watch fer Sssegine Avenue. Should be comin' up any sssecond. The fuckin sssign ain't hardly big enough ta sssee."

Sure enough, only a few moments later, they spotted the sign and Snake turned carefully into Segine Avenue before switching off the headlamps.

"This it?" Stanley asked.

"Almost," Snake whispered. "Keep yer voice down. We'll sssit here 'till our eyes get used ta the dark, then we'll go down the road 'till sssomebody meets usss."

Before Snake switched off the headlamps, Stanley had seen what he called, "the road." It was little more than tire tracks in the dirt, with trees and thick shrubs on either side. He could not believe Snake, or anybody else, could drive it without lights. But within less than five minutes his eyes had adjusted to the darkness and he found there was enough light coming from the stars for him to see the tracks twenty-five or thirty feet ahead of them.

Snake put the motor in gear and they began to creep forward. After about two hundred feet the road began to swing off to the left and angle down an increasingly steep grade. Turning off the engine, Snake let the down hill grade and the weight of the truck carry them. Almost immediately Stan began to see flashes of silvery water through breaks in the foliage, then, a moment later, as the tracks began curving back to the right he realized they were in the process of making a loop. A few feet further on, as the grade began to flatten out, Snake stopped the truck and set the hand break.

"What now?" Stanley whispered.

"We wait."

The words were hardly out of Snake's mouth before they heard two soft taps on the front fender followed seconds later by two similar taps on the driver's side door. The truck tipped slightly then a blur, Stanley took to be a face, materialized in the window next to Snake's shoulder. Starlight or not, it was impossible to make out the features of the man who seemed to be dressed all in black.

"Right on-a time," the blur told Snake in a whispered voice that wasn't friendly or unfriendly, just flat, emotionless, business like.

"Ya got somebody in dere wid ya?"

"Yeah," Snake whispered back. "New guy. Helper."

"Any changes you suppos-a to let us-a know." This time the voice was definitely unfriendly.

"Yeah, well it was sort of a last minute thing." Once again Snake's voice was devoid of sibilant esses. "Walt thought wid two of us it would go quicker. He's okay."

"You got-a da money?" The voice asked.

"Yeah. Behind the seat."

"Gimme it."

Stanley felt, rather than saw, Snake reach for the package his brother had given him, then pass it out the window.

"Okay. He come wid-a me," the blur told them. "You bring da baskets." The blur disappeared.

"What do I do?" Stanley whispered.

"Do like he says," Snake answered as he opened his door and started to climb down. "And don't make no noise neither. Just ease the door closed."

Suddenly, unexpectedly, the door behind Stanley opened. The hand that grabbed his arm didn't pull him out, it lifted him out. Stanley was not a big man, five-foot nine, about one hundred forty pounds, still it was hard to believe anyone could actually lift him off his seat with one hand...

"Come wid me." The hand gripping his arm pulled him towards a tiny path through the bushes.

Twenty paces along the dark pathway the shrubbery began to thin out and starlight returned. A few feet further on, Stanley could see a wooden walkway leading out over the water to where a boat was tied. As they got closer he could make out another shape standing on the deck. The blur released his arm and handed Walter's package to the shape on the deck. "Dis here's a new guy," the blur told the shape. "Snake says Walt sent him ta help."

"Ain't never needed help before," the shape replied. "Keep yer eye on him while I check the money."

A hatch of some kind opened and a dim light spilled out. Jesus Christ! It was him. The guy who opened the door. The guy who found them. The guy who hit him while the bitch chewed off his cock.

Slowly, carefully, Stanley pulled the pistol out of his pocket. His hand trembled slightly but he steadied it with his left hand and with both thumbs pulled back the hammer. In the silence, the sound of the pistol cocking was like the snap of a dry branch breaking. At the same instant Franco saw the barrel of the gun glisten in the starlight.

"Hugh! He got a gun!" Franco lunged towards the man as the gun went off with a defining explosion.

Franco's body slammed back into Hugh, just as Hugh pulled his own pistol and returned fire. Stanley pitched backwards onto the small dock where blood spurting from his head quickly began to darken the wood planks.

Hearing the roar of the two shots, Snake dropped the fish baskets he was carrying, drew his own pistol and ran towards the boat dock. He could see the boat below him but he could not make out what was happening. From his position on deck, however, Hugh could see Snake silhouetted against the night sky. Taking careful aim, he fired, then watched as Snake collapsed.

"Stay bellow." Hugh whispered to Mary Kate as he crouched behind the gunwale... Watching...waiting... After several seconds he called softly to her, "It's all right. Come look after Franco." Jumping to the dock to untie the mooring lines, Hugh realized his arm and hands were wet... sticky with blood. Quickly throwing the lines onto the ship, he jumped back onboard and ran to the wheelhouse.

The engines started quickly. He eased the ship forward, pointing her towards the mouth of the cove and the open sea beyond. As he increased her speed he was aware of Mary Kate arriving next to him. "How's Franco?"

"He wants you Hugh."

Telling Mary Kate to take the wheel and keep her heading straight out, Hugh went to Franco and knelt beside him.

"Hugh..." his voice was shaky, scarcely above a whisper. Hugh bent closer to hear. "You take care... Rosa... the boys..."

"Like they're me own, Franco. Like there me own." Hugh was never sure that Franco heard him.

Part Two

The Musician

1.

NEVER MIND THE VERNAL EQUINOX, if you live in Joliet, Illinois, as I do, you know the shortest days of the year are in January and February when the wind blowing down from Lake Michigan brings clouds that blend the gray of morning into the dusk of evening and you can go for days without a sight of the sun. Days when the temperature never gets above freezing and the sound of sleet makes an almost continuous hiss as it strikes the Chicago River Canal which runs through the center of the city.

About forty miles south and east of Chicago, Joliet is what they call a "blue collar town." It isn't very big. I learned in Sophomore American History that in 1673 a French Canadian explorer named Louis Jolliet (yeah, two "L's") was paddling down the Des Plaines River and pitched his camp on a hillside near where our city is located. About sixty years later a man named Charles Reed built a cabin in the same area and before long other settlers began arriving and they decided to call their new town Joliet. (Yes, one L.) Nothing in our history told him why Charles Reed decided to settle there, or how Reed and his companions knew Louis Jolliet had camped there sixty years earlier, or why they decided to name their town after him, or why they didn't know his name was spelled with two L's.

Last I heard the population of Joliet is right around forty thousand. The main industry is steel. Steel, and railroads to carry the steel, and ships to bring ore down the river and carry steel back up the river.

Maybe I should put all that in the past tense, because the depression has made a lot of the mills close down and there are not very many trains or ore boats coming here these days. With mills closing down almost every day probably now Joliet is best known for the State Prison just outside of town.

We talk a lot about the depression in school, and about F.D.R. My dad thinks he will be our next president and will get the country back on its feet.

I know a lot of people are hurting, but the truth is things haven't seemed that bad to me. I guess I'm lucky! My dad still has a job and we have a nice home up on Raynor Avenue. I suppose when you're seventeen years old and in the middle of your senior year in High School, you don't think much about anything other than passing grades and having some fun. I'm getting good grades, I have an after school job and, best of all, I have my drums.

Saturdays are sort of good/bad days for me. Dad has to be at work by eight-thirty, so we get up at seven o'clock, but because the man next door works nights, I'm not supposed to touch my drums until at least ten. Before that I have to make my bed, clean my room and wash the kitchen floor. Since I have to leave for work at eleven-thirty, Saturdays don't give me much practice time. That's the bad part.

The good part is my job at the State Theater. The State is the second largest theater in town. It's located just two blocks away from the Rialto, our biggest theater, and just around the corner from the Hotel Joliet. The hotel is eight stories high and it's our tallest building.

I started working at the State as an usher when school got out last May. Then, in October, I was moved up to Doorman and I got a raise from fifteen cents an hour to twenty. I work after school on Tuesday, and Thursday from five until the box office closes around nine. Saturdays from when we open at noon until the last feature goes on sometime between ten and ten-thirty. Once a month I have to stay until closing, which is always a couple of minutes before midnight. On Sundays I work from one until six. In Illinois, theaters are not allowed to open until one o'clock on Sunday.

All tolled, I put in twenty-three hours a week. At twenty cents an hour, I'm making a neat four sixty a week, plus mom and dad can come see the show for free any time they want to, which is mostly on Thursday nights. They usually come for the early show and then the three of us take the trolley home. Each week I pay twenty-five cents for a student trolley pass that's good for as many rides as I want.

When I was moved up to Doorman, I got to know Millie Novoczech, our box office cashier. She has dark hair and a pretty face. I thought she was beautiful. It didn't take her long to let me know she was twenty years old and I was much too young and naive to interest her.

Millie sits in a glassed-in booth in the outer lobby and sells tickets. Tickets are numbered and come in big rolls. Each day our manager, Mr. Oliver, loads the ticket rolls into the machine under the counter, behind the ticket window, then he and Millie check the number of the first ticket on each roll. When Millie sells tickets she puts the money into the cash drawer, then she pushes a key, and the machine spews out as many tickets as she tells it too. At the end of the night Millie and Mr. Oliver check the last ticket number, figure how many tickets have been sold, then count the money in the till. The money and the number of tickets should come out even. There's always a chance for making mistakes with change, so sometimes the numbers aren't exactly in balance, but Millie brags her cash is ahead more often than behind. I remember once hearing Mr. Oliver tell her she was the best cashier he ever had. Little did he know.

Millie was what my friend Hammy Richardson calls a "cock teaser!" But, like the moth and the flame, I couldn't keep away from her. When things were slow I would walk out to the outer lobby and talk with her for a couple of minutes.

Millie loves to tell me things about her sex life. For instance, she will stretch and yawn and say something like, "I'm so sleepy. Me and my boy friend did it all night long." Then she'll ask me if I like to "do it?" I always try to sound mature and sophisticated and say something like, "Who doesn't?" I don't tell her a lie, but I'm not going to let her know I have never "done it."

Whenever I talk to Millie her skirt is almost always up above her crossed knees and sometimes I can see the tops of her stockings. When you're seventeen years old that sort of thing can give you a hard-on. It can also make you agree to do a lot of stupid things you might not normally agree to do.

A couple of weeks after I started working as a doorman, Millie told me she knew how I could increase my income by as much as a buck-fifty, maybe even two bucks a week. My job as doorman is to tell people "hello" and take their tickets when they came in. I try to make them feel welcome, tell them where they can find the best seating, or how long they'll have to wait for seats, things like that and I tear their tickets in half, put one half in the ticket box and give the other half, the "stub", back to the person who handed me the ticket. But lots of times, especially when people were late for a show, they are in too much of a hurry to take their stubs. Millie told me if I didn't tear their tickets in half, and they didn't ask for their stubs, I would have perfectly good tickets in my hand. Tickets I could give back to her to sell again. That meant money that didn't have to match up with the ticket numbers. Money Millie and I could share.

2.

THIS JANUARY HAS BEEN THE WORST one I can remember. It's been really cold and I don't think there's been a single day since New Year's when we haven't had at least some snow. A lot of times you hear people say "it's too cold to snow." Maybe that's true, but not in Joliet.

On Saturday, January 11th, when I finished washing our kitchen floor, the thermometer outside the door was registering 11 degrees; it was snowing hard and we had a super double-feature scheduled: "Tarzan of the Apes," with Johnnie Weismuller and Maureen O'Sullivan, and "Red Dust," staring Clark Gable and Jean Harlow. It's hard to tell how weather will affect our business. Some days when it's snowing, or just plain awful, almost nobody comes to the movies. Other times, same weather, we have lines all day long.

I was pretty sure with Tarzan and Clark Gable playing this was going to be one of the "lines all day" kind of days and on bad weather days Mr. Oliver doesn't mind if I let people into the outer lobby to keep warm before Millie opens the box office. So, looking at the thermometer and the snow coming down outside, I decided to cut a couple of minutes off my practice time and catch the eleven fifteen trolley.

My prediction turned out to be right. We were so busy that most of the afternoon our Chief of Service, Tom Kravitz, was working the lobby rope helping me try to keep people in line until seats were available. With him that close, I didn't have a chance to "kipe" any tickets until after five o'clock when he gave himself a short break. Then I got four fifteen-centers, and handed them to Millie.

Our prices go up to twenty-five cents at six o'clock, so there is usually a rush just before then and I figured Millie would be able to re-sell the four tickets with no trouble, but she was unhappy about my not having given her more tickets earlier in the afternoon. I guess I was sort of apologizing to her when I looked up and saw Tom Kravitz, just a few feet away, looking at me. I had heard about people getting so scared they pissed in their pants, but until that moment I had always thought it was just an expression. Finding out it actually might happen was too close for comfort.

"There probably won't be any seats until the show breaks," I told Millie in a loud voice, while with my eyes, I tried to let her know Tom was watching us.

"Okay, thanks Charles." Millie and my mother are the only two people in the world who call me "Charles." From my mother it's okay. From Millie... She knew damn well I didn't like it. She only did it to get my goat.

I watched her give a little wave to Tom and calmly push the cover plate back in place over the open part of the ticket window to stop the cold draft that wanted to get into her cubical. Even with the heater she had inside, I knew it got pretty cold in there. She was always telling me about the woolen panties she wore to keep her "you know what" warm.

Hammy's right. She is a cock teaser! But why is she teasing my cock?

It was only a few minutes after Tom Kravits saw me talking to Millie that he asked me to come see him when I took my seven o'clock break.

I said, "Okay." Then there was nothing I could do but worry until seven o'clock.

In a way I was surprised he hadn't fired both of us right when he saw us. Then I realized he couldn't do that. First he would have to tell Mr. Oliver, and second, on a busy night like this, they couldn't very well operate without a cashier and a doorman. He would have to get somebody to take our places first. So I was going to have to wait until my break before he would tell me I was fired. What was I going to tell mom and dad?

Tom's "office" was a worn out wooden desk pushed against the basement wall, just past our lockers, down next to the furnace room. He had a swivel chair with a worn out leather seat, and one plain, straight back wooden chair somebody else could sit in if he told them it was okay. Usually, when he called the staff to a meeting, he would sit and all of us would stand. Not that he was a bad guy, in fact he was really great to work for. We all liked and respected him. Once, when I was telling my dad how Tom insisted we had to be quiet and taught us how to use hand signals rather than call... "shout". My dad said he thought Tom ran a "tight ship" and it was a good thing. Not only for the theater, but for all us kids as well.

Tom told me to sit down. I guessed this was it.

"Chuck, I've got some news for you but I'd like you to keep it to yourself for a couple of days. Okay?"

What was I supposed to say to that but, "Okay. Sure Tom. Anything you say." All I could think of was it didn't exactly sound like he was about to fire me.

"Okay. Good." Tom had a way of tapping his

finger when he was thinking. At least I guess he was thinking because he wasn't saying anything, so I sat and watched his finger and wondered if he ever played the drums. Finally he took a deep breath, twisted his head around like his collar was too tight, and looked right at me.

"Chuck, I'm leaving the State at the end of next week."

"Wow!" I think I said it out loud, I'm not sure. But news like that certainly deserved a "wow". "What happened?" I finally managed to ask.

"I'm going over to the Rialto. They offered me an Assistant Manager job."

"Wow," I said again. I was really articulate. "Gee, Tom that's great!"

The Rialto was Big Time. Mr. Oliver called it "The Big House." The Rialto played vaudeville, real live acts, and about once a month, usually on a Wednesday, one of the famous orchestras came in for a "one nighter". I saw The Dorsey Brothers band there, and Vincent Lopez. Best of all, last summer Cab Calloway and his All Negro Review. My mother would drop dead if she knew I like the black bands better than the Dorseys, or Vincent Lopez.

"My leaving means an opening here at the State, Chuck. Would you be interested in taking over my job?"

Me?" I could not have been more surprised.

Maybe "shocked" is a better word. I came down to his office expecting to get fired and instead Tom Kravitz was asking me if I wanted his job.

"Wow," I said it again. No question, I need to expand my vocabulary. I knew he was waiting for something more concrete than "wow."

"Gosh Tom, I don't know what to say except I can't take your job. I've got to finish high school, then I'm going into music."

"I understand you wanting to finish school, Chuck, but the job here will start you out at fifteen dollars a week. That's a pretty good salary, and if you do as well as I think you will, I'm sure you can expect a raise in six months. Besides, if you want to, you can probably work out a way to go to school half days and get your diploma."

Tommy was right. Fifteen dollars a week was a damn good salary. He also was right, I could work out a way to get through high school on a half-day schedule. Lots of guys who were lucky enough to find jobs were doing that. But I wasn't really interested in being the Chief of Service, or a manager for that matter.

My folks wanted me to go on to junior college after I graduated from high school, but I wanted to go into music. I had already put together a trio: piano, clarinet, and me...drums. We played Friday afternoons for the weekly school "social" and a man, who's son was in my class, told me come summer he would give us five dollars a night to play Fridays and Saturdays at his restaurant.

That would be great for a while, but I really wanted to join one of the bands I listened to on the radio or went to see at the Rialto, so I told Tom, "I don't want your job here, but I'd give my shirt for a job at the Rialto where I could see all the bands that play there. Someday I'm going to get a job with one of them."

"Okay, Chuck," he smiled at me. "I told Mr. Oliver I didn't think you'd want the job but I promised him I'd give it a good try."

"Gee whiz, Tom, I'm really flattered he would want me for the job. Is it okay if I tell him thanks?"

"Sure. He would like that. He thinks a lot of you. And listen, about the Rialto, I'll see what I can do, but meantime you keep at it here. With me leaving, Mr. Oliver is going to need you more than ever."

3.

EXCEPT FOR ONCE A MONTH, when I have to work late, Saturday night is when Millie and I split our week's take. After the last show starts, as soon as Millie and Mr. Oliver go to his office to check the tickets and money, I'm off. Well as soon as the "late man" comes to take my place, that is. The ushers and I take turns being "late man."

If anybody still wants to see what's left of the show after the box office closes, they pay the late man. They don't even have tickets for late admissions; it's just, "take the cash and let them in." Since Millie and I already had a deal for extra money, I always turned in all the late admissions I collected, but I wondered how much money Mr. Oliver got from the other guys, and how much they maybe kept.

Harold finally got there and I took off. I walked slowly across the lobby. Tom Kravitz would have a fit if any of us were to run, or even walk fast, across the lobby. But once I was through the door to the basement, I was like greased lightening.

It took me about four seconds to slip out of my swallowtail uniform coat. I could unclip the bow tie so fast you couldn't really count the time that took, and I could unbutton the collar that held the stiff shirtfront on almost as fast. My high top trousers were too big for me, so I had suspenders to hold them up. When I slipped the suspenders off my shoulders, I didn't need to unbutton the fly to take them off. What did take time was hanging up my coat and those pants so they would hold their creases. Tom was always giving demerits for trousers that didn't have good, sharp creases.

It never took me long to put on my own clothes, except tonight I had shoe trouble... a pretty big hole in the sole of my right shoe. If there had been an H-O Oats box top around the house this morning everything would have been okay. I don't know what it is about H-O Oats box tops, but they are almost waterproof. I have worn an H-O Oats box top in my shoe for two, maybe three days at a time, but this morning there was still a lot of cereal left in the box, so there was no top I could use and I had put some newspaper in my shoe. By the time I got to the theater the paper was soaked through and I took it out. Now I needed something to replace it with.

There was nothing in my locker that would

work, and nothing I could find on the floor, so I just had to walk on my heel until I got to the White Tower at the corner up the street... I sort of knew a guy named Don who worked at White Tower because I ate there a lot. Sometimes Don would give me a free hamburger and sometimes I let him into the theater for free. I was pretty sure he would give me one of those bags they put burgers "to go" in. I don't know what those bags are made of, but they are really good. Almost better than H-O Oats box tops!

When I got to the White Tower, Don gave me a bag. "Gee, thanks Don," I told him as I took my shoe off. Of course that is exactly when Millie arrived...

"If you're undressing for me Charles, I'm not interested so please don't bother." She said it loud enough for Don and everybody in the place to hear. Someone laughed and I started to blush. Then, of course, the more I blushed, the more I blushed, if you know what I mean. Almost everybody was laughing or at least grinning by then. Naturally Millie made it even worse by saying, "Stop blushing Charles." Millie seemed to enjoy embarrassing me.

I didn't say anything to her. I just kept my head down and carefully tied my shoe before I straightened up. Then I took a sip of the hot chocolate I had ordered and bit off about half my oatmeal cookie. When you order a hot chocolate at White Tower you get two oatmeal cookies with it. It cost a nickel but it's worth it.

I guess Millie decided she'd had enough fun because she didn't make any more remarks. Instead she slid onto the seat next to me, ordered a cup of coffee, then swiveled her body towards me. All of a sudden I could feel her knee pressing against my leg and sort of moving up and down gently. She is a cock teaser! I told myself while my cock began to grow what Hammy calls a "lazy hard-on."

"What did Tom want?"

"Nothing much," I tried to cover my surprise at her question. "Just a couple of new signals he wants us to use," I lied.

"It must have been more than that," she insisted. "I'm sure he didn't call you down to his office on a Saturday Night unless it was for something important." Then she got "that" look on her face. The look that tells you she is much smarter than you are. "Did he tell you about his new job?"

I'm sure my eyes got wider. Tom had told me his new job was a secret and Millie already knew. "How?" I started to ask how she knew, but I promised Tom I wouldn't talk about it.

"You look surprised, Charles. You don't think me and Tom have any secrets do you?"

"I don't know about any secrets," I told her. Then, trying to change the subject I asked, "How much did we make?"

"Not going to talk?" She looked at me for a couple of long seconds, then her leg stopped rubbing mine and she turned her body away. "Okay. Your share is a dollar and twenty cents." She reached into her coat pocket and pulled out a handful of money.

"I was thinking it would be one-fifty, " I told her.

"Oh Charles. It could have been, but you were too late giving me those last tickets this afternoon. I couldn't sell them before the price change."

"Okay," I said slowly. "A dollar twenty is pretty good." In my mind I was finding it hard to believe she couldn't sell the four tickets I gave her. She had practically an hour. After about three beats I added, "I would have thought you could sell a couple of them anyway."

She turned back towards me again and "batted" her eyes. I mean she really did. Before that very moment I never knew what it meant, "bat your eyes." I remember reading that expression once and asking my mother what it meant. She told me it meant to blink. That's like calling Lake Michigan, "water". I mean it is water, but that doesn't really describe it.

"Charles, do you think I'm cheating you?"

For a minute I wasn't sure how to answer, then I decided to tell her the truth. "I think it should be more."

"Well, if that's what you think..." She swiveled her seat away from me, got up without finishing her coffee, and headed for the door. And without paying for her coffee either!

I watched her walk past the White Castle window all hunched over against the snow. When she was out of sight, I put my second cookie in my mouth and thought about her and Tom Kravitz. What did she mean about them having no secrets? She was always telling me how much she and her boy friend "did it." Was he the boy friend?

Why is it that whenever I think about such things I began to get a hard on? I finished my hot chocolate and put down a nickel for her coffee.

"That's okay Chuck. On the house," Don told me. "Us guys gotta stick together against them dames."

Outside the White Tower it was cold and snowing hard. I realized I should have told Don thanks again for the sliders bag but I wasn't going to go back. Why do people call them "sliders" anyway? I asked myself. What's wrong with "hamburgers?"

There were only a couple of people on the

trolley. I sat down in the middle of the car, half way between the front door and the back door, where it's warmest. I didn't want to think about Millie and Tom but I couldn't help it. Were they "doing it?"

"Fucking", Hammy would say?

I wondered how Millie would look with no clothes on.

I wondered if Tommy used a "rubber" when they did it.

I wondered if she bit his ear when she was coming. Hammy told me hot girls always bite your ear when they do it. Tomorrow I would look at Tom's ears. No, I wouldn't look at his ears. What the hell did I care if they are doing it? Why in hell do I keep saying "doing it?" Fucking is what they're doing. Just plain fucking!

Geeze, I wonder what it's like?

It wasn't a lazy hard on anymore; I was having a genuine erection! Shit! I looked around to see if anyone was watching me. No body was. Thank God for that!

I pulled my Ludwig Drum Catalogue out of my coat pocket and opened it on my lap. With this week's pay, I now had the eighteen dollars I needed for the tom-tom I have been wanting. In the morning I'll give the money to my mother and she'll write a check for me to "Goldrich Music

Store" in Chicago. Then, in a couple of weeks, I'll have the drum I needed to fill out my set.

Looking at drum equipment and thinking about the really professional set I'll have once I get the tom-tom will usually take my mind off almost anything, but it wasn't working tonight. I wonder where they do it? I wonder what it's like? I wonder how a tit feels?

I don't know how we traveled so far so fast, but before I realized we were even getting close, I heard the conductor shouting, "Raynor Avenue. Next stop North Raynor."

I looked up and saw him looking right at me. Gee Whiz! I still had a big goddamn erection! I jammed my hand in my pocket, made a big fist, and went out the back door.

I walked the two blocks to my house slowly. I knew my mother would be awake, waiting for me, and I couldn't go in with a stiff pecker. Walking slowly, snow began to blow under my collar and leak over the tops of my shoes. There's nothing like snow and wet feet to calm an erection. By the time I climbed up the front steps I probably looked like a snowman, but I didn't have a bulge in my pants anymore.

4.

SUNDAY WAS COLD, but for a change, no snow. Well, I mean it wasn't falling anymore. Before yesterday's storm there had been a foot on the ground, and now there was another two inches on top of that.

Shoveling our walks is another one of my jobs. So I shoveled snow and thought some more about Millie. I decided not to give her any more tickets to re-sell. I knew she would be sore, but the way she acted last night, I didn't care if she was. Besides, if I was practically gunna take over Tom Kravitz's job for a while, I couldn't really do that again. In fact, I should probably tell Mr. Oliver what Millie was doing... well no, I couldn't do that either.

When I finished shoveling I had about an hour left for practice before going to work. I don't guess my mom and dad liked "the noise" very much but the truth is, I never play real loud. I've always thought drums should be subtle. I learned that from my mom, she told me was not to play loud all the time. She said, "Play softly, then when you want to make a statement you have someplace to go!"

So, I played softly for almost an hour then headed for the State. I got there about quarter to one, put on my uniform and was on the floor when Millie and Mr. Oliver came walking across the lobby to the box office with the ticket rolls and cash box.

"Hi, Mr. Oliver." He smiled and waved back. I didn't say anything to Millie and she didn't even look at me. I guessed she was still sore but that was okay, I was mad at her too.

I didn't give her any tickets Sunday. I didn't even talk to her all day.

I didn't talk to her on Tuesday, or on Thursday either, except when I had to tell her something about seating. By Saturday I guess everybody knew we were on the outs, but nobody cared very much because Saturday was Tom Kravitz's last day and everybody was thinking about that, not about Millie and me... Everybody felt bad Tom was leaving and we were all going to meet after work at the White Tower for sort of good bye party, only I couldn't go because it was my late night.

Tom took the door when I went for supper and I told him how sorry I was that I couldn't be at the party. He said business comes first and besides, we were going to be working together again as soon as a spot opens up at the Rialto. That he remembered I wanted to work there made me feel good.

When I got back from my supper break, one of the ushers, Teddy Dodge, handed me an envelope, "It's from Millie." He grinned that kind of grin you hate to get from anybody. "I though you two were mad at each other. What's up?"

"Wouldn't you like to know?" I stuck the envelope in my pocket.

"Ain't ya gonna read it?"

"Not while you're standing here. It's probably a hot love letter."

"Oh sure. I bet." Teddy walked away. Sometimes if you tell a guy too much he doesn't believe anything.

We got busy then and I didn't have time to open Millie's envelope until my break, then I sat down in front of my locker, opened the envelope, and read the note inside.

Chuck. I'm sorry you can't come to Tommy's party and I'm sorry you are mad at me because I like you a lot. If you come to my house when you finish work tonight maybe we can make up. 284 East 9th Street # 4B. Top Floor. Don't tell anybody if you come.
M.

Gee Whiz! I said to myself. What's this all about? She never called me "Chuck" before, and why does she want me to come to her house?

Hammy once told me sometimes a cock has a mind of it's own. I never believed him, but now I know it's true. I wasn't even thinking anything and all of a sudden mine was getting stiff.

5.

GUESS WHAT? IT WAS SNOWING AGAIN by the time the show ended.

Saturdays, when I close, I really have to rush because there is a trolley at about ten minutes after twelve. I think it's timed for the end of our show and if I miss it, it's nearly an hour until the next one. I made it to the corner just about the same time the trolley did. There was a bunch of people waiting, most likely people who had been to the show. By the time I got on board all the seats were taken so I grabbed a straphanger and hung on as the trolley started up with the usual lurch.

For the past three hours I had been trying not to think about Millie's note, but now I had to. 9th Street was the third stop. I knew she was just teasing me. Getting even. If I went to her house she probably wouldn't even be there. Or if she was, her boy friend would probably be there too. What if Tom Kravitz is her boy friend? Well, I could always say Millie told me, since I couldn't go to the party, I should stop in...

But maybe Tom isn't her boy friend. Maybe she hasn't even got a boy friend. Come to think about it, I have never seen anybody with her. If she has a boy friend you would think he would come by once in a while to take her home or something. I bet she hasn't got a boy friend.

I got off at 9th Street and walked east to number 284. I half thought there wouldn't even be a number 284, but there was. Just as she said, 284 was an apartment building. I looked at it from across the street for a while then decided, what the heck, I'd call her bluff.

In the vestibule, just inside the front door, in a small metal frame, there were buttons with apartment numbers next to them,. You could push somebody's buzzer, and if they wanted to let you inside the locked inner door, they would buzz you back.

I pushed the button next to the number 4B.

Almost before I took my finger off the button I got a buzz back. She must have been watching from upstairs. I opened the inner door and went in.

Half way down the hall there were stairs. I climbed to the third floor and looked up. Millie was leaning over the railing.

"Shhh." She put a finger up to her mouth.

When I got to her floor she whispered, "Don't

talk until we get inside." Millie was wearing something I think they call a "kimono." I couldn't tell for sure what she had on under it. A nightgown maybe.

As soon as we got inside, she closed the door. "You're covered with snow. Come on, I made some hot chocolate."

She walked past me and I followed her to the kitchen. There were two cups and a dish holding some cookies sitting on a little oilcloth covered table. "Take off your coat and sit down, Chuck," she told me. Then she took the cocoa off the stove and poured some into each cup. "Don't you like me any more Chuck?"

I didn't know what to say, so I just looked at her.

"Cat got your tongue?" Her voice was beginning to sound like a little girl's.

"I don't know what I'm supposed to say," I told her honestly.

"You're supposed to say you like me."

"I do. I like you, Millie."

"You're supposed to say it like you mean it, Chuck."

"I do mean it. Except you tease me a lot, and I was mad at you after last Saturday. But I like you."

"And I like you, Chuck." This time her voice was not little girl. It was soft and sort of husky. "I guess I tease you because I like you so much."

I suppose that makes sense, if you're a woman.

She tilted her head and looked at me for a couple of seconds. "Now you're supposed to say you like me a whole lot and you want me."

"I don't think I know what that means exactly..."

She put her cup down and stood up, then took a step towards me. Suddenly she was standing so close my face was practically against her stomach. "You've never 'done it' have you Chuck."

Before I could say anything she put her hands around my head and pulled my face against her. "I think you are a really wonderful boy Chuck and I want to be your first woman. Would you like that?"

Holy Moses!

Before I knew it, Millie was leading me out of the kitchen. Then we were in her bedroom and she was unbuttoning my pants. She put her hand on me and I had an orgasm. I mean I came right in her hand.

"Oh shit..."

"It's all right, Chuck. I'll get a towel."

I just stood there with my trousers down around my ankles until she came back with a warm washcloth and a towel and started to wash me. I don't think I ever stopped being hard but if I did, I got hard all over again.

"Let's get in bed together and do it."

The next thing I knew she had turned the light off and I heard some rustling sounds, and then she was in bed next to me. I could feel her skin against mine... her breasts against me. Her "you know what" against me.

I came again!

"My goodness Charles. If you keep on like that we won't ever get to do it."

This time when she washed me, the wet cloth was almost cold. That seemed to make me even harder. Then, before I knew what she was doing, she was on top of me and I felt the most wonderful feeling I ever felt as my cock went inside her.

We did it together twice and she seemed to like it too. After the second time she put her head on my chest and one arm half way round me. I was practically falling asleep.

"Oh gee!" I sat up suddenly. "I've got to get home. My mother will kill me!"

Two weeks after my night with Millie I got a phone call from Tom Kravitz asking me if I wanted to work three days a week at the Rialto. When I told Mr. Oliver he shook my hand and said he knew how much I wanted to work there but if I ever wanted to come back to the State, he would always have a job for me. That made me feel pretty darn good.

6.

TWO WEEKS AFTER I STARTED at the Rialto, Paul Whiteman and his Orchestra came in for one day. I had read a lot about Paul Whiteman. He called himself "The King Of Jazz," but his music wasn't really jazz even though he hired a lot of top jazz musicians. The orchestra he was bringing in today had a trumpet player named Bunny Berigan in it, and a trombone player named Jack Teagarden. Both those guys are great!

Whiteman got his start in San Francisco. He began as a classical viola player and played with the San Francisco Symphony. When the war came along he joined the Navy and led a navy band.

After the war he started his own orchestra and they began playing at the Fairmont Hotel. In 1920 he made his first recording: "Whispering" backed by "The Japanese Sandman." The record sold something like ten thousand copies and Whiteman was a star.

During the 20's, he had musicians like Red

Nichols, Tommy Dorsey, Joe Venuti and Bix Beiderbeck playing for him and Bing Crosby got his start with the Whiteman orchestra back then, singing in a trio called "The Rhythm Boys." In 1930 they made a movie called, "The King of Jazz." I saw it at the State Theater before I even started to work there.

Usually orchestras came in on Wednesdays and did four shows. One-thirty to two-thirty. Four-thirty to five-thirty. Seven-thirty to eight-thirty and ten-thirty to eleven-thirty. My regular schedule at the Rialto is Monday and Wednesday from six until nine-thirty and Sunday afternoons, one to six. But when we have a stage show I start right after school, at four o'clock, and work until the last show begins.

When Paul Whiteman finished his third show, Tommy told me I could have a ten-minute break and, if I wanted to, I could go back stage and try to meet Mr. Whiteman. He knew the main reason I wanted to work at the Rialto was to have a chance to meet some real musicians.

Mr. Whiteman was in his dressing room. The door was open and I could see him sitting in there, looking at a magazine or something. He had his tuxedo coat off and his tie undone.

All of a sudden I got cold feet.

Paul Whiteman was one of the most

important men in the music business. I wanted to meet him in the worst way, but what gave me the right to bother him?

I stood outside his door, trying to work up nerve enough to knock when suddenly he looked up and saw me.

"Hello young man..."

"Hello Mr. Whiteman," I tried to say, but my voice didn't seem to want to come out.

"Come in, come in and tell me what's on your mind."

I took a deep breath, cleared my throat, and took four steps through the door into the dressing room. "I don't want to bother you, Mr. Whiteman. I'm a musician and I just wanted to meet you."

"It's important for us musicians to know each other. What's your name?"

"Chuck, sir. Chuck Stacey."

"Hello Chuck Stacey. What instrument do you play?"

"I play the drums."

"Drums." He nodded his head and beckoned me to come closer. "The drummer is a key member of the orchestra. Are you good?"

"Yes sir. I think so."

"That's fine. Confidence is important. Can you read music?"

"Yes sir. I took piano lessons from my mother

for seven years before I switched to drums. I can sight read."

Mr. Whiteman smiled, "What happened to your piano playing?"

"I heard a record by Art Tatum when I was twelve and I knew I was never going to be able to play like that, but at the same time I discovered the drums. I'll be as good on the drums as he is on the piano as soon as I get through school and start playing regularly."

"Art Tatum may be the best jazz piano player in the world. You will have to be very good indeed to equal him."

"Yes sir. I'm going to be."

Mr. Whiteman pulled a watch out of his trouser pocket. "We've got a little time before the last show. Why don't you get your practice pad and show me what you can do."

"I can't Mr. Whiteman." I was so embarrassed my voice was leaving me again. "I don't have my sticks and my pad with me and I'm only on a ten minute break," I finally managed to say.

Mr. Whiteman gave me another smile. With a smile like that it's no wonder people like him so much. "That's too bad, Chuck. I'm afraid I've got to leave immediately after the last show. Maybe the next time we come through town you can play for me."

My meeting with Paul Whiteman taught me a lesson I wasn't going to forget. When I came to work on Sunday, I brought a practice pad and a pair of sticks and put them in my locker. I was never going to miss another chance like that.

A month later in March, Ben Bernie and "all the lads" came in. Ben Bernie was a lot different from Paul Whiteman. I've heard him on the radio and I've read about him too. He was from New York City but you would never know it to hear him speak. He sounds almost southern. He called himself "The Old Maestro" and he was kind of a comedian. He talked with sort of a drawl, said "Yowsa, Yowsa" a lot, and told some jokes. When he ended his show he would say, "This is The Ol' Maestro Ben Bernie, and all the lads, saying Good night... Cherie Oh... A bit of a pip-pip, and pleasssant Dreeeams."

As a kid Bernie was sort of a violin virtuoso. When he got out of school he started doing a vaudeville act, telling jokes and playing the violin. People seemed to like his jokes and his voice better than his music and for a while he teamed up with a comic named Phil Baker. Their act went over pretty well but he liked music better so around 1923 he put together an orchestra. They got a "temporary" booking at the Roosevelt Hotel where the crowds liked them so much it turned into an exclusive engagement - from 1923 to 1929! In '29, he lost all his money in the market crash, but he managed to keep the orchestra together and somehow he got a radio show. Now, between the radio and touring with his band, I guess he's getting rich again.

I wasn't so nervous when I went to see him. His dressing room door was only slightly open, but a radio was playing inside, so I knocked.

"Who dat knockin' at my door?" The voice was just the same as it sounded on stage. When he said "door" it sounded like "dough-ahh."

I pushed the door open wide enough to be heard. "My name's Chuck Stacey, Mr. Bernie. I work here, but I'm a musician and I wanted to meet you."

"Sho-nuf Mr. Stacey. Yowsa, you-all come right on in here."

"Here" sounded like "he-ah."

Mr. Bernie had his coat and his trousers off and was laying flat on his back on the floor, smoking a cigar. I had never seen a famous orchestra leader lying on the floor in his underwear before. I guess I looked pretty surprised.

"It's my poe ol' back... it kills me, yowsa. Yow! Sa! This is the only thing that helps." He turned his head and looked at me. "You're a handsome young man Mr. Stacey. What instrument do you play?"

"I play the drums Mr. Bernie."

"Well what about that. I used to play a bit of the drums myself. Turn down that radio and let me hear you play something."

Gee Whiz, this was great! "I'll go get my sticks and pad." I told him.

"No-sa, no time for that. I is needin' a nap. You just use yo thumbs and play somethin' on the back of that old chair over there." He inclined his head towards a wooden chair standing in front of the makeup table.

This wasn't exactly what I had in mind, but the chair back would do fine. I'd spent half my life drumming on things with my thumbs and fingers and I wasn't going to pass up a chance to have him hear me.

I did a few paradiddles to sort of warm up then I closed it into a single stroke roll. I started it real soft them built to a crescendo, then switched to a rhythm beat.

When I finished, Mr. Bernie took a big drag on his cigar, then sat up and let the smoke out. "Mr. Stacey, yo pretty good with those thumbs. Yowsa. If I was to need a drummer in my band I think I'd give you a chance. But I got a fine lad on the drums just now, so you are out of luck tonight. But keep after yo music, hear me? One day somebody's sho to need yo services."

"Thank you, Mr. Bernie."

"Aw-right. Yowsa. Now you run along like a good lad and let the ol' maestro have a bit of a nap."

"Yes sir."

"Ben Bernie thinks I'm good enough to play with his orchestra," I told Tommy.

"That's great, Chuck. One of these days you'll be sitting up there on the stage instead of out here in the lobby taking tickets."

7.

ACTUALLY, THERE ARE SOME DAYS in Joliet when the weather is very nice. May 5th was one of them. The sun was shining, the temperature was about seventy degrees, and flowers were blooming all over the place. May 5th was a Wednesday and Henry Love and his Romance Orchestra were scheduled into the Rialto.

Henry Love came from a town in western Canada called Calgary. From what I've read, Calgary is kind of a wild-west place and not at all where you would think a man who looks and sounds like an English Lord would come from. He was a kid who started out playing the violin. His father owned a hotel in Calgary and when Henry decided he wanted to be an orchestra leader, his father hired him. People liked his music well enough that he got an offer to take his orchestra to Toronto where he played at the Hotel Prince and, as they say, the rest is history.

Henry Love plays "society" music and older people love it. I would have to say his music is pretty corny, but he has a real live orchestra, and I couldn't wait for school to end so I could go to work.

I was in Geometry Class when an office messenger came into the room and handed a note to Mr. Halleck. He read it then looked towards me, "Miss Lane wants to see you in the office." Miss Lane was an Assistant Principal. "Take your books, it sounds like you won't be back today."

You know getting called to the Principal's office is not something anybody likes. "The office" usually means just one thing. Trouble!

I told the office secretary who I was and she said I was to go right in to Miss Lane's office.

"Chuck, Mr. Kravitz from the Rialto Theater called. They have an emergency and he asked if you could be excused for the rest of the day."

"Gee whiz Miss Lane!" I was really surprised. "Did he say what's wrong?"

"No. He just said they needed you, and it was very important." She looked at something on her desk, "Let me see... you have Geometry and Latin this afternoon. If you promise you'll make up whatever work you miss today, I'll let you go."

"Sure, I promise Miss Lane."

"All right. You're excused for the rest of the day.

"Thank you Miss Lane."

It was just a couple of minutes before noon when I got to the theater. Most of the crowd for the first show was already inside and Tom Kravitz was waiting for me on the sidewalk out front. "What's up, Tom?"

"Chuck, come over here." He put his arm over my shoulder and led me away from the entrance doors. "Henry Love's drummer didn't show up and Henry says he won't do a show until he gets a new drummer down from Chicago. We have a big crowd inside and Mr. Simon doesn't want to start refunding tickets, so we told him you could fill in for the first show."

"Me?" I couldn't believe my ears. This was like something I dream about... something I make up when I'm waiting to go to sleep. Me! On-stage, at the Rialto. Henry Love's Romance Orchestra might not be the first band I would pick to play with, but they're famous, they're big time.

"Yeah, if Mr. Love goes for it. Mr. Simon is talking to him now. I know you can do it, Chuck. Come on."

"Is this the young man?" Henry Love asked.

He was a lot shorter than he looked in his pictures... maybe five feet seven or eight. He was skinny, he wore a skinny mustache and his kind of English accent did not sound the least bit friendly.

"Yes," Mr. Simon told him. "Chuck, this is Mr. Love."

I started to say "How do you do" but he cut me off.

"You've had professional experience?" His tone of voice said he wasn't going to believe whatever I said, so I decided to make it good.

"Yes sir. I work with a dance orchestra here in Joliet and Ben Bernie offered me a job when he was here last month."

"Hmmm. Why didn't you take it?"

I was ready for that. "I'm a senior in high school and I want to finish my final semester."

"I know the young man can do it, Henry."

Mr. Simon is probably the smoothest guy you will ever meet. He's a big, friendly looking man and he has a way with people. Somebody starts demanding a refund and before you know it he has them buying advance tickets for next week's show. That's what I call a manager!

"You know, Henry," Mr. Simon's voice got very confidential, "Without the first show we will have to refund a great deal of money. They don't like that up in Chicago."

I think that was what they call the "velvet glove."

The Rialto Theater is part of a big chain with headquarters in Chicago. We only book orchestras for one day, but the Chicago Rialto books them for three or four weeks, and the chain has theaters in Cleveland and Pittsburgh and Boston. That's a lot of good dates not even Henry Love can ignore. He thought for a moment then turned to me. "Get your sticks and I will audition you right now." I thought there was a little less antagonism in his voice.

The score he gave me was just like his music. Dull and simple. Boom-chick. Boom-chick. Boom, boom, boom-chick. "What tempo would you like Mr. Love?"

"Are you ready?" I guess I surprised him. I suppose he thought it would take me a while to study.

"Yes sir."

"Like this, then," he made like a conductor with his right hand and counted, "A-One, and-a two, and-a three and four."

Boom-chick, Boom-chick, Boom, boom, boom-chick. I taped my foot on the floor for the bass drum "boom" and made a cymbal sound with my mouth. After two eights of boom-chicks, there was a three count press roll and a cymbal splash. Boy oh boy! To think somebody gets paid good money for doing this.

"Well that was quite well done Charles."

Charles. My God, I thought, only my mother called me that. My mother and Millie Novochech,

I remembered.

Henry Love turned to Mr. Schimer. "All right, Lou, we'll give him a try. After all, as you said, the show must go on."

Then, turning to me, "Charles, you take this book and look over the scores. We'll cut the tap dance, drum duet from the first show, and the Polynesian number with all the tom-tom work. The rest of the show is not too complicated. I trust you can handle it."

The way he said, "trust you can handle it," made me angry but I don't think it showed. I'm going to be in the band, I told myself, so be nice. "Thank you, Mr. Love. I won't let you down."

"I hope not. Now I want you to sit right here and go over the score for the show. If you have any questions at all, you ask me. Meanwhile I'll have Howard find you a uniform. Perhaps you can wear the one Ronald Ede wore. You'll be using his drums. They are all set up on stage.

"Yes sir."

There was nothing difficult in the score he gave me but I studied it carefully anyhow. I wasn't going to make any mistakes.

"Mr. Love, what tempo for Whispering'?"

He looked up from something he was reading. "Very good, Charles. I'm glad to see you are concentrating. We play 'Whispering' at this tempo." He lifted his arm and did the conductor thing again: "A-One, and-a Two, and-a Three and Four."

"Thank you."

Gee, the note on the music said "bright." If the tempo Mr. Love just set was what he called "bright," I wondered how slowly he played tunes marked "slow".

After a while Howard brought in a uniform. I put it on while Mr. Love watched. The collar was tight and the shoulders were kind of snug but it didn't fit too badly and he decided I looked all right.

At quarter past one, Howard came back to help Mr. Love put on his tuxedo jacket.

"All right, Charles," Mr. Love looked towards me. "Let me see you again."

I stood up and he looked me over once more while Howard fixed my tie. "Very good," he said. "Follow me, it's time for us to go to work."

I followed Henry Love out of his dressing room and on to the stage where the band was setting up on three risers. The piano on the first level along with orchestra desks for three violins, two of whom were girls, and four saxophones. On the stage floor itself, in front of the saxes, there were chairs for the two vocalists, "Handsome Hunter Valentine" and "Lovely Dorothy Darling."

The second level was for a banjo, a tuba and two trombones. The third level was for three trumpets and me!

"Ladies and gentlemen," Mr. Love said as we walked on stage, "This is Charles who will be replacing Ronald for this performance." He turned to me and made a gesture with his hand that told me to take my place behind the drums.

There was almost no reaction to his announcement. The piano player sort of waved his hand and said, "Hi Charles." The two violin girls smiled, and a couple of other people looked at me without much interest. Boy oh boy! I was certainly making an impression.

After everybody got into place, the two vocalists made their entrance. And I mean "entrance." They reminded me of something Hammy said a lot: "They think their shit don't stink." The vocalists obviously did not have anything to do with the rest of the orchestra. They went to say something to Mr. Love, then took their seats without so much as looking at anybody in the band.

Ronald Ede's drum set was like a picture in my Ludwig Catalog except his set was Slingerland. A snare drum, a bass drum, three tom-toms, four cymbals, plus a hi-hat, a cow bell, a wood block and a set of temple blocks. He had an equipment tray on top of the bass drum with three pairs of sticks, two pairs of wire brushes and two pairs of tympani sticks with felt covered heads. Nothing in the score called for even half of all that equipment but it sure looked impressive. I sat down and decided I needed to raise the seat and change the angle on the snare drum slightly, but aside from that everything seemed all right.

While I was adjusting things I heard the newsreel starting. Six minutes later the newsreel end title music came up, the stage lights went down and we were in total darkness, waiting. Then I could hear, more than see, the main curtain starting to open... A pair of spotlights focused in on Mr. Love and he spoke into the microphone, "Ladies and Gentleman... It's Time for Romance." He looked up at me and gave a sweeping down beat with his violin bow.

The first note of his theme music was a big splash from the eighteen inch Ziljian Cymbal mounted on the floor stand to my right. That was the most exciting cymbal splash I ever played!

Fifty-five minutes later I played the same splash again as the curtain closed. I guess I had been more nervous than I thought because my jacket armpits were soaked with sweat.

"Nice job, kid." The voice surprised me. It had come from the trumpet player who sat next to me. "Thank you," I started to say but he was already out of his chair and half way off the stand.

"Charles." Mr. Love called me. "Come to my dressing room in five minutes please."

When I knocked on the door I reminded myself to be sure to ask him for a note confirming I had played a show with his orchestra. I didn't know if references counted for much in the music world, but I figured it might help next time if I had something to prove I actually did play for him. It would be better than saying Ben Bernie offered me a job.

Howard opened the dressing room door when I knocked. Mr. Love was seated at the makeup table reading something. He made a slight gesture with his left hand that I understood meant I should wait quietly until he was ready to talk to me. Finally, after what seemed like forever, he looked up. "Charles, Howard has given me some rather bad news. It doesn't seem we will be able to get a replacement for Ronald Ede before tomorrow so I would like to have you play the rest of the shows today. Can you do that?"

I think I blinked. I know I tried to say something but at first nothing came out.

"Mr. Love," I finally started making understandable sounds with my voice. "I don't know if you remember your first real job when you started out..." I swallowed a couple of times, "Right now there is nothing in the world I want to do more than to play the rest of the shows with you today."

"Very good Charles... I like your spirit."

Just at that moment the door opened and Mr. Simon walked in. "It went very well I thought Henry."

"Yes Lou, it did. Your young man acquitted himself very nicely. In fact I've just asked him to continue on today. If that's all right with you of course."

Mr. Simon looked at me. I think he winked before he turned back to Mr. Love. "I believe we can work that out Henry. I'll ask Tom to find a replacement. But of course Chuck won't receive any pay from us for today, so I'll expect you to compensate him appropriately."

Gee Whiz! Now Mr. Simon is my agent!

"Yes, all right Lou. I'll have Howard take care of that."

Mr. Love didn't sound particularly pleased at the idea of paying me, but I don't think he had much choice. "Charles," he turned to me, "The Romano's are unhappy that we left out their drum duet number. I would like you to go with William Dubin and spend some time with him and Norman and Patti. Perhaps the four of you can come up with something that will satisfy them."

"Yes sir." I started towards the door. "Oh," I

turned back. "Who is William Dubin?"

"William is our pianist and rehearsal conductor. I've asked him to wait for you. He should be somewhere nearby."

In fact, he was standing right outside Henry Love's dressing room. He was the man who had said "hello" when Mr. Love introduced me. William told me, "Hi, let's go see the Romano's."

The Romano's specialty number was done to "I Got Rhythm". Up-Tempo. The thing about it, the thing that made if fun, was that in the second chorus the drummer does a series of two bar breaks on the snare drum, then, in unison, the Romano's tap the same breaks. It's kind of like the drummer is daring them to do what he does. Then the Romano's turn it around and do some longer breaks the drummer copies. Finally they do something that is supposed to be so complicated the drummer can't keep up with them. He shrugs hopelessly and the band comes back in with music for the "big finish".

I worked with Norman and Patti for about half an hour, while William Dubin watched over us, then all three of them agreed I could do it fine and the Romano's went out for coffee.

"Wait a second," William said as I started to follow them. He handed me some more sheets of music. "This is our famous 'Polynesian Number'. You think you can handle it?"

I took the sheets and looked at them. The tune was, "The Hawaiian Wedding Song," and the two singers did a dance to it. William said Henry Love always made a big thing of it by introducing it by its Hawaiian title, "Ke Kali Nel Au." It had been written way back in 1926 by somebody named Charles King. I don't know if Charles King ever went to Hawaii. My guess is he didn't.

The arrangement was a slow kind of muffled tom-tom beat that gradually increased in tempo the way Ravel's Balero does.

"You're kidding, right?" I no sooner said it, than I realized I shouldn't have. But something about the way he said "our famous Polynesian Number" made me think he didn't take Henry Love's music too seriously. It was too late anyway, I had already said it. William rolled his eyes upwards. "No my boy, I only wish I were, but that's about as complicated as it gets around here."

"Thank God for the Romano's," I said without thinking. Geeze, me and my mouth. Why couldn't I learn to shut up?

"All right, Stacey." His voice was jokingly serious. "Let us not bite the hand that feeds us. The Romance Orchestra may not play the worlds jazziest music but the pay checks come regular."

"I wouldn't know about that," I told him. "I'm only here for the day."

"I hope not."

It took me about two beats to realize what he had just said, but before I could ask him if he thought there was any chance I could stay with the band, he was out the door.

We had about thirty minutes left until the next show. Most of the orchestra members had gone off somewhere. What I wanted to do was get to a telephone and call my mom. I was still wearing my band uniform trousers but I had taken off the coat and shirt and put on my own sweater. I decided I looked okay to go outside, around the theater and in the front to Tom's office.

When my mother answered I asked her if she and dad were still coming to the show tonight. She said they were and why was I asking. "Well," I told her, "I want to be sure you'll be here to see me playing with Henry Love's Orchestra. I'll ask Tom Kravitz to save a couple of good seats for you right down front."

I suppose it's just the mean streak in me that made me tell her that way. I could have counted to a hundred before she said anything.

"Charles. What are you telling me?"

"Honest mom. Henry Love's drummer didn't get here and Tom Kravitz and Mr. Simon fixed it up for me to play with him. So, you and dad are coming for sure?"

"We certainly are! You know your father likes Henry Love but I'm not certain he will be ready for this." Then she thought for a moment. I have been known to sometimes joke around about things. "Charles, you are telling me the truth. You are actually going to be on the stage with Henry Love?"

"Yeah, mom. Honest Injun."

Another pause. Then, "When is the next performance?"

"We go on in just a couple of minutes, then again at seven-thirty."

"Your father and I will be there at seven-thirty."

"Great! Tom will have seats for you."

For the four-thirty show, we did the Polynesian Number. Mr. Love smiled at me twice and gave me a nod that said he was pleased. Then the Romano's came on and we did the "I Got Rhythm" tap dance and drum duet. When we finished, they got really big applause. They bowed twice then turned and pointed to me. One of the spotlights swung away from them and focused on me. Wow! When a spot light shines on you, you can't see a thing.

"Take a bow stupid!" a voice in the dark next to me said. I stood up and sort of half bowed then pointed back towards the Romano's and clapped for them.

Just before the seven-thirty show Tom Kravitz came back stage and told me my mom and dad had arrived. "They're in the front row. I was in the lobby when you took your bow but Jimmy told me that was the biggest applause in the show." I honestly think he was as excited as I was. "You gonna do it again?"

"Gee, Tommy, I don't know. It wasn't scheduled. The Romano's just did it. I don't think Mr. Love was very happy about it."

"He should be."

"Yeah maybe, but I kind of get the idea Mr. Love likes to keep most of the applause for himself."

As it turned out, Mr. Love didn't have much choice. In the seven-thirty show the applause for the Romano's went on so long Mr. Love had to call them back for a second encore. We did another few bars of the "I Got Rhythm" duet and they pointed to me again. So I stood up and bowed. You think I wasn't excited? Gee Whiz!

Wholly Mackerel! Applause is something I'll never get enough of! And my mom and dad were in the audience.

After the seven-thirty show Tom brought my folks back stage. Dad looked a little stunned; mom was so thrilled she had tears in her eyes. We were hugging and kissing when Mr. Love appeared. "Is this your mother and father Charles?"

"Yes sir." I introduced them to him.

"I'm most happy to meet you both," Henry Love's accent sounded even snootier than usual. "The fact is I was hoping to contact you this evening. I wonder if we could step into my dressing room?"

Mom and dad looked at each other then at me. I shrugged back at them. I didn't know what Henry Love wanted.

"May I offer you some tea?" was the first thing Mr. Love said when we got inside his dressing room.

"No... no thanks," my dad answered. Then he looked at my mother, "Do you want some tea Edith?"

Mom shook her head "no".

"Ahhh..." Mr. Love glanced around at nobody for a second... "We've been playing in Canada recently... I brought back a tiny bit of Scotch whiskey. Would either of you care for a drop of that?"

"No thank you, I don't think so Mr. Love."

My dad is the impatient type. I guess Henry Love made ten times as much money as my dad did, maybe twenty times as much, but my dad wasn't going to let Mr. Love intimidate him. "Perhaps you could just tell us what it is you want. Edith and I would like to get back and see the movie."

"Yes, of course Mr. Stacey." Mr. Love put his hands together, palm to palm, with his fingers extended. I remembered seeing our minister do the same thing when he was giving a sermon.

"Your son Charles," he angled his head towards me, "Seems to be quite a talented young musician." He paused and nodded his head up and down as if agreeing with himself. "Perhaps he's told you I must find a new drummer." Mr. Love looked towards my dad, but my dad didn't answer.

"Yes...well that is what I must do, and I think Charles could very well be the person to step into that position."

Dad looked at my mother for a second, then looked at me, then he looked back at Mr. Love. "Are you offering our son a job, Mr. Love?"

"Yes. Yes I am, Mr. Stacey."

For a minute I just tuned out. Gee Whiz! A job as a real musician! Golly! Then I tuned back in as my dad was asking, "What would the job pay, Mr. Love?"

"Thirty-five dollars a week."

"Thirty-five?" My dad reached up and scratched his head. "Mr. Love, I know Chuck wants a career in music, but I'm afraid that isn't a career opportunity. He's been offered Twenty-five a week as an Assistant Manager at a theater here in town where he would be living at home. I assume if he were to join your orchestra he would be responsible for his own living accommodations and meals?"

For half a second I started to correct my dad. It was only fifteen a week Mr. Oliver was going to pay me. Then I realized I should keep my mouth shut and learn how to negotiate.

Mr. Love started to answer, but before he said anything my mother told him, "We want Charles to graduate from high school and go on to college, Mr. Love. He can be a musician after that."

"I appreciate your feelings Mrs. Stacey. Education is very important. But, and I stress *but*, if Charles wishes to pursue a career in music, it is not likely he will receive many opportunities like this one. I'm sure you realize my orchestra is world famous. Playing for me can do nothing but enhance his education and reputation as a musician."

"I'm sure that's true," my dad jumped in before mom could say anything more. "But the simple fact is we can't send our son out on the road without sufficient money to ensure he can eat and live decently. I don't think that's possible on thirty-five dollars a week, Mr. Love, and we're not in a financial position to subsidize him."

"I understand, Mr. Stacey. These are difficult times." Mr. Love put his palms together again and looked up at the ceiling. Maybe he was asking God what to do? After a moment he looked back at my dad, "I'm willing to pay forty-five - the same as I was paying his predecessor, Ronald Ede. Although I must point out Ronald is an experienced professional."

My dad nodded his head up and down, "Is he the 'experienced professional' who left you in the lurch today Mr. Love?" Dad cocked his head slightly and looked into Henry Love's eyes. "That is something Charles would never do. I think he should receive fifty."

"I'm afraid that's out of the question, Mr. Stacey, but I'm willing to split the difference with you. Forty-seven fifty. That's the most I can offer."

"That doesn't sound unreasonable, Mr. Love. Would you mind if my wife and I talk this over with our son? We can telephone you in the morning with our decision."

That seemed to surprise Mr. Love. He blinked a couple of times then told my dad, "All right Mr. Stacey. I don't suppose that will be a problem. I'm staying at the Hotel Joliet, but I've got to leave for Chicago promptly at ten in the morning. I'll have to know before then."

Dad reached out to shake Mr. Love's hand. "We'll definitely call you at nine o'clock."

When we left Henry Love's dressing room, I walked with my folks up to the front of the theater. We didn't say anything, I guess we were all thinking about Henry Love's offer. Mom and dad were going to stay for the final stage show, then we would all go home together. We were standing in the lobby looking at each other when a kid came up to me.

"You're the drummer!"

Maybe I just wanted to believe there was excitement in his voice. "Yeah.. Yes, I am," I told him.

"Gee. Can I have your autograph?"

If nobody ever asks you for an autograph, you will never know the feeling that went through me.

As soon as the curtain closed on the last show I jumped down from behind the drums and caught Mr. Love before he left the stage.

"Don't worry Mister Love," I told him. "I'll be here tomorrow."

"I hope so Charles. I believe you'll do very well with us."

Outside, Mom and dad were waiting for me in our old Plymouth. I climbed into the back seat and even before I sat down I asked, "Can I go?"

"Ummm." My mother made a sort of sound. Not a word, just something between a sigh and a groan.

I leaned forward so my head was in between her and dad. "What do you think? Can I?"

Dad put the car in gear and pulled away from the curb before he answered. "We have been talking about that."

"Chuck. What about your school?" I can't remember when my mother ever called me "Chuck" before.

"There's only two weeks left mom, and I'm sure I can work out something to graduate."

"Yes, I suppose you can do that," dad said quietly. "The thing is son, your mother and I have been expecting you to stay there for college..."

Joliet Township has a two-year college in the same buildings as the high school. Mom and dad couldn't afford to send me away to college, but I knew they wanted me to take advantage of that.

"Dad..." I hesitated for a second. I knew what

I wanted to say, but I wasn't sure just how to say it. "Dad, I'm going to be a musician. I know you and mom don't think that's such a good idea, but it's what I'm going to do. You can make me stay here and go to college if you want to, but a chance like this... well I don't think they come along every day."

"I suppose not," dad said.

Mother sniffed. I hadn't realized it, but she was actually crying. "Honey you're so awfully young to go off like that..."

"Well Edith," Dad glanced at her, "It wasn't very many years ago that boys Chuck's age were going off to war."

A little shot of excitement went through me. Dad was on my side. We talked about it some more on the way home, and before we went to bed, but I knew dad had already made up their mind. I could go.

In the morning I packed my drums while mom packed a suitcase for me, then dad drove me to the Joliet Plaza Hotel where I was going to meet the band bus. Mom had decided not to go with us. She said goodbye to me at the back door and started to cry.

8.

IT'S ONLY A FIFTEEN-MINUTE DRIVE down the hill and across the Chicago Canal to the Joliet Hotel. Dad made a couple of tries at things to talk about, but after last night we were pretty much talked out about being careful and being sure to eat properly. Then, when we pulled up in front of the hotel, he sort of cleared his throat. "Son... You'll probably be meeting a lot of girls once you're on the road. We haven't talked much about girls..." He reached into the breast pocket of his suit coat, pulled out a small book and handed it to me. "This is something for you to read."

Men and Women by **Dr. E. J. L. Brown.**

I read the title twice trying to think what I should say. "Thanks dad," was the best I could come up with. I mean my dad was never much when it came to talking about things like sex. I wondered what he would say if I told him about Millie Novoczech.

Before either one of us could say anything else a bus pulled in behind us. I looked back at it and saw the sign across the top of the front window:

Henry Love's Romance Orchestra

Dad helped me carry my stuff over to the driver. While he started putting my drums into the luggage bin, dad took out his wallet. "I didn't ask Mr. Love about when you get paid. Probably not until the end of the week so you'll need something to tide you over 'till then." He took out two ten-dollar bills and handed them to me.

"Gee, thanks dad. I'll pay you back first payday."

"That's all right, son. I wish I could give you more."

Talk about awkward moments. It was always easy to talk to my mom, but somehow it was different with dad. I didn't know what to say; neither did he. To make things worse, the driver was standing there sort of waiting to see what to load next. Dad and I looked at each other for a couple of seconds, then we tried to help him. Finally dad looked at his watch. "Well, I expect I better get to the office." He put out his hand to shake mine, then, as our hands gripped, he pulled me close to him and put his other arm around my shoulder in a real hug. "Your mother and I are very proud of you son, and we love you very much. We're going to miss you like the dickens, but we know this is what you want to do and we know you'll be successful."

"Thanks dad. I love you and mom too." I hugged him back. I think there was a tear in dad's eye as he headed back to the car. I know there were several in mine.

I watched him drive away until he reached the corner and turned up Cass Street. I kept looking at the corner thinking maybe, like in the movies, everything will reverse and dad would come back. But that didn't happen and suddenly I felt very much alone. I watched the corner for a few seconds more, then I turned, walked over to the bus and got on.

I was the first one on board so I took a seat in the middle like I usually did on the trolley. Pretty soon the two girl violinists got on. Their hair was done up in rollers and they looked like they were still asleep. They sort of nodded at me and one of them said something, I think it was "Hi."

In the next few minutes the bus began to fill up. It was supposed to leave at eleven o'clock, but it was ten after before William Dubin and the trumpet player who had talked to me showed up. They climbed on board and headed down the aisle. Just as they were passing me the trumpet player grabbed my shoulder.

"Come on, kid. The back-a the bus with us."

I got up and followed them to the bench seat in the rear. They sat down and made room for me in between them.

"Chuck, my friends call me 'Bill'," William told me as I sat down. "And this nut is 'Wacky' Marvin." His real name is Richard but when you get to know him you'll understand why everybody calls him 'Wacky'."

"Fuck you, Dubin," Wacky growled then he turned to me with the brightest smile you'll see this side of a toothpaste add. "It's a pleasure to meet a real musician, Chuck. I don't pretend to understand why Henry hired you. Three musicians in his band is about two more than he knows what to do with, but lucky for us he doesn't really know how good you and me are."

"Actually, Wacky is a musician in name only," Bill Dubin sighed and shook his head. "He doesn't play the trumpet at all, but Henry thinks an orchestra needs three trumpets so when we found Wacky standing in the middle of Michigan Avenue a year ago I felt so sorry for him I brought him in and handed him a horn. I write all the arrangements for two trumpets so Wacky can just sit there making believe he's playing. Henry doesn't know the difference."

"Yep." Wacky slapped his knee and laughed, "Old Henry doesn't know the difference." Then he turned to me. "Who's your favorite drummer?"

"Right now it's Sonny Greer," I answered. "And I like Wally Bishop, but there's a lot of guys

I haven't heard that much. There's a guy named Joe Jones I've only heard on one record but what I heard was really good. Really subtle."

Wacky slapped his knee again. "Dubin, you right, this man is definitely hip."

By the time the bus got to Chicago I knew Wacky and Bill loved jazz as much as I do. They told me how they would go listen to jazz almost ever night after work.

"The best thing about working for Henry is only old farts like his shit and they go home early," Wacky told me. "So we start early, finish early, and hit the joints."

"We've got a rehearsal tonight," Bill said quietly. "A couple of new arrangements to go over. Then we're gonna dig Earl Hines, you wanna come along?"

"Are you kidding?" Did they think I might not want to. "Yeah I want to."

"You better bunk with us then," Bill added. "No point rooming with any body else. You'll just wake them up coming in late."

"I dig that!" Wacky did another knee slap. "You pay a third and we all save money."

9.

THE CHICAGO PAPERS CALL Henry Love, "the King of Chicagoland Dancing." Henry and his Romance Orchestra had been booked into the North Shore Hotel's Lake View Room from the end of December through January, then again for the entire month of June since before Wacky and Bill had joined him and nobody thought that schedule would change for a long time to come.

Since we were going to be playing at the North Shore Hotel, I expected we would be staying there too. Not so. Musicians couldn't afford the North Shore Hotel. Most of the guys in the band were booked into a place called the Star Hotel, a couple of miles away just off Rush Street. Wacky said it was a "theatrical hotel." The rooms went for two or three bucks a night and the toilet was down the hall. The Star wasn't exactly fancy, but you have to realize it was the first time I ever stayed in a hotel without my folks so the Star Hotel seemed like the Chicago Hilton to me.

"I think I'll have my dinner now," Wacky

announced after we got settled in our room. "Charles, you'll join us of course?" Wacky has a way of sometimes talking like my old English teacher, the rest of the time he talks like a black guy.

I told him "most assuredly old boy," which got a laugh, and we went to an Italian restaurant across the street from the hotel. As soon as we sat down Wacky pulled a flask out of his inside coat pocket.

"Rye whiskey my boy." He didn't ask if I wanted any, he just poured some into my water glass, then poured some into Bill's glass until Bill said "enough," then poured about twice as much into his own.

"Let us drink to the exciting new arrangements maestro Dubin is going to present to us tonight." Wacky sort of tipped his glass towards Bill, then he drank about half of it in one swallow. Bill rolled his eyes upward then took a sip from his own glass. I made the same kind of move towards Bill with my glass, then I put it to my lips.

I had only tasted whiskey once before. One time before the depression, when I was seven or eight years old, my dad had taken me fishing and we got caught in a rainstorm. When we got back home I was wet and shivering and mom and dad decided I needed a "hot toddy" to keep me from catching cold. As far as I knew, "hot toddy" meant cocoa. What it turned out to be was some whiskey in hot water. Where dad got the whiskey from I don't know, I guess like everybody else he had a bootlegger. Anyway, even before I tasted the toddy the smell was enough to make my eyes burn. One sip was all I could handle. I didn't care if I got double pneumonia and died, but if I lived I knew I would never drink whiskey again and here I was with two guys I wanted to be friends with and I didn't want to seem like a kid, so there was only one thing to do, drink it.

It tasted just as awful as I remembered but I managed to swallow one sip. I don't know what I would have done if the waiter hadn't brought our spaghetti at just that minute. I was darn glad I didn't have to find out!

The rehearsal room in the basement of the Star Hotel was okay. I suppose it's the room where they held dances, or parties if they ever had such things. Howard had everything set up for us when we got there. "Us" didn't include Delightful Dorothy or Handsome Hunter. They didn't rehearse with the orchestra even though one of Bill's three new arrangements was a duet for them on a song written a couple of years ago by Dorothy Fields and Jimmy McHugh titled, "Exactly Like You."

His second new arrangement was of an old song titled, "Chicago." It was written in 1922 by a man named Fred Fisher, who wrote a lot of popular songs after the end of the war. Bill said Henry wanted us to be ready to play this one for our opening tomorrow night. The third was what in Henry Love's book was an "Up Tempo" arrangement of another old song, "Dinah." It had been written in 1925 by Sam Lewis and Harry Akst. I was getting the idea Henry Love's orchestra never played anything new. No wonder I thought his music was corny.

We took a few minutes to look over Bill's music before he had us play each one a couple of times. Then he said everyone except the reeds and strings could take five while they worked alone.

"The awful moan of the saxophone," Wacky muttered to me as he shook spit out of his horn and put it on his chair. "Come on, let's go see my aunt." He pronounced it: "*ount*," not "aunt," like I have always said.

I followed him to the elevator and up to our room. He unlocked the door and with a big bow and a sweeping arm made like the butler in one of those English movies indicating the way inside. "Grab a glass," he angled his head towards the little wooden table against the wall. "I'll find 'Ahhntie'."

The rooms in the Star Hotel, or at least our room, didn't have any running water, so there were three glasses and a pitcher full of water on the table. Bill told me they didn't have running water and basins in the rooms because if they did, everybody would piss in them rather than walk all the way down the hall to the can.

"Ountie," it turned out, was tonight's name for his flask, which he pulled out of his pocket with the same English butler flourish.

"Only time for a short visit. Billy won't take long with the moaners."

"Ah... Wacky. I don't think I'll have any this time. My stomach seems to be having an argument with that spaghetti."

"Oh-ho. In that case you gonna need a double. Best thing for a sour stomach." He grabbed one glass from me and poured what seemed like a lot of whiskey into it, handed it back to me and took a glass for himself. "Soften it if you wanna." He nodded towards the water pitcher while he poured about twice as much into his own glass. "I like mine neat."

I didn't know what else to do but put water in my glass and try to drink a little of it. Maybe, I thought, if I get him talking about music, he won't notice I'm not drinking.

"Where's Henry Love tonight? How come he isn't at the rehearsal."

"Henry don't come to no rehearsals man. He leaves all that to Billy."

"Oh yeah?" It hadn't occurred to me that a bandleader would not rehearse his own band. "So how long will the rehearsal last?"

"Maybe another hour." Wacky pulled his watch out and looked at it. "Ought to be done about nine thirty. Then we'll get the clowns out-a there and jam a while. No point in heading out 'till eleven or so."

I think my eyes must have opened to twice normal size. "You and Bill and me?"

"Yeah, the three of us. Maybe Jimmy will hang around too. He ain't great but he likes to try."

"Who's Jimmy?" Without realizing it I took a sip of the drink I was holding in my hand.

"Tenor sax."

"Which one? The guy with the short blond hair?" I took another sip. Somehow it wasn't as bad tasting as it had been at dinner.

"Yeah, Jimmy Thompson. Nice guy but he ain't no Coleman Hawkins."

"Who the hell is?" I laughed.

I'd heard Coleman Hawkins on the radio, playing with Fletcher Henderson's Orchestra lots of times. I even have a couple of records the band has made. Hawkins was from St. Joseph, Missouri. In 1920, when he was sixteen years old, Mamie Smith heard him play and hired him. He worked in Kansas City with her "Jazz Hounds" until 1923 when Fletcher Henderson hired him and he's still with Henderson's band. According to what I've read, it wasn't until Louis Armstrong joined Henderson's band in 1924, that Hawkins and the entire band really got into jazz. They say Hawkins made the tenor sax a solo instrument. These days there are a lot of other great tenor men around, Ben Webster, Lester Young, Chu Berry, but "Hawk" most always gets credit for making the sax what it is today.

"You right. You right." Wacky agreed. "Nobody like 'Bean'."

"The Bean," was another nickname for Hawkins. I don't know where that one came from.

Wacky polished off his drink and put his glass down on the table. "Ahhh yes. Thank you auntie. Now," he turned to me, "We best get back before old Billy has a shit fit."

I was surprised to find my glass was almost half empty.

Wacky's prediction was accurate. We played Billy's new arrangements of "Dinah," and "Exactly Like You," twice, and did "Chicago," three times, then Billy had us run down a couple of old ones he said we were having trouble with. About nine-thirty he said "Okay, Good enough," and told us all to remember we were due on the bandstand at 7pm tomorrow night so he expected everybody to be in the dressing room not later than six-thirty, and there would be a two dollar fine for anybody who didn't make it. Then he told everybody, "Thank you, enjoy Chicago, and goodnight."

Eleven men and two women were out of that room in nothing flat and Billy, Wacky, Jimmy Thompson, the tenor sax player, and I had the place to ourselves. Then I realized Howard was still there. "You mind if I start collecting music and stuff Billy?"

"Hell no, Howard. You do anything you want to."

"Okay, thanks. Maybe I'll hang around and listen for a while too, if it won't bother you."

"Howard," Billy walked over and put his hand on Howard's shoulder. "You do more for us than any three people I know. There is nothing you could do that would bother me or anybody else."

"Gee. Thanks Bill."

I guessed Billy was right. I hadn't really paid much attention to Howard before but he did do everything. He made sure our instruments got where they were supposed to get. He set up my drums. He put out and collected all our music. Then, like he had nothing else to do, he ran errands and did things for Henry Love.

"Okay Chuck," Billy sat down at his piano. "You're the new kid in school. What-a you wanna play?"

Now I'm the first one to admit there are times when I don't know what to say, but when it comes to music I never have any trouble. "Don't Be That Way," I answered. It's a tune Fletcher Henderson wrote and I've heard Earl Hines play twice on radio shows from the Grand Terrace Ballroom, where we were going later!

"Dig!" Wacky did his knee slap thing. "Start it off my-man."

I did.

Billy came in after four bars and four later, Wacky came in over him.

I don't have the words to tell you what a thrill that was. Working with them in the orchestra, I had no idea what Billy and Wacky could do and I guess they didn't have much of an idea about me either. From the moment we started it just seemed like the three of us were reading each other's minds.

We jammed until about eleven-thirty, when Billy stood up and said, "I'm goin' to hear 'Fatha'!"

I would have been happy to stay there jamming all night. Seeing Earl Hines would be great but I had never played with musicians the caliber of Billy Dubin and Wacky Marvin before. Not that Jimmy wasn't okay, but I've played with guys as good as him. Billy and Wacky though, wow! What were they doing playing schmaltz with Henry Love? And me. I realized I could play with them. What were we doing working for Henry Love?

Billy had already answered that question on the bus. Henry Love paid well. Henry's orchestra played extended engagements in only the best places, very few one-nighters. The music might not be exciting, but the job is one of the best in the music business and "you don't bite the hand that feeds you!"

Yes, okay, I told myself. But there isn't any reason a band can't play like we were just playing and be successful. Earl Hines, Fletcher Henderson, Jimmie Lunceford, Duke Ellington... they seem to be doing all right. How come most of the white bands play the kind of stuff Henry Love plays? Why can't a white band play jazz like Hines and Henderson do?

After Earl Hines finished for the night, when I thought we would head back to our hotel room, the night was just beginning. We went to a speakeasy Bill and Wacky knew about called the "One-Two-Three Club." It was on Rush Street, not far from our hotel.

Wacky knocked on the heavy looking street door and a couple of seconds later a little window popped open.

"Good evening, my good man." Wacky was using his English Teacher voice again.

"Hello ass-hole," a muffled voice answered. "Come on in."

Four black guys, up on a tiny little stage crowded into one corner of the room, were playing. Piano, tenor sax, string bass and drums. And they were good!

Bill and Wacky knew the guys and as soon as we were inside Wacky took out his horn and went up on the stand to join them. (Something I was learning about Wacky, he never goes anywhere without his horn.) A minute later Billy walked up there too. He sat down next to the piano player and they started playing together.

I didn't believe what I was watching. White guys and black guys playing together, I had never seen anything like that before.

After a couple of minutes Wacky said something to the drummer, then waved to me to come up on the stand. Wacky told the drummer I was Chuck and told me the drummer was Freddie, then the drummer said, "If you cova fo me I got a chick would love fo me to be home early." He got up from the drum case he used for a seat and handed me his sticks. "You be good now." Before I could say anything he was headed off the stand. I looked at Wacky who nodded his head at the drums and told me to sit down.

At some point between then and five AM, when we decided to go home, I found myself thinking about my mother and what she would do if she knew I had been drinking whiskey with a Jewish guy, then jammin' all night with a bunch of black musicians. In one day all her worst fears about my leaving home had come true!

Well not quite all, I reminded myself. Thanks to Millie Novacheck, one had come true a long time ago.

10.

I HAD NEVER BEEN IN A PLACE like the Lake View Room before. One entire wall was windows that looked out over Lake Michigan. Through them you could see strings of electric lights running along both sides of the hotel's two, boat docks. It seemed as if there were always lighted boats, yachts really, tied to the piers or sailing by.

The three-tiered bandstand was located in the middle of the window wall. I was on the top tier, so all I had to do to see the view was turn my head a little. And for a drummer that's an easy thing to do.

I also had a perfect view of the oval-shaped room itself. There was a dance floor right in front of the bandstand surrounded by three tiers of candle lit tables, covered with gold tablecloths. I couldn't imagine there were very many rooms as magnificent as this one. We played the Lake View Room for four weeks and almost every night, after work, Billy, Wacky and I went some place to listen, or sit-in. Chicago was alive with clubs and "speakeasy's."

Our closing night in Chicago was June 25th, my eighteenth birthday. Mom and dad came up from Joliet on the train and had dinner in the Lake View Room listening to us play. During our first break, I got an okay to go sit down with them.

Joliet is only forty miles or so from Chicago but, with train fare and taxies and meals out, it costs a lot to make a trip like that, and this was the first time I had seen my folks since I left home, so we had a lot to talk about. I told them about my roommates and how we had been "sittin'-in" with other groups around town... I didn't tell them there were black guys... I think they could tell how excited I am about everything. Then just before we were due back on stage, Henry Love came to the table to say hello and wish me Happy Birthday. My folks were very impressed.

The day after my birthday, the 26th, we left for St. Louis. Henry Love and his Romance Orchestra are very big in St. Louis and the 4th of July Ball in the River Room is the high point of the St. Louis summer social calendar.

In August we were in Atlantic City where we sort of got ready for the "new season" which officially began in September at the Waldorf

Astoria in New York.

After New York, we went to Philadelphia, then on to Cleveland, Cincinnati, Richmond, Atlanta and Detroit. Henry's "moaning saxophone music," as Wacky called it, had admirers in every city we went to. We were back in Chicago when Prohibition officially ended.

Tuesday, December 5th, 1933. Repeal Day - The end of Prohibition!

It was a day... well, a night to remember! Even Henry Love's usually reserved audience cut-loose and we stayed on the bandstand until two o'clock Wednesday morning.

Wednesday night, after work, the three of us went to the One-Two-Three Club. It had still been Prohibition time when we were there last. I couldn't see much difference in things now that drinking was legal.

By the time we left town last summer I knew all the guys who played there. The leader, "Little George", played string bass, Freddie Washington the drums, Ernie Jones on tenor sax, and his brother David, played both piano and guitar. When Billy sat in, David usually switched to his guitar, which he said he liked best anyway, and Freddie was always anxious to go home early if somebody would take over for him, so as we walked in he gave me a big wave and held his sticks out towards me.

As soon as we got our hats and coats off we headed for the stand and picked up right in the middle of what they were playing. Well, Billy and I did. Wacky's horn was so cold he had to stick the mouthpiece in a cup of warm water and wrap his arms around the horn itself until it was warm enough to put to his lips. Chicago winters. Man oh man...

When we were sitting in at the One-Two-Three Club it always seemed like the people who were there would stick around to hear us as long as we wanted to play, no matter how late it got. About one o'clock, which was more or less "official" closing time, Little George started putting his bass away .

"My wife is sick," he told us. "I got-a get home. You boys have fun, hear?"

"Gee, sorry to hear that George," I told him. "Tell her to get well quick."

Little George said "thanks" and "Goodnight," but before he could leave the stand J.J. arrived. "J.J.", which stood for Joshua Jordan, was the club manager. He was a young, good-looking guy, with the highest pitched voice I ever heard from a man. When he was excited it got even higher, and tonight he was real excited.

"Little George, where you goin'?"

"I told you before, J.J. My wife is sick."

"Yeah, yeah, I know George, but I just got word the boss is comin' in with a party that wants to hear some music."

"Well that's all right J.J." George grinned, "Look what you got here. Two black guys and three white ones. They can make plenty of music." Before J.J. could come up with an argument, Little George headed for the back door.

"Motherfucker!" J.J's voice hit a new high even for him. It was a new high for me too, it was the first time I ever heard the expression "Mother-Fucker!" I wondered who thought it up. Maybe it was original with J.J.

"Guys." JJ turned away from watching Little George leave and looked at the five of us who were still playing at the same time we were tuned in to him and Little George. "I just got word the owner and some friends are comin' in. You guys got to stick around." It wasn't exactly a request.

Ernest and David nodded "yes", then J.J. looked at me. "You guys too."

"Okay by me man, I'll stay all night." I mean he was nice enough to let us sit in whenever we were in town, it was the least we could do. I looked to Billy and then Wacky. They both said sure and we went back to playing while J.J. went to the front door and put his eye to the peephole. With Prohibition over I don't know why they still had a peephole, but they did.

We went on jam-in' and I sort of kept an eye on JJ. I really don't know how long it was, maybe five minutes, maybe ten, when all of a sudden J.J. straightened up, ran his hand through his hair and opened the door. A couple of beats later four people came in.

It had been freezing when we got here, by the look of them it had gotten a lot colder since then. The four were so bundled up, and there's so little light in the club anyway, I couldn't tell if they were men or women. Well, one was a guy, he was big as a house. You couldn't miss him, he looked like a professional wrestler or prize fighter but it wasn't until the other three began to get out of their coats and mufflers that I could make them out. There was one other man, who walked with a limp - I knew he had to be the owner, Tony Belinni, and the other two were women.

There's a story that somebody once asked Louis Armstrong about his playing without a music score in front of him. Louis is supposed to have replied, "If you got to read music to play, what chu gonna do if the lights go out?" Well, the lights weren't out in the One-Two-Three Club, but it was not what you could call brightly lit either and It was pretty hard to tell much about the two women. I thought one was a bit older than the other. From where I was she looked pretty. The younger one, even in the dark I could tell she was a knock out!

While J.J. was getting everyone settled I started an easy tempo with my brushes and Billy came in with something nice he had written but didn't have a name for yet. Wacky picked it up, then Ernest and David figured out the chords and came along with some thoughts of their own. It's such a nice, pretty tune, we worked it around for about five minutes. When we finished, the owner and his friends gave us a nice hand.

"Anything you want to hear?" I called out to them. Nobody answered, but I saw the young girl turn to the big guy and say something to him.

Since no one asked for anything, David started something on his guitar that we all picked up on. Then I saw J.J. and the young girl walking towards us. The closer she got the more beautiful she became Dark hair. Dark brown with maybe just a touch of auburn.

"Fellas, this here lady wants ta sing a couple-a songs." J.J. didn't say it like, could she? He said it like she was gonna, and we better know what she wanted to sing.

"Hi," I said to her. Well, somebody had to say something.

She smiled at me. Oh man, her smile lit up the room like a spotlight! There's a line from a song: "Five foot two, eyes of blue, but oh what those blue eyes can do..." She was taller than five-two but man, them eyes!

"What would you like to sing?" I asked her.

"Can we do, 'Mood Indigo'?"

Her request floored me. What does this girl know about Duke Elington's music?

"Duke's 'Mood Indigo'?" I asked.

"Is there another one?" She laughed.

"There surely is not!" Wacky proclaimed. "I'm hip."

"About like this?" I started a slow beat.

"Pick it up a little."

I did, and she told Billy "D sharp." He came in with an intro and she sang. I mean she sang!

She might not be more than fifteen maybe sixteen I told myself, but she's good! Watching from in back of her, I couldn't see what her face was doing, but the way she used her arms and her hands was surprising, expressive, and very sensual. She was poised. She knows her music, and she has talent.

When she finished "Mood" everybody in the room applauded, but quietly. It wasn't that they didn't like what she did, it was just they were too moved to make a lot of noise.

"That was great," I told her. "Do some more."

"How 'bout, 'I'll Take You Home Again Kathleen'? That's daddy's favorite."

This time Billy picked it up almost before she finished the title. Slow. Beautiful. I didn't know if she was always this good, but with what Billy was doing behind her, she could really bring tears to your eyes.

When she finished "Kathleen" there wasn't any applause until the big guy said, "That was beautiful darlin'... Thank you." Then suddenly everybody started clapping.

I decided it was time to brighten things so I started an up tempo with my brushes. "Let's do somethin' like this before everybody breaks down cryin'," I told her. She listened to my beat for a couple of bars, began snapping her fingers and sang to Billy, "I'll Be Down To Get-chu in a Taxi Honey."

After that she did "Honeysuckle Rose" and that brought the house down!

"Thank you for letting me sing with you. Thank you very much." She wasn't kidding, she honestly appreciated singing with us, and maybe she didn't even know there was no way we could not have let her sing with us, even if she didn't know note one. But she did. Man, did she ever!

"It's almost my birthday," she told us. "And we're having a sort of party. Come on over and have some cake and a drink if you want."

The word "drink" definitely got Wacky's attention. "Yes ma'am. Don't mind if I do." He put his horn down, took her arm and escorted her down off the stand.

I looked at Billy; he looked at me and shrugged. "I guess we're going to have a drink," he whispered. We got up and started to follow Wacky and the girl when I saw Ernest and David were not moving and realized they didn't think the invite was meant for them. Well, if they weren't included, I wasn't going either, but before I could sit down, or say anything, the girl saw what was happening. She slipped away from Wacky and came back to the stand. She looked first at David then at Ernest. "Aren't you coming?"

"Us?" David asked.

"Yes, us," she told them. "It's my party. Come on."

When J.J. realized what was happening, he whispered something to his boss then straightened up and signaled his waiters to bring over an extra table. Then, with a head nod and a finger point, he let David and Ernest know they were to sit at the end of the table. That didn't go over too well with me, so I managed to grab a seat in between them and Billy sat down next to Ernie. That made it black-white, black-white rather than two black guys at the back of the bus.

11.

FRIDAY NIGHT IS BROADCAST NIGHT for "The Bright Smile Toothpaste Hour."

"It's time for Love!
Bright Smile Toothpaste,
For your Most Beautiful Smile,
Brings you the Music of
Henry Love
For your most Romantic Evening!"

John Ashton, "Mr. Toothpaste" himself, and his wife were at a table down front along with a young, college type guy, I later found out was John junior, and a cute looking girl who was his date. The way Henry Love treated John Ashton you might think he was the King of England which, I suppose, was understandable because, since our September opening in New York, we had been doing a weekly, coast to coast radio show for his company - two broadcasts actually, one for the east coast and mid west, and a second one, later at night, for California and what ever else was out west. Henry's picture, complete with a big smile, was showing up in toothpaste ads and people could get a special record of our theme song by sending in a couple of box tops.

Since the end of Prohibition, every night had been a special night, with people drinking champagne and getting ready for Christmas and New Year's. Christmas week was even more so.

John Ashton junior and his date were not the only college kids in the audience this Friday night, half the people in the room had brought their kids with them. I didn't think Henry Love's music was exactly what kids liked to dance to and, as it turned out, it wasn't.

Our first set after the east coast broadcast, John junior and his date came up close to the bandstand and the girl called out, "Hey Mister Leader this stuff's corny. How about something jazzy?"

"How about a drum solo!" the loud, "I'm the boss' son" voice of John Junior added, with a laugh that said a drum solo was the last thing he thought Henry Love could produce.

Henry tried to pretend he didn't hear the request, but with Junior and this date leading them, a half a dozen other kids started chanting, "Drum Solo. Drum Solo."

What's a leader to do? I mean his sponsor's

son, the son of the man who is paying him a lot of money, wants to hear a drum solo.

"Charles..." Henry leaned over the saxophones towards me, "Charles, ehh, do you think we can do something?"

"Yes, sure Henry." I had now progressed to the point where I dared to call him by his first name. "Billy and Wacky and I can do something." I loved to call the guys "Billy" and "Wacky" when I spoke to Henry because he always called them William and Richard.

Henry nodded and went to the microphone. "All right Ladies and Gentlemen. Here's our drummer Charles Stacey, together with pianist William Dubin and trumpeter Richard Marvin." He turned back towards me with a flourish, "What will it be Charles?"

"Don't Be That Way," I called back. For a moment Henry was confused by my answer, but the kids out front heard me and knew it was the name of a tune, not a comment on Henry's inquiry. Their applause covered Henry's temporary confusion.

We sounded good. I did a thirty-two bar solo with brushes and Wacky played with a mute in his horn so we kept it pretty soft. Even the older crowd seemed to get a kick out of the number. When we finished there was a general demand for an encore so we did "Maple Street Rag" with more from Billy and Wacky than from me. After that Henry called for the moaning saxes and the rest of the orchestra to do "Charmaine," a song another drummer named Lew Pollack had written with a guy named Erno Rapee back in 1927. As I said, we don't play very many new tunes, but I like "Charmaine." It's a great song. We played it then took a break.

In the Lake View Room, like most of the places we play, musicians must leave the bandstand during breaks, but we are not allowed out in the audience. The same did not hold true for the leader who has a certain amount of celebrity and is, therefore, in some demand by patrons who felt they gain a bit of notoriety by having him stop at their tables and say "hello." As we went backstage "celebrity" Love was making his way to the Ashton's table. Neither Billy, nor Wacky, nor I knew we were the topic of much of their conversation until next morning... well, if you call one o'clock in the afternoon "morning," we did!

Saturday morning, Billy, Wacky and I had breakfast as usual in the Star's Dining Room. For fifteen cents they served a great breakfasts: orange juice, a couple of eggs with bacon, potato pancakes, breakfast rolls and all the coffee you could drink, which Wacky always drank five or six cups of.

While we were eating, I couldn't help thinking about all the people I had seen yesterday afternoon standing outside in the cold waiting for a hand out. I was getting ready to slip a couple of our rolls into my pocket to give to someone when Howard came in looking for us. "Hey fellas, Henry says he wants to see you... his room at the hotel. Okay?"

"Okay, thanks Howard," Billy answered.

I wasn't surprised to find Henry's "room" was a suite in the North Shore Hotel, with a great view of Lake Michigan and the shoreline half way to Canada...

"Come in, come in boys." As he opened the door for us, Henry was more cheerful than I could remember seeing him before. He directed us into the sitting room and pointed to a silver tea pot and cups on a table.

"Help yourselves to tea..."

"Thank you, Henry," I told him and went to pour a cup. I didn't know what else to do, besides I like tea. Billy and Wacky followed my lead, although I knew the only "tea" Wacky liked came in cigarettes.

"May I pour some for you Henry?" I asked. My mother hadn't spent all those years teaching me manners for nothing.

"Thank you no, Charles." He waited until the three of us had successfully filled our cups, then he pointed to the sofa and chairs. "Sit down boys, sit down." We did, and he continued, "First, I want to tell you how pleased I am by the way you three performed last evening." We all sort of nodded and told him thanks. "And... Not only was I pleased,' he continued, "Mrs. Ashton thought you were wonderful."

That's good if the Ashtons liked us, I thought. The way Henry had been kissing their asses it couldn't hurt to have them like us.

"Mrs. Ashton thinks we should have you do a number on our radio show each week."

"Holly Moses!" The words were not out of my mouth before I realized it was a pretty juvenile expression, but what the hell! Henry Love had just told us we are going to get a featured spot on a coast- to-coast radio show. Holly Mackerel!!!

"That's wonderful, Henry." It was Billy's voice of reason speaking now. "I hope this is something you're comfortable with."

"Thank you for expressing that, William. Yes. Yes, I think it's a splendid idea."

Henry's voice told me he wasn't completely sure it was quite that splendid. I remembered Henry Love didn't like to share the spotlight, so I suspected the idea of three members of his orchestra having a featured spot on his radio show might not be exactly the thing he most wanted to have happen, but that's the way this tune goes Henry.

12.

ONE OF THE THINGS that was particularly nice about working for Henry Love was the way we traveled. Something I really began to appreciate as we left Chicago for our "western swing." On short trips, like from Chicago to St. Louis we had a private bus, but when we made a big hop, like Chicago to Los Angeles, we went by railroad, in a private Pullman Car. For a musician on the road that's pretty high class travel!

We were booked for four weeks at the Coconut Grove, in the swank Ambassador Hotel on Wilshire Boulevard. After L.A. we began a slow journey east: Phoenix; Dallas, Texas; New Orleans; Washington, DC, then Atlantic City.

Every Friday during the long trek Bright Smile Toothpaste gave us Love Bugs a chance to show off and we heard the show had been gaining audience which made Mrs. Ashton very pleased. But other than the radio show we did not have much chance to play. Henry's regular audience was mostly older folks who preferred Henry's usual, I call it "schmaltzy", music.

By the time we reached Atlantic City I was ready to look for a job with one of the swing bands that were beginning to get popular playing music I like. And Wacky felt the same way I did. Practical Billy did too, but suggested,

"If we find something better we'll leave. "But right now we're getting paid very well. So let's not screw it up."

Atlantic City claims to have the longest boardwalk in the world. I don't pretend to know if that's true or not, but they have a nice boardwalk. It attracts a lot of people.

There was a brochure in our hotel room telling us "Welcome to Atlantic City," and giving some history of the place. Atlantic City is on an island... Absecon Island. Way back in 1670 some guy named Thomas Budd got title to it from the British Government... I don't believe anybody talked to the local Indians about that. Fifteen years later a man named Jeremiah Leeds built a house on the island. Apparently he lived there until he died in 1838, then his widow decided to turn their house into a tavern. She called it, "Aunt Millie's Boarding House."

In those days the beach was probably even more beautiful than it is now and pretty soon when people started visiting the island someone decided to call it Atlantic City. It wasn't long before they built a railroad track from Camden, New Jersey to the place.

Where tourists want to visit is where entrepreneurs want to build hotels and in no time Atlantic City became a tourist Mecca.

One trouble the hotels had was sand. It blew into their lobbies, it blew into the railroad cars, it blew everywhere.

Then a man named Alexander Boardman came up with an idea to build a wooden walk out over the beach, as a way to control the blowing sand. In 1870 they opened an eight-foot wide, one-mile long "Boardwalk," named for him, not because it was made of boards.

When we arrived in Atlantic City Henry's business partner and manager, Ira Bernstein, was waiting for us at the station. Well, I guess he was waiting for Henry, but at least he waved to the rest of us and said things like "Hi" and "Hello" as we walked past him. Of course Henry didn't ride in our Pullman, he had a private state room several cars behind ours.

Our final radio show for this season would be Friday night so I assumed Ira had made one of his rare visits to be on hand for a get together with the Ashton's, who were also going to be here.

Thoughts and plans for next season were no doubt on everyone's mind. Thoughts Wacky, Billy and I learned more about next morning.

I can remember Ira Bernstein's words like it was yesterday:

"Boys, boys... How do I begin? You're so popular now, already you're stars! But that's a problem for Henry. He thinks the world of you three boys. He really does, but business is business, and what you boys play is... not Henry Love. You know, the Romance Orchestra, that's Henry. Not so much the Love Bugs. Henry is worried he could begin to loose his audience with your kind of music...."

I hated to see a grown man cry, so I had decided to finish it for him. "So Howard has my drums packed up?"

"Yes, yes, Chuck. absolutely." It was like a drowning man suddenly getting a fresh supply of air. "Howard's taking care of everything. And here," he had reached in his breast pocket and pulled out three envelopes. "An extra week's pay and tickets back to Chicago. Henry and me, we're business men, but also we got a heart."

The day before we left Atlantic City Jimmy Thompson, the tenor sax player, told us we should forget Chicago and head for New York.

"There's lots-a work in New York," Jimmy said, and he knew a sort of agent up there named Fred Young who could get us work. "Go see him. He's got an office on 48ᵗʰ Street."

"New York sounds good to me," I told Billy and Wacky. "We could cash in these Chicago tickets for some money to live on while we see if Fred Young can find us work. What-a ya think?"

New York City **is** like no other place in the world. There was a Nedick's Stand at the corner of 7th Avenue and West 48th Street in New York where you could hear music from four different directions while you order a Hot Dog. The hot dog is a nickel but the music is free and comes from eight or ten rehearsal halls in the area.

48th Street had more music stores than any other street in the world and the city had more music in clubs, hotels, theaters, ballrooms and dance halls than any other city in the world. If you're a musician, New York City was a magnet. There wasn't any place else in the world where you would rather be! At least there was no other place I wanted to be.

And so, when we reached New York, carrying my drum cases and Wacky's horn, Fred Young's 48ᵗʰ Street office was our first stop

Young's office was on the third floor, over

Manny's Music Store. The reason he had his office there, he told us, was because when he needed a musician, all he had to do was call out the window, "I need a trumpet," or, "I need a sax," or whatever else he wanted.

Fred Young had greeted us with, "Christ, there ain't no room in here for all that shit. Leave it in the hall."

Young was right. The office wasn't as big as my bedroom back home in Joliet and he had it stuffed with a huge desk, three large chairs and a big file cabinet. Also himself. Old Fred must have weighed in at well over two hundred pounds and he wasn't all that tall.

"You clowns must be Henry's Love Bugs Jimmy called me about," his voice wasn't exactly unfriendly, but on the other hand, it didn't sound like he had been counting the hours until we got there. "Come in... sid-down."

Part 3
The Lovely Young Lady

1.

NOT LONG AFTER Frank's and Peter's father died, Hugh Crawford took his daughter on his knee one night and told her they were going to move away from their home over the restaurant to a big, wonderful new house.

"What about Peter and Frank, daddy?" Kathleen wanted to know. There were other children in the neighborhood, children she played with, but, except for her mother and father, her older "brothers" who lived across the street were the most important people in her young life.

"Ah, Kathleen darlin', don't chu worry about Franco and Peter. Them and their mother is goin' with us."

The "wonderful new house," was located in the tiny village of Arrochar, just next to Fort Wadsworth Actually there were two big houses, located on one large plot of ground, surrounded on three sides by a wall, and protected in front by a thick privet hedge behind which her father installed a chain link fence. The house in front, on the left side, was theirs; the house farther back on the right was for Frank, Peter and their mother, "Aunt Rosa."

Shortly after they moved in, two men named Howard and Kenny and their wives moved into the apartments over the big garage at the back of the property. From then on, until she was ready for high school, it seemed to Kathleen, she was hardly ever allowed to go anywhere and when she did it was only with her father, or Howard or Kenny. Then, to her surprise and absolute delight, she was allowed to go to the Laura Roberts School for Young Ladies, a private school located in Manhasset, Long Island.

To visitors from the city it seemed impossible that such a beautiful campus could exist so close to midtown New York. Less than half mile away from Manhasset Bay's pristine beaches, LRS' ivy covered buildings were surrounded by beautiful, tree covered hills, and looked down on lovely Leed's Pond, which, in winter became a frozen ice rink for skating and the snow covered slopes perfect for tobogganing and skiing.

In addition to the physical beauty of its campus, LRS boasted an excellent scholastic reputation and a proud history of educating young women. Parents were confident there could be no finer place for their daughters than the Laura Randolph School.

She told everyone she was anxious to go to LRS because the school had an exceptional music program. To herself she admitted just as strong a reason was the chance it would give her to get away from what she considered a stifling environment at home. To her dismay, she found life at the school was not much less restrictive than it had been at home. None of the girls were permitted to leave the campus without a chaperone and when she went home on weekends and holidays she was always escorted to and from the school by one of her brothers or one of the men who worked for her father.

But the LRS music program had made up for all that. From the time she could first remember, she loved to sing and as she grew, singing became her passion, and her ambition. She had studied voice and music on Staten Island, but nothing there compared with the program at LRS.

It was late October in her Senior year when the school's Music Director, Paul Van Votagraven came up with the idea to stage a shortened version of the new Broadway musical, "45

Minutes From Broadway," as a Thanksgiving present for the students and their visiting families. The title song could have been written as the theme song for the Laura Randolph School. Train travel from the nearby Long Island Rail Road Station in Manhasset, to Pennsylvania Station in New York City, took almost exactly forty-five minutes.

Dutifully, Paul Van Votagraven had conducted open auditions for all girls interested in performing in the play, but he, and just about everybody else knew who would win the lead roll. She won, hands down. This did not surprise Van Votagraven, who considered Kathleen to have the best voice he had ever worked with. Nor was his confidence in her talent misplaced as the audience's reaction to her performance testified. She was called back for six curtain calls.

On her second call back she asked if she could sing a special song for her father. Having alerted him of her wish to do this if an opportunity presented itself, Van Votagraven had already seated himself at the piano and immediately struck the opening chords of, "I'll Take You Home Again Kathleen."

As she finished the song she blew a kiss to her father, half whispered, "Thank you Daddy." and a very proud Hugh Crawford hugged his wife as he returned his daughter's kiss.

Now Christmas and her birthday were less than a week away and it was only three days until the Holiday Dinner and the beginning of the Christmas vacation. Daddy, Mother, Aunt Rosa and brother Peter would be back again and maybe even brother Frank, if he could break away from what ever he was always doing since he got his law degree.

She loved both her "brothers" but Pete was the special one. Frank was wonderful but Pete was her pal, He had been named for his Uncle Pietro. It was always fun having him for her escort because he was more like her best friend than a brother. They shared everything from what he did on dates, to secrets about their families. Secrets she did not share with anyone else. It was from Pete she learned her father, and his father, had been rum runners during Prohibition. It was also from him that she learned his father had not been lost at sea but had been shot in a gun battle. Her father and mother and Aunt Rosa and Uncle Pietro had taken his body far out into the Atlantic Ocean and buried him there. From that time on, her father had tried to be a father to Frank and Peter as well. It was then they moved to the compound in Arrochar, where her father, and men who worked for him, could watch over them.

Waiting was never something she liked to do and waiting for Christmas was hardest of all. The Staten Island Advance Daddy had given her a subscription to sometimes helped pass the time, especially when her roommate Gladys had long telephone calls with her secret boy friend. She didn't have a boy friend so she read the Advance.

Island Life
by
Phyllis Jenkins
Plans for the Bay View Yacht Club New Year's Eve Ball are just about complete. This year the Chuck Stacey Orchestra will provide music for dancing from 8PM until???
Members are advised to get their tickets early... a large crowd is expected.

"Oh my goodness."
Kathleen's gasp caused Gladys to look away from the telephone and ask if she was all right.
"Yes, I'm fine. Just an article here in the paper I'm reading."
Gladys grunted something and returned to her phone call.
Chuck Stacey, Kathleen thought. He can only be the drummer from Chicago. What is he doing

on Staten Island?

Memories came flooding back: That wonderful night in Chicago when she and mother and daddy went to celebrate her birthday at Uncle Tony's "One-Two-Three Club." That night when she sang with Chuck Stacey and Billy and Wacky. Was it possible Chuck Stacey's coming to play on Staten Island was more than coincidence? Was it fate? Was it his band she was destined to sing with?

"I have got to go to that dance," she told herself. "I wonder if we belong to the club. Oh well, it doesn't matter, Daddy can arrange it." All she would have to do is get Pete to take her. That shouldn't be too hard, she thought. Pete wasn't like his brother Frank. Pete would usually do anything she asked.

2.

BEARING GIFTS GALORE, Mother and Daddy, Aunt Rosa, Pete and, surprisingly, Frank, all arrived Friday afternoon in plenty of time for the Christmas Dinner Party. All their gifts were wonderful but one was very special. It was from Pete. He would "escort" her back to Staten Island by way of the Paramount Theatre. WOW!!!

True to the song lyrics, forty-five minutes after they left LRS, Kathleen and Pete stepped off the Long Island Railroad train and climbed the stairs into Penn Station where they caught a subway to Times Square, If there was ever a magical place in the world, Kathleen thought, it was Times Square. And the restaurant she though was the most exciting restaurant in the world. Toffenetti.

Pete told her Toffenetti wasn't the best restaurant in New York, but she didn't care. She loved Toffenetti! From it's windows overlooking Times Square she could see the Paramount Theater marquee: and she could imagine some of the people hurrying by were musicians from Rudy Valley's orchestra, or one of the other big bands playing up the street at the RKO Palace, or the Capital or the Strand.

She supposed Pete considered her a pest the way she kept asking him what time it was, but the stage show started at two o'clock and she did not want to miss a second of it. And If they were going to be sure of getting good seats they would have to be in line not later than one forty-five.

The Paramount Theater had opened in 1926 and with 3,664 seats was the biggest theater in town until the Roxy, with almost twice as many seats, opened three years later.

She had been to the Paramount Theater four times before today, but she knew if she went a hundred times she would still be overwhelmed by it. The entrance was just like Alice's looking glass... Once you stepped through, you were in wonderland.

The Paramount's lobby was modeled after the Opera House in Paris, with Grecian statues, beautiful white marble columns and balustrades and a magnificent chandelier hung so far above them she could not imagine how anyone could reach it to clean and polish the crystals or replace the light bulbs.

The lobby floor was covered with thick, red

carpeting that matched the beautiful red velvet drapes hanging on the walls. But to Kathleen, the most beautiful feature of the lobby was the curved, grand staircase with polished brass railings that seemed like open arms wanting you to climb up to the balconies above. She loved to climb to the top of that stairway just to have the thrill of gracefully walking down it, feeling like the Queen of England herself.

Ushers, dressed in handsome uniforms, made you feel like royalty as they took your coats and hats to the check room and guided you into a line for the either balcony or main floor seating.

Grandest of all was the auditorium itself. Grecian niches lit by soft yellow and red lights adorned the walls. Another huge chandelier hung high above the two thousand seats on the main floor and a slightly smaller version was suspended above the mammoth balcony. For Kathleen the beautiful Paramount Theater was the magic land of her dreams.

An usher showed them to their seats just as the lights dimmed for the Newsreel. Six minutes later as the "Eyes and Ears of the World" looked back at the audience, the great curtain closed over the movie screen and a spot light centered on a man, in a white tuxedo, seated at the giant Wurlitzer organ just to the left of the proscenium.

As he began to play, Kathleen could feel excitement in every nerve in her body. In just a few more minutes the spotlight would leave the organ, then, "My Time is Your Time," Rudy Valley's theme, would lead the orchestra up out of the pit, on to the stage.

She had no idea what kind of motors it took to lift an entire orchestra up from below the floor and put it on the stage where, just a couple of minutes ago, there had been a movie screen, and she didn't care. The motors worked. Rudy Valley and his orchestra appeared, and for the next hour she was in a world of her own.

"My Time is Your Time..." Rudy Valley sang his theme song more slowly than when the show opened and a single spotlight followed him as the bandstand began to disappear below the stage. "Thank you everybody... Thank you... and remember, "My time, Is your time..."

The spotlight went out... He was gone.

She was fulfilled and ready to leave, but Pete said he wanted to see the movie, which was okay with her. The picture was "Jimmy The Gent." Its stars were Jimmy Cagney and Betty Davis. She didn't much like Betty Davis and she didn't find the story interesting, but that was no problem for her. Just sitting there in the Paramount Theater was a treat, and her imagination carried her to a dressing room, where she was preparing to go on stage.

...A makeup man did her eyes.

...A wardrobe woman helped her into a dress.

...Rudy Valley knocked on her door to ask if she was ready.

No, it wasn't Rudy Valley. It was Pete. The movie was over. She had no idea what it had been about but, yes, she was ready to leave.

Back out on the street the fantastic, running lights on the theater marquee had almost replaced the light from the sun which was now well down below the surrounding buildings. She couldn't believe how cold it had become. Her excitement kept her from feeling the cold before the show and inside the theater it was warm and comfortable. Probably it was the theater's warmth that made it seem so cold outside now. But even if it was cold, it was okay. She was in New York. She was on Broadway surrounded by crowds of excited people leaving the theater or waiting in line for the next show. Someday they would be waiting to see her.

The subway ride to South Ferry, the boat ride to Staten Island and the rail road trip to Arrochar should have given her more than enough time to "suggest" Pete take her to the New Year's Ball but somehow she didn't get around to it until the last minute. Pete's answer was almost a disaster. He already had a date with Ann Harris, a new girl friend. Oh well, any port in a storm. Frank would be home, he could take her.

3.

IT HAD BEEN COLD ALL DAY but sitting on a bench on the Staten Island Ferry Chuck Stacey was quite comfortable and his mind drifted away from the famous views to thoughts of their un-famous orchestra. Two years in New York and what did they have to show for it. Fred Young had done a good job for us: Friday and Saturday nights in a Hotel lounge for the three of them and the radio orchestra for the once a week "Music Just For You Hour."

That was where they met Carl and Bob Walker, the sax playing brothers, and guitar playing Richard 'Rich; Green. Then, out of nowhere, Jimmy Johnson turned up. He had finally had it with Henry Love and decided to follow his own advice and try New York. Sure enough, he wound up with the same studio orchestra Billy, Wacky and he were in. Playing together once a week it wasn't too long before they all decided it was time to start up their own "big band" and go forth to make a fortune. If

Tommy Dorsey could do it and Benny Goodman could do it, why couldn't they

The two years since then had been up and down years. Mostly down. Swing Bands were dime a dozen and unless you were Benny Goodman or Artie Shaw or one of the other big names. If you didn't have a record contract and radio time and dates at the big night spots, life could be tough. But, you never know, he kept telling myself, tonight might be the night. The night when things would begin to go our way. He was determined to be at his best and he knew the rest of the guys were too. Besides, when they were playing you couldn't feel bad. Playing together was just too much fun.

They arrived "fashionably late," as people who are usually late were prone to say. Frank had been away all day on some sort of business thing with her father and they had not arrived back home until nearly seven-thirty. He had come in for a moment to tell her he would hurry before running across the yard to the house where he and Pete and their mother lived.

"Don't worry about it, Franco," her father called after him as he started out the door. Every so often her father called him Franco. "We tried the easy way now we do it the other."

Things Pete told her from time to time made her father's words sound ominous. Someday she was going to have a long talk with her mother, someday soon. There were too many things about her family she didn't know, things she was almost afraid to know... but needed to know.

It was eight o'clock when Frank re-appeared, now dressed in a tuxedo and looking very handsome indeed. She asked him to please not call her "sis." As long as no one thought they were related, she would be the envy of every girl there.

Decorated with hanging balloons, multi colored streamers and lit mostly by candle light, the Bay View Yacht Club was far more beautiful then Kathleen had expected.

Frank, being Frank, had reserved a table towards the back of the club's large ballroom but even from that distance she immediately recognized Chuck Stacey. The band was swinging "One O'clock Jump" and the crowd on the dance floor loved it. A crowd mostly of people Frank's age, even her age, rather than the white haired gentlemen and blue haired ladies she had seen at other clubs.

"What do you want to drink, sis? A coke?" were the first words out of his mouth after they were seated.

"Frank..." she scolded. "You promised."

"I'm sorry sis... I mean Kathleen. Would you like to dance?"

"I certainly would and I want you to order champagne."

Without Frank realizing she was controlling their direction, she let him lead her to the front of the bandstand. "Look, Frank, there's some of the fellows I sang with in Chicago." Without waiting for Frank's reply she raised her voice, "Hi Billy, Remember me, Kathleen? I sang with you at the One-Two-Three Club in Chicago." She looked up to the leader, "Hi Chuck... Can I sing a number with your band?"

She had seen people look surprised before, but nothing to compare with the expression that popped onto Chuck Stacey's face. She thought his eyes were going to come out of their sockets.

"Kathleen. Wholly mackerel!" were the first words out of his mouth. "Yeah, yes come sing."

Second maybe to having Tom Kravitz tell him Henry Love needed a drummer, seeing Kathleen here on Staten Island was probably the biggest surprise Chuck ever had. A lot of water had gone under the bridge since she sang with them in

Chicago. All told he didn't think they spent more than three-quarters of an hour with her. She sang, they had a glass of birthday champagne with her and her family, and that was it. But somehow she would turn up in his thoughts every now and then. And all of a sudden, here she is, on Staten Island.

"Is this the reason you wanted to come here, sis?" Frank broke in. He didn't exactly sound mad, she thought, more like resigned. Before he could say anything else, Pete and his date joined them in front of the bandstand.

"Hi Frank... sis. Say hello to Ann Harris."

So much for not being the little sister who couldn't get a date. But that was okay. She was here, the musicians actually remembered her and before anyone said much else the tall skinny trumpet player, who had escorted her back to her table in Chicago, was at her side.

"Madam, your subjects await your pleasure."

To Frank's surprise, she took his arm and let him help her up onto the bandstand. "What would you like to sing this evening your highness?"

She sang "The Isle of Capri," in a slow, romantic tempo, then slid into an up beat "Red Sails in the Sunset."

We had no arrangements for her, so mostly she was accompanied by Billy's piano, my soft brushes, and Wacky's muted horn. The enthusiasm of the applause she received when she finished surprised her.

When she turned to tell us "thanks" before heading back to her "date" I called to her, "Kathleen, wait a sec, I need to talk to you. Can we get together after this set?"

"Sure Chuck," she answered. "We're sitting towards the back, stage left. I'll keep an eye out for you."

I went to their table as soon as we finished the set. She introduced me to her brother, Frank Tucci, who seemed a bit "reserved," He wasn't exactly unfriendly, but he certainly didn't exude charm and warmth. So, what the hell? It was Kathleen I wanted to talk to.

"Kathleen, you were absolutely great!" I told her. "Your voice was good when you sang with us in Chicago but it's a thousand times better now."

She seemed surprised and pleased by what I said but the way she kept glancing at her brother made me wonder if maybe I was treading where I shouldn't. Well, in for a penny, in for a pound.

"Kathleen, our agent says we've got to find a girl singer. I've been looking and listening, but until tonight I hadn't heard anyone I thought could sing with us but you sure could. Would you like to?"

That got a reaction from her brother, but before he could say anything Kathleen "shushed" him.

"My gosh, Chuck..." I thought she was blushing slightly. "You do know how to take a girl's breath away."

"I'm not trying to embarrass you. The simple fact is, we need a singer and you're great. With a voice like yours you have to be thinking of a career in music. I think with our band backing you, you could go a long way."

"This is ridiculous," Frank spoke at last. "Kathleen's going to school. She isn't even thinking of a career yet."

She gave him a look that said, "don't be so sure," and asked me how she could get in touch. I gave her Fred Young's card and told her Fred was our agent.

The brief conversation with Chuck Stacey left Frank with a bad taste in his mouth. He watched Stacey head back to the band stand then stood and told Kathleen, "It's time to go."

Without saying a word she let Frank escort her to the door where the valet quickly brought Frank's new Duisenberg.

The doorman opened the door and Frank

helped her in. At least we're making a decent exit, she thought as she noticed several other couples looking somewhat enviously at Frank's car and his "date".

"That was fun, Frank," she told him as he got behind the wheel. "Thank you for taking me."

"Kathleen!" He ignored her thanks. "What was all that about in there?"

"All what about?" She tried to sound sweet and innocent.

"You know damn... I mean perfectly well what I'm talking about. Why did you tell Stacey I'm your brother? Why did you take his card? You certainly aren't thinking about singing with that band." It was a statement not a question. Then, when she did not answer he turned to look at her and made it a question. "Sis... you're not... are you?"

"Stay on the road, Frank."

"Kathleen!" He corrected his steering. "You're not!"

"And what if I am?" She kept her voice low. Calm and, she thought, mature

"Your father will have a fit."

"Frank, I'm not exactly sure what I'm thinking right this minute, nor do I know what daddy might or might not say about it, but one thing is sure, the subject is not one for you to discuss with him. When I decide what I want to do, I will talk with my father. Not you."

Frank did not reply.

"I'm going to be a singer. No, I am a singer. That's what I'm going to do with my life. I haven't decided if this is the time to start singing professionally, but it's really none of your business. When I make up my mind, I will tell my mother and my father and I will consider it a serious breach of our friendship if you talk about it with either of them."

"Jesus Christ!" Frank almost never used profanity in her presence and it surprised her. "The acorn really doesn't fall very far from the tree does it."

"Like father, like daughter you mean?"

"Yes. When your father gets serious his voice has that same tone."

"And when it does, people take him seriously don't they?" She watched Frank nod his head up and down.

4.

SINCE SHE HAD GONE AWAY TO SCHOOL, when she was home morning walks with mother and daddy had become something of a ritual Even in cold weather like today, they would walk until it was time for lunch, then, after lunch, Frank or Pete would escort her back to Manhasset. But this morning was different. She would not be returning to Manhasset. Her mind had been in such a state of excitement last night that it had taken her at least an hour before she could get to sleep, an hour during which she had made her decision about Chuck Stacey. Now all she had to do was tell daddy and her mother.

As always, when they went walking, following some fifty paces behind, Howard and Kenny came with them. She had decided they were going to be the "wedge" she would use. Carefully taking hold of her mother's hand, she took a deep breath, looked up at her father and began.

"Daddy, Howard Quinn and Kenny used to be policeman didn't they?"

"Yes." Her father was surprised by the question.

"Now they're sort of our bodyguards?"

"Well yes, darlin'." He glanced over her head at her mother. "I guess you could call 'em that."

"And when Frank or Pete take me to school, they carry guns don't they?" She heard her mother take a little gasp of air and felt her squeeze her hand.

"'Tis nothin' fer you to concern yourself about if they do." Her father was becoming irritated. She would have to be careful. If he got angry he might not pay attention to what she had to say.

"Daddy, mother. Please don't get angry. I need to talk to you. I need to have you listen." The urgency in her voice had a sudden calming effect on her father.

"All right," he put an arm around her and pulled her to him. "I'll not be gettin' angry. Now what is it you've got to talk about?"

"Daddy, I know you don't think so, but I'm a grown woman, almost eighteen. When you were seventeen you and mom were..." She couldn't finish her sentence...

"Jesus Christ!" Her father exploded. "Yer not with child?"

"No daddy. It's nothing like that." She watched him take a deep breath, then reach for his handkerchief to wipe his forehead.

"Someday I would like to have children but I don't know how that can happen if I'm going to have bodyguards with me all my life."

"What are ya leadin' up to Kathleen?" Her father's voice was no longer angry, just exasperated. She realized he had about reached the end of his patience. Time to fish or cut bait, as Uncle Pietro always said.

"Daddy," she began slowly, "I love you," she looked to her mother again, "And mom. You know I love you both, but I don't want to live the rest of my life the way we do. I can sing. I can sing very well and I want to be a singer." She waited for them consider what she had said as they walked on. "I am a singer and I want to sing with Chuck Stacey's band. You both met him at Uncle Tony's club in Chicago. His band was at the Yacht Club last night."

In his mind, Hugh heard his mother's words, "He's so young, Tom" and his father's reassuring response, "Not to worry mother... no danger there." No danger he had said, but there was danger. Could there be danger here in the compound too? Danger for his daughter? Was it possible Kathleen would be safer if she were to leave home? And if she didn't, was it right to keep her almost a prisoner? No, it wasn't.

"Alright, you want to be a singer. But why with

this Chuck Stacey outfit? Who ever heard of them?"

"Nobody," she answered slowly. "But you could fix that, couldn't you daddy."

Her answer...her question surprised him. And delighted him.

"Well now," there was a smile on his face as he spoke, "Perhaps... And just when do you propose startin' all this?"

"Tomorrow." She replied.

5.

THE RINGING TELEPHONE woke him up.. Calls before 10AM were not common and never much appreciated.

"Shit! Go 'way," he told the ringing phone, but it wouldn't go away so he climbed out of bed and went to the phone.

"Yeah, hello."

"Chuck, it's Fred..."

"Jesus Fred, you gotta call this..."

"Listen," Fred cut him off. "I got a man in the office who says he neds to talk to you. Name is Frank Tucci. He says you know him. Says it's very important!"

It took a second then he remembered, Kathleen's brother. And he was no longer half asleep. "Oh. Oh wow. Did he tell you what it's all about?"

"No. He said you would know. He wants to meet you for breakfast."

"OK. Great. How 'bout the automat right near your office. Half an hour?"

He could hear Fred asking Tucci, then, "He says fine. He'll see you there."

Billy, Wacky and I ate half our meals in the automat. The food is good and I am still enough of a kid to get a kick out of sticking nickels into the slot and watching the little door swing open for me to take the food out. Also, Horn & Hardart is about the only place in the country that made Tapioca Pudding as good as my mother's. Almost as good anyway. Most days I eat Tapioca Pudding for breakfast along with an order of bacon and a bagel with cream cheese. The bagel and cream cheese I learned from Wacky, only Wacky put Lox on his. Lox I can't take.

"Hello Chuck. I'm Frank Tucci."

"Yeah, sure Frank. I know who you are for gosh sake, we just met New Year's Eve. How's Kathleen taking all the applause she got?"

"I believe she liked it. That's more or less why I've come to see you. Kathleen's father would very much like to talk with you. Could you come over to Staten Island for a meeting with him?"

This guy Frank, hard to figure. He's built like a bull, but he talks like a businessman and he dresses like a lawyer or something.

"Yeah, sure," I agreed. "When?"

"Well, now, if it isn't too inconvenient," Frank

answered

"Wow," I couldn't help laughing, "Nothing like long range planning."

When we took the ferry to Staten Island for the Yacht Club dance I hadn't paid much attention to the view. Today, trying to keep my mind from worrying about the man I was with and where he was taking me. I did. By the time we were passing the Statue of Liberty I was mesmerized. I kept wondering how could I tell mom and dad about it, and knowing I couldn't. There are no words. Well there are, I just don't know how to put them together.

When we reached the Island I began worrying again.

We took a train to some place named Stapleton, then walked a few blocks to a restaurant called Original Angelo's. It wasn't a very big building, but it looked nice. The kind of place a guy would take his wife if he wanted something good but not too expensive. We walked through the parking lot next to the building and up a flight of stairs to the second floor... the top floor. Frank knocked, somebody inside opened the door and a voice said, "Come in."

To me the office looked more like a living room in a comfortable house, or maybe one of those clubrooms you see in magazines like Esquire. Two big rugs, a leather sofa, a coffee table and a couple of chairs in front of a huge window looking out over the waterfront and New York harbor beyond. A pair of very nice looking desks and some more chairs on the other side of the room and two doors on the far wall that, I guessed, led to other rooms at the front of the building.

I nodded to the wiry looking guy holding the front door for us and said "Hi," when a voice from across the room called out, "Hello Chuck Stacey."

The voice was as big as the man it came from. There aren't many men his size, I recognized him right away, Kathleen's father. "Hello Mr. Tucci."

"Mr. Tucci is it?" He laughed. That's something we best clear up," he continued. "Me name's Crawford. So's Kathleen's. Tucci here," he nodded towards Frank, "Him and his brother call her 'sis', and all, and they're like son's to me, but they're no kin." He nodded to a chair and said, "Take a seat Chuck Stacey, we got some talkin' to do." Then he looked towards the doorkeeper. "Jeff, I'm sure ya wont take no offense. What me and him has ta discus is... you know, a kind of family thing."

"Sure Hugh, I was just leavin'."

Frank, I noticed, was not asked to leave. He

was family regardless of not being Kathleen's brother and being a Tucci not a Crawford. It's too damn complicated who all these people are, I told myself. Just sit back and see what's on his mind.

"So then Chuck lad," he began after Jeff left, "You've been talkin' with Kathleen about singin' wid-chure orchestra and she tells me that's what she wants ta do."

Oh wow! Kathleen wants to sing with us. I know my eyes widened, then I realized that might not be what her father wants. He was expecting me to say something and I was trying desperately to think of something to say.

"Mr. Crawford." I found my voice at last. "Kathleen's a fine singer. She has a marvelous voice and I think she can be a star. My band needs a singer and if she would sing with us... I tell you the truth, she would make my band a success, too."

"Would she now?" He put his hands together with fingers extended, placed them in front of his chin and began rubbing them up and down so that his forefingers kept bumping into his nose. "Then am I right thinkin' you'd be payin' her a great deal of money to sing with your band?"

"In time," I told him. "My band isn't making it yet. We have a great bunch of musicians, but some of our bookings haven't been good. The other night there were people the right age for us and they liked our music... and they loved Kathleen. I think now, maybe we can expect to land better dates in places where we belong. If we have a singer like Kathleen with us I know we'll go right to the top. Then we could be talking about a lot of money."

Hugh sat quietly for a moment, then turned to Frank "What did you think of this fellow's band, was it any good?"

"I don't know, Uncle Hugh. I don't have an ear for music. Everybody at the dance seemed to like them pretty well and when Kathleen sang there was a lot of applause. I think Stacey may be right thinking she could be a success." He hesitated a second then added, "With the right promoting of course, the right bookings and all that."

"Is that something we could do?"

All of a sudden I was not part of the conversation.

"Maybe Uncle Hugh," Frank answered. "If we want to. The new place you and Tony have in Chicago could be a good start..."

"The Paradise Club?"

"Sure. Tony's been booking top entertainment. They do a radio feed three nights a week. It's the big time. If you wanted to build somebody up, that wouldn't be a bad place to do it, but you would be taking a chance... if they aren't what the audience wants it could hurt the club."

"Oh hell, Frank. What goes on in the ballroom don't mean nothin'." Hugh spread his hands apart and laughed. "The money's upstairs."

"Uncle Hugh!" Frank glanced towards me, obviously he thought his uncle was saying things I shouldn't hear.

"Yes, all right Franco." Hugh stood up and walked towards Frank. "Now about this booking business. The Paradise is a good start. Where else? Seems like Tony and me got a few friends here and there. Could we find some more work fer her?"

I understood "her" was Kathleen, and understood it was Kathleen, not our band that was of interest to Hugh Crawford and his make believe son Frank Tucci, but I didn't care how we got where we wanted to get, as long as we got there. I also knew Fred Young was going to get involved and I wasn't sure just how Fred would take to having somebody else booking "his" band.

"Mr. Crawford," I broke into their conversation. "You're talking about booking our band, but we have an agent who books us.

"Oh?" Hugh looked at me. "Who is this agent you got bookin' you."

"Fred Young, One of the guys who's with us knew him. When we got to New York he took us on and he has been booking us ever since. If we have a chance to make it big, Fred needs to be part of it.

"I see." Hugh Crawford scratched his chin, then looked back to Frank Tucci.. "You think we could work with this Fred Young guy?"

"We could probably do that," Frank looked up from something he had been writing. "We could set up a company, maybe hire this Fred Young to run it...If we think he knows what he's doing. It might be a good new business for us." With that he held up whatever he had been writing and showed it to Hugh.

"Not a bad idea, " Hugh smiled, "Not bad at all. Show him" he nodded towards me:

CATHY CONNERS
With the
CHUCK STACEY ORCHESTRA

Oh my, I thought. First, who is Cathy Conners and how come we get second billing? But I kept my mouth shut for a change. If this guy could get us big bookings we could deal with that, but Cathy Conners? So I asked. "Cathy Conners?"

"Yeah," Hugh Crawford answered, "Good idea. Crawford's not a very good name to put out there." Obviously deep in thought he picked up his pencil and began tapping it on the desk top, then, "Matter of fact it might be better to turn that around. Put Stacey first. He's been around a little. Let people think more about him than Kathleen."

I didn't ask why but I was beginning to have an idea.

"All right." Frank agreed.

"And you'll talk to this Fred fella?"

"I'll take care of it," Frank assured him.

'Good!" Hugh nodded. "Now, I better talk to Tony." He picked up his telephone. "Long distance," he told the operator.

I listened as he spelled out the name, Belinni and then announced the call would go through in ten minutes..

"It just don't seem possible," he said shaking his head. "Ten minutes and I'll be talking' to Tony a thousan' miles away."

"One of the wonders of the twentieth century Uncle Hugh," Frank told him. "Without the telephone I don't know where business would be today."

"I don't know either," Hugh agreed, then lapsed into silence as he thought about the call he was making to Tony Belinni. Unconsciously he picked up the pencil and began tapping again.

Laughing, Frank asked, "You taking up the drums too Uncle Hugh?"

"What? Oh," he looked down at the pencil in his hand and grinned, "Well maybe I best do that if I expect ta see me daughter anymore."

I knew the grin was covering an ache in Hugh's heart. He was going to miss his daughter.

Almost exactly ten minutes later the phone rang, Hugh picked up the receiver, assured the operator he actually was the Hugh Crawford who had placed the call to Anthony Belinni in Chicago, and a few seconds later said, "Hello, You hear me okay, Tony?" He listened, grinned, then, "Good here. Real good. How bout out there. Things okay with you?" A short pause, then, "Tony, I got a band we need-a book inta the club. Chuck Stacey and Cathy Conners. You know Cathy Conners a little better as me daughter Kathleen."

7.

I STILL HAD TROUBLE BELIEVING IT when I got back to New York and got the guys together to tell them the news. "Tuesday, February tenth, with our new singing star Cathy Conners, we open at the Paradise Club in Chicago."

For three, maybe four seconds there was absolute silence, then all hell broke loose.

I had expected Hugh Crawford would want us to rehearse on Staten Island but that was not the case. "The less connection you have with Staten Island, the better," he told me.

Frank Tucci got together with Fred Young over the weekend and by Monday we were set to rehearse in a studio on 48th Street, just across from Fred's office.

And that was the day a blond Cathy Conners" showed up for rehearsal along with a pretty girl named Shirley Winter. Shirley, it turned out, was a teacher who was going to play chaperone and also keep "Cathy" up with her school work because Kathleen's mother wanted to be sure her daughter got a high school diploma so she could go to college "if this singing business doesn't work out."

Well, I figured that wasn't so bad. Instead of one, we'll have two good-looking girls traveling with us. Shirley is probably in her early twenties. When Billy first met her I thought he was never going to be able to get out the word, "Hello." I think her reaction to Billy was not that much different.

Cathy's arrival, for her first rehearsal with the band, was when I made the announcement that starting then, we were all getting rehearsal salary.

At the end of our first day of rehearsal, Billy, Wacky and I decided to celebrate by taking Cathy and Shirley up to Harlem to hear Duke Ellington at the Cotton Club. Cathy didn't have to tell me she dug the Duke, ever since she sang with us at the One-Two-Three Club I knew that. What I didn't know was how much she liked Ivy Anderson. When Ivy sang "Mood Indigo," Cathy got real tears in her eyes.

The Cotton Club is located way up in Harlem at 644 Lenox Avenue, right at 144th Street. It was opened in 1923 and has always been a great place to hear music. Duke Ellington's band became the "house band" in 1927 and stayed there until 1930. Since then he has been back for extended engagements every year. He started getting to be well known because of the weekly radio shows they did from there.

Like the Grand Terrace in Chicago, the Cotton Club is on the second floor of a three-story building and is owned by a gangster named Owney Madden. Everybody knows he's a gangster so you wonder why he isn't in jail. I guessed New York wasn't that much different from Chicago.

The showroom is decorated to look like an old southern mansion and it's a wonderful place to hear music and see great entertainment. They do two shows each night, one at Midnight, the second at 2AM.

The performers are all black, but only whites are allowed in the club to see them. I know there is something wrong with that, but that's the way it is at the Cotton Club.

Billy, Wacky and I got to know most of Duke's men from sitting in with them at jazz places all over town, so before the first show we took the girls back stage. Meeting Duke and some of his guys was a thrill for both of them, but for Cathy, meeting Ivy Anderson was monumental. She told Ivy the thing she wanted most in the world was to sing like her.

We stayed at the club until the first show ended at ten minutes after one, which in a musician's life is early evening, but Shirley felt compelled to act like a proper guardian. I'm sure Cathy wanted to stay longer, and I know Wacky, Billy and I would have stayed until the band went off, then probably we would have gone somewhere and jammed with some of them until morning, but Shirley said it was time for us to take them home.

January weather in New York is about as predictable as the Chicago Cubs. You think spring is almost here and next thing you know, you get a blizzard. In the four hours we spent in the Cotton Club things had changed from a comfortable evening into a snowstorm. Fresh snow falling past shining street lights making everything look clean and new is hard to beat. With the Duke and Ivy still echoing in our heads, it seemed too beautiful to believe.

In New York City, anything more than twenty feet above sea level is called "a hill" and using that yardstick, the girl's hotel was on a hill where a bunch of kids were sleigh riding. Just what kids were doing out sledding at two o'clock in the morning I don't know, but I guess if you're a kid in New York you've got to sleigh ride when there's snow because by mid morning, what's snow tonight will be nothing but slush from all the traffic.

So, I'm still a kid, I admit it. When we got out of our taxi, I took a quarter out of my pocket and grabbed Cathy's hand. "Come on." I led her to a kid who was pulling his Flexible-Flyer back up the street. "Two-bits for a ride," I told him.

"Okay, sure mister."

Cathy started laughing, but she didn't resist when I helped her sit down in front of me on the sled. I put my legs around her so I could get my feet on the steering bar. "Give us a shove," I told the kid.

I suppose our ride was no longer than half a city block, and our top speed wasn't much faster than you can walk, but I never had a roller-coaster ride that was more fun. Cathy whooped and squealed and when we slowed to a stop she leaned back against me with such force we both fell off the sled into the snow.

. "Oh Chuck." She was laughing so hard she could hardly talk. "You are such a nut." She rolled over until we were face to face. "I think I'm going to like working for you." Then she gave me a quick kiss on the nose.

For a second I wondered exactly who was working for who, but having a beautiful girl lying on top of you in the snow can put a lot of other thoughts in your mind very quickly.

8.

IN SOME WAYS our opening in Chicago was anti-climatic. We had been living with the dream for so long it just seemed like another rehearsal. My mother and father had come up from Joliet. Cathy's mom and dad along with her two brothers were there too. So was Fred Young. But we were sort of oblivious to it all. It wasn't until we finished our last set and collected in the band room, where Toni Belinni had set up several dozen bottles of champagne that it all began to register.

I took a glass of champagne and held it up to Cathy. "Know what I wish?" I asked her.

"What?" she answered.

"I wish there was some snow outside and a slay so we could go for a ride."

"Don't worry," she clicked her glass against mine. "We'll have a lot of sleigh rides together."

Staten Island

THE END